PRAISE FOR *PRETEND WE ARE LOVELY*

"A family must navigate the secret currents of guilt, obsession, loss, and—most dangerous of all—hope in this pitch-perfect examination of two Southern seasons in 1982. In prose that ambulates between stark, hallucinatory, fuddled, and chewy according to the guiding character's point of view, Reid masterfully denies her novel the impulse to solve its characters' problems, leaving the reader with the brutal task of lingering within their experience."

—**KIRKUS**, Starred Review

"An outstanding, unflinching novel about starvation and indulgence, family and self. Noley Reid writes profoundly raw characters with guts and grace. This is one of the most moving novels I've ever read."

—**SHARMA SHIELDS**, author of *The Sasquatch Hunter's Almanac*

"In *Pretend We Are Lovely*, Noley Reid captures what it is to have to be a parent while still a child in the most true and perfect way. Even more magically, she captures the reverse, calling on the children inside us with so much empathy that we come away able to laugh at the pain that makes us wise."

—**TUPELO HASSMAN**, author of *Girlchild*

"A novel that will make you laugh and also break your heart in all the right ways . . . Told with wit and charm and compassion, this novel resonates with all that we hunger to have and all that feeds us."

—**LEE MARTIN**, author of *The Bright Forever*

"A book fat with love, full of tender absurdity and absurd tenderness, a story that artfully depicts the first aches and thrills of adolescence while also unmasking the unslakable thirst that slips with us into adulthood."

—**ALETHEA BLACK**, author of *I Knew You'd Be Lovely*

"Hunger shapes the intertwined narratives of Noley Reid's searing and clear-eyed novel, wherein no one escapes unscathed the emotional starvation of a family."

—**LESLIE DANIELS**, author of *Cleaning Nabokov's House*

"Readers will be spellbound by this intimate portrayal of a family told in a symphony of voices—each member of the Sobel family's search for redemption equally urgent and compelling. Like the best love songs . . . sad but hopeful, raw but tender, shocking but, ultimately, deeply comforting."

—**JULIA FIERRO**, author of *The Gypsy Moth Summer*
and *Cutting Teeth*

PRETEND WE ARE
LOVELY

PRETEND

WE ARE

Lovely

noley reid

TIN HOUSE BOOKS / Portland, Oregon & Brooklyn, New York

Published by Tin House Books, Portland, Oregon, and Brooklyn, New York

Distributed by W. W. Norton & Company

Library of Congress Cataloging-in-Publication Data

Names: Reid, Noley, author.
Title: Pretend we are lovely : a novel / by Noley Reid.
Description: First U.S. edition. | Portland, OR : Tin House Books, 2017.
Identifiers: LCCN 2016056391 (print) | LCCN 2017011472 (ebook) | ISBN
    9781941040669 (alk. paper) | ISBN 9781941040676
Subjects: LCSH: Family secrets--Fiction. | Domestic fiction.
Classification: LCC PS3618.E5453 2017 (print) | LCC PS3618.E5453 2017 (ebook)
    | DDC 813/.6--dc23
LC record available at https://lccn.loc.gov/2016056391

First US Edition 2017
Printed in the USA
Interior design by Diane Chonette

www.tinhouse.com

for my two
best boys

Todd,
who feeds me
and knows every hunger

&

Tolen,
who I hope
never will

&

for my mother,
whose only language
is love

1

Enid

I'm her girl, the second. The baby. Or third, if you count my brother.

We live in Blacksburg, Virginia, on a dead end by the old, paved-over railroad tracks. The calendar page hanging in Ma's kitchen is a fluffy dog, white and black like a cow, with her paws on her snout like she was naughty. Little muddy paw prints spell out *July 1982* across the top. I like the calendar even if Vivvy thinks it's for babies.

Vivvy is Vivian, because even her nickname is beautiful. She is older by almost three years. I'm ten and she's almost thirteen. Ma wanted us separated three years perfect, but I was preemie. Vivvy says I'm squishy dough because Ma didn't cook me long enough but I'm not smaller than she is. I'm thick like Daddy, who says that's a sturdy way of living.

Vivvy says it's being fat. Once she started to blow away in a wind tunnel in Chicago, pulled up into the snowy air. Vivvy likes thinking of herself as someone who can easily blow away. One time she said if I were with her there again in that wind tunnel, the two of us holding hands, I'd be her anchor and keep her safe.

•

Vivvy and I play in the pines off the side of the house, the ones that make a wall marking where we end and the Thomsons' yard begins. Sometimes we climb them. More times, we swing or dangle from the thick branch, our yellow pigtails or ponytails hanging down.

Clint Thomson crouches small behind the corner of a shed, watching us. Like we don't see him. Vivvy and I laugh.

He comes out, says, "I'm coming up."

"The hell you are," says Vivvy.

"Hell you are," I say.

She tips back her head, eyes rolling.

Clint kicks the trunk of our tree. He touches the branches but doesn't know which is the one to grab. He holds on to two thick ones and walks his feet up the trunk but then he's scrunched like a ball, stuck.

He drops back down in the dead needles. "I'll come up," he says to Vivvy.

She hooks her chin on a branch over us. Her ponytail hangs straight down her back, smooth and perfect. Clint has this way of looking only at Vivvy when he talks, and I don't know why but it makes my stomach feel homesick.

His dog Basey trots over from underneath the bushes at his back door. A beagle mix with a coiled tail and a scruff of hair at the base of his neck for when he's feeling ornery, which is almost all the time but especially when our dog Floey's out playing too. Today Floey's inside because Ma's making her a fairy costume for Halloween. This is only July but Ma likes an early start.

Clint tries again. He grabs another branch but it's wrong, too, and there's nowhere to go from there, so he just sort of grips at the sticky needle tufts coming at his face and leans there. Basey's sniffing around every inch of forsythia and brambledy blackberry bush we've got, peeing every step of the way. He's got funny short legs and, when one springs up in the air, Vivvy calls it peeing *with gusto*. It about tips him over when he lifts his leg so fast and high.

"He's doing it again." I nudge her to look down at Basey in the currant bush.

"Stupid dog," she says.

"He can't help it," I say.

Sun spots Vivvy's face through the needles. It falls across her eyes but she doesn't squint or move away. "That's the trouble with being stupid, Enid," she says.

We're carrying on this conversation loud enough for Clint to hear it but we are high up enough he can pretend not to hear if he doesn't want to, and he must not because he hops off and Basey follows him back into his yard.

"Stupid boy," says Vivvy, watching him go. She drops down to hang by her knees.

"Stupid," I say, and she flicks my big toe.

The screen door slaps shut and out comes fluffy white Floey running her happy-dog run that's more like a horse's gallop. Right to our tree she comes. I see her catch on that Basey was here and she's so smart that she turns her head and looks into the Thomsons' yard.

3

"Good girl," I tell her. "Smart girl."

Then she's off walking the bushes, sniffing everywhere he's been, stuffing her nose right into all those drips of pee.

"Do you ever wonder what it's like," says Vivvy, pulling herself back up on the branch to sit by me, "to think about things or do things that other people don't know you do?"

"Like what?"

"You know, *secret* things."

"Bad things?"

"Oh, never mind. You're too young."

"What did you do?" I say and shove her once.

"Don't be stupid."

"I'm going out," Ma calls from the screen door. She's in her tennis togs. She's clutching her tennis satchel. But she doesn't go get in the car; she heads back into the house. She never takes her racket. And you can't play all by yourself, but no one ever calls her to *reconnoiter*—that's one of Ma's favorite words—and she never calls anyone.

"Bye," she says to us once she's made it out the door twirling her keys, and still I don't answer because I'm watching the sun catch in the pleats of her white skirt, the pink balls bouncing from the backs of her ankle socks. Her ponytail tied with a lemony bow to match her yellow hair combs.

She backs the Datsun out the gravel drive.

Vivvy swings upside down again, says, "She lies to us."

My stomach drops and now I'm afraid. Of being up high. Of Vivvy falling and landing on her head. Of Floey gone to find Basey. Of this being the start to the end of summer. Of Daddy not knowing the particulars of this day for us, because this isn't one of *his* days—it isn't a spend-the-night day and it isn't a barbecue-grill day and it may not turn out to be a phone call day.

•

Daddy doesn't live here anymore. And we don't live with him because Ma said "no" and Vivvy said nothing and I said "yes" but that was that. He's in an apartment over by the university—which I guess is convenient, because that's what he says. Vivvy says, "At least it's not Christiansburg," and we laugh because everybody knows what you get when you add hot water to Christiansburg: instant grits, and our daddy is *no* gap-toothed, shiny-shirted, greasy-haired grit.

First time we visited, Daddy made Chicken Hot as the Devil, which is his specialty. We had strawberry ice cream after supper. When he handed me the bowls to take out to the patio, I chose the bigger scoops for me. Ma says I'm a creamy girl: mashed potatoes, yogurt, pudding, oatmeal all make my head spin.

I took a big bite of ice cream.

"Easy, sister," said Daddy.

•

Clint's at the base of our tree again. Basey's sniffing around after Floey, who was here a minute ago but now's gone off exploring. Ma's back home and Vivvy's inside getting the pins stuck in her Bambi costume. She'll have a tail sewn on some brown shorts and white patches on the insides of tan leg warmers, a thrift store brown turtleneck, and an old Easter basket with twigs for antlers

5

on her head. What she wants is what I want. Something in a kit, store-bought. Something brand-new.

"I saw you," he says to me, looking up but into the angles of the tree limbs, not at me.

"Saw me what?" I call down.

"Which branch to start with."

"Did not," I say. "Prove it."

"It's this one right here," he says, and makes like to start climbing. The silver clip jingles on his Scouts shorts.

"You don't know anything," I tell him. I rip off a hank of needles and toss them at him. He blinks, this time looking up at me.

"Come on, Basey." He pats his side and that dumb dog sort of turns his way but then thinks better of it and keeps on with my yard. "Come on now," says Clint. He goes after him and takes hold of Basey's loose red collar and starts dragging him home by it.

I swing from the branch. I swing upside down. I swing right side up. I swing and swing. Ma'll make me a pirate next.

Francie

I drive the same route to the tennis courts each day. Windows rolled tight so the air wraps me in heat. I smile and breathe the sun. The girls can hang like monkeys in their tree all they want.

I go out of my way, go into downtown. I wouldn't drive to tennis any other route. This is my path.

Midway, I slow to pass Carol Lee Donuts but keep my face forward, my eyes in front of me. It doesn't matter. Even just seeing it peripherally, I know the scene by heart. Inside the big picture window, an imposing mixer pipes batter rings that drop into hot oil below. They float and sizzle and then the pretty girl with the thick red braid flips them. One by one she dunks soft yellow edges and the fried rings bob up golden brown.

I know who she is. To Tate. And for how long—at least part of last quarter. I tidied a set of papers he left spread across my porch table after watching the girls in April. On principle, he has never given a student a *100%*, yet there it was.

The name on her tag, the name on her essay.

On the days I see her here, turning the rings, I run 20 more laps around the courts.

On the days I don't see her, I run even more.

Tate

On the first day of my July aesthetics class, I give a brief lecture to open the course and now the students are filling thirty minutes on who is the better artist: Warhol or Michelangelo. I set my notes aside and, on the back of a piece of scratch paper, begin a grocery list:

milk
o.j.
bread
popcorn
pitas
sp. sauce
lasagna noodles
ricotta
salad stuff

I look up and she stands in front of me at the desk. "Yes?" I say and slide the roster over my list.

Holly smiles. So I smile back—I go for a *please move it along, what do you need?* kind of smile.

•

Holly sits up next to my freakishly fuzzed knees. She looks toward the covered window. I lie on the bare top sheet. There is some vestige of covers in a mess down at the end of the bed just beyond her pink-nailed toes, but the rest must have hit the floor some time ago. Stark naked, she is just as poised as she was when handing in her essays and exams all last spring.

I'm not quite old enough to be her father and that is a comfort. Holly scoots back up here and nestles against me, her head in the crook of my arm. Her hair splays all across the mattress and her skin and mine.

I grab her arm and kiss it, bring her to me and kiss her between the eyebrows and down the freckled slope of her nose. I track a line, kissing as I go.

"So," I say.

"Me hungwy," she says like Cookie Monster. She jaws my chest over and over again, as if I am made of cookies.

It is 4:22 PM. Not officially time for food but no one here cares about that. I go pick up a sausage-and-pepperoni at Angelo's and we eat it back in bed.

Vivvy

"Ow."

"Then hold still."

Mom rocks back on her knees. "You want this or not?" she says.

"No," I say.

She knows what I want. Princess Leia, the one from *The Empire Strikes Back*, with braids hanging in loops and a lightsaber. Enid and I saw the costumes at Leggett and we decided we could both be Leia—only Enid would have to be Leia with the buns and I could be new Leia with braid loops. And a saber.

We found Mom in the dressing room, saying, "Why don't they make these small enough? Who wants blue jeans that sag?" She spun around and grabbed at the empty fabric hanging down from her butt. "And look at this waistband." Then she saw what we were holding. She dumped the jeans on the floor, slipped her own pants back on, and walked out. She didn't speak again until we were on the white aisle heading out the door.

"You don't expect those horrible *things* to go home with us, do you?" she said over her shoulder.

We had already laid the costumes down.

Now I am on Sheldon's locked toy chest in the hallway outside the door to his old room. I'm being measured and stuck, wearing an upside-down egg basket on my head—so she can get the "full effect": twigs poking through the top to make antlers. The little old ladies on our block will ask if I'm a *tree* this year.

"At least let me go as the hunter and Enid can be Bambi's mother. I can shoot her every time we ring a bell."

2

Enid

Summer days all drift together and I lose track. So when I see Daddy pull up the driveway in the old Plymouth, which is long and sleek, I almost think it's someone else.

He's in his blue shirt today, almost every day, pretty blue like the sky and like snow cones. He sees me first and I'm sure that's a sign.

"Bug!" he calls, and I'm running, feeling the pine needles crawl up in between my toes and wedge in the straps of my sandals.

Vivvy's slower; she was up in the tree. I squeeze him big, around the middle, best I can. He squeezes me back.

"Rabbit!" he calls out past me.

"Dad," shouts Vivvy, getting down and finally coming to him.

"Where's your mother? The car's gone."

"Who knows," says Vivvy.

"Tennis," I say.

Vivvy's face is to him, saying she's not so sure but all right, she can go along with it.

Daddy doesn't like it. It seems to make him tired. But all of a sudden he stands up straight and happy. "Get your things," he says. "We're headed for Williamsburg."

"Busch Gardens?!" I say. "Does Ma know?" I don't know why I ask it. I don't even care. But now Daddy is rushing and Vivvy's getting in the car and there's something in me wondering how easy they could be gone without me and not even notice before I'm back with my knapsack.

"We'll be back so fast—sooner than she can make peanut butter fudge," he says. "What's there to know?"

Vivvy hangs out the car window with her head and arms draping down like someone shot dead in a movie. "Get the show on the road!" she yells.

I get in the Plymouth. Vivvy and me squeezed into the front seat, me in the middle because I'm younger. But this is where I want to be. He's in brown shorts and sandals and I can't help liking the way his thick legs glow orange from so much sun. Golden curls of baby's hair all over them and I'm getting carsick from not watching the road. I let my hand sit on the slimiest little strip of black Naugahyde between us.

"Would you look at that?" He elbows me but shoots his eyes over to Vivvy.

There's a car we're coming up behind on 81 and its side is all smashed up and it's turned on a funny angle into the ditch along the shoulder of the highway.

"Shut your eyes," he says as we pass it.

Vivvy yawns because she gets sleepy in car rides, but we both spin around for a better view: a deer, half of it under the front of the car and the other half on top of it. All smashed up. The hood of the car is crunched and the windshield is caved in like a slack spiderweb.

"Oh," escapes me and my mouth stays open.

"Cool," says Vivvy, staring.

A bit later, Daddy starts to whistle. That way he has with his tongue at the roof of his mouth. Vivvy is grog-eyed, leaning into the door. It's ninety-two degrees out there—I know because the bird feeder thermometer said so—but all the hairs on her arms are goose hairs; she's freezing cold just like Ma.

•

"Get off." I barely say it because I don't truly mind. But I know if it were me drip-jawed on *her* shoulder, Vivvy would be the first moaning about it. She's awake but not by much. She shifts back into the corner of the seat and door.

"Sug," says Daddy, patting my knee.

I look up at him.

"Why not just be smoother with your sister?"

"I didn't mean . . ." I put my fingers through Vivvy's but Daddy can't see it because her hand's dropped down between us on the seat. She's back to sleeping already.

The road goes by pretty fast, even in this old car. Roanoke, Cloverdale, Waynesboro. Already we're past these, and I start to wonder if Busch Gardens is really where we're headed. Because why? Why would we be going there without Ma knowing it, without us having a whole week of looking forward to it? Vivvy's worked her bent knee up onto the seat, up onto my lap, and I hope Daddy sees that I'm letting it be.

"What are you looking at, goosey?" Daddy pats my knee once but I don't think he's listening for an answer.

I turn to the backseat once more, see my knapsack slipped partway beneath some old paper sacks with their tops gone soft-shiny for having been rolled up and down in his big hands so many times. "What's in the sacks, Daddy?"

He blows his bangs out of his eyes, says, "Huh? Oh, things. See that plate, duck? Arizona . . . Now, they're a long way from home."

I think about that. The white Ford pickup and big-haired lady sitting smack in the middle, like me, because of her man's arm around her shoulder, holding her to him.

I want to pull my knapsack out.

"Is my girl hungry?" he asks me, low-voiced like a secret.

I only nod yes.

He takes the next exit and pulls us into a Pizza Hut—we never get burger fast foods with Daddy because McDonald's and Wendy's won't serve him a beer. Pizza's plenty yummy for me.

Daddy and I want Personal Pan Pizzas because that way yours is yours and nobody can grab hold of a slice before you're ready. Daddy gets extra cheese and ground beef. Me too. Vivvy just wants a plain with pepperoni.

We're not talking too much. Daddy swigs his beer and I can smell it on him. Vivvy nibbles at her second piece of her pizza. I'm on my last, picking off the little meaty balls with my fingers and setting them on my tongue one by one.

"Slide out," says Vivvy. "I have to pee."

I do. Daddy and I smile at each other. We don't look at Vivvy's pizza, the two pieces left, the barely touched slice on her plate, the slicks of orange oil puddling in her pepperoni slices, the blobs of cheese stretching over the edge of the crust turning to sublime, crisp-edged goo.

He moves first. Takes the third piece. I take the fourth. We both scarf these down, not wanting her to catch us—as if she won't notice the second half of her pizza is gone, double gone. We finish our bites at the same time. I've got a sore place in my throat now from too big a hunk of crust going down. Daddy hiccups. I smile-laugh. He doesn't smile. He doesn't look at me. He looks at the window, or through it. He pushes the table out of the way to slide himself from the booth and goes to the front to pay.

"Round up your sister," he calls back. "I'll be at the car."

I turn away from him and the door. I take Vivvy's nibbled-on slice and jam it into my mouth, keep chewing chewing chewing until my cheeks ache.

Vivvy comes out of the bathroom.

I look away and gulp, feel my eyes watering.

She rubs circles into both cheeks and she looks pinker, more awake. She didn't see.

I push the table back over to Daddy's side so I can get up. "Come on," I say, trying to shoo her out, away from the table. "Let's go," I tell her. "He's waiting, we have to go."

But she stands at the booth. She reaches for her cup and takes another drink of Pepsi. She stands here sipping so slow on the straw and looking at our three empty pizza pans. And now, even her plate is clean. She turns around with her hands on her hips just like Ma. "Revolting," she says.

•

15

We get into the car and Daddy yawns once, then again. "You girls tired? Enid, you look tired."

"Unh-uh, Daddy."

"I'm good," says Vivvy, bright-eyed.

"I'm gonna dip my hands in the stripy candle wax," I tell Vivvy. "Remember how it stripes? And the petting zoo. I'm doing the petting zoo."

"All those yaks and goats jumped all over me," she says. "They're stupid."

"You weren't feeding them fast enough."

She puffs out her front. "You may not expect manners at the dinner table, but Mom and I do."

She's mad at me. About the pizza.

I put my hand on Daddy's shorts cuff and sort of tug it. He keeps on driving. Staring ahead.

Later on, Vivvy and I have climbed over the seats to lie down in back. When she's asleep, I snitch a saltine from my knapsack and let it turn to mush on my tongue. I take a second one. Vivvy sighs. I hold still, my mouth too dry now to melt the cracker.

"Maybe," says Daddy, starting up again. He has us in the far right lane and we are slowing down. "I'm not sure, but maybe this isn't the smartest thing . . . Francie, well . . . Francie will worry." His fingers drum the wheel. It's getting dark.

"This is so stupid," says Vivvy, her eyes still shut. "This is the stupidest thing ever."

•

Ma stands in the driveway shaking her finger at us when we pull up. Daddy jumps out of the car.

"Completely unacceptable!" she says to him.

"I wanted to surprise them," he says.

"You certainly surprised me."

Before we're out of the car she turns her back and goes into the house, letting the screen door slap shut on Floey, who wants to follow her in for supper. Daddy gets there next and Floey sneaks in before him.

I don't feel like going in, I don't feel like sitting here. Neither one is good but here is where I am, so I fold my arms below the window and stare at nothing and no one on the porch.

Vivvy comes to sit close beside me.

"Raaaaahr!" she screams into my ear and yanks both of my braids.

I grab at her. We're turned together now and shrieking. I throw my bag over the front seat and then I throw myself over the front seat. But Vivvy has my leg and is pulling and digging her nails into my skin so I have to hold on to the seat belt buckle and tug myself over. I'm sweating and hot. My sandal pops off in Vivvy's hands when I drop down into the seat. I turn to see her. So she can't sneak up on me again. My knees scrape on the buckle but I swing the door open and she can't grab me anymore.

I stand on the gravel in one shoe, shouting, "What is wrong with you!" back into the car.

"What is *wrong* with you?" she mimics, shaking her head and grinning at me. She pulls two sections of her ponytail to either side to tighten the band.

I slam the car door shut and run, nearly dumping out all my stuff again from the knapsack, which I guess is upside down and wide open. So I turn it around, pull the ties, and hold on tightly. I have to limp, too, going fast but jumping faster onto my sandal foot when little rocks poke up in between my toes. From out here, the house looks empty.

I wipe my hands on my shirt, wipe at the sweat stinging my eyes and soaking my bangs. I try to feel where my hair is weird, before Ma sees. Two skinny french braids still hang down my back but all my little too-short hairs have popped out. I poke at a big loop standing right at the top of my head, where the braids begin. I tug at the next crossing of the braid, and feel for whether the loop is smaller or gone.

Once on the porch, I see the kitchen light on, so I go through the other door, the one into the eating room. Ma tries to call it the family room but it's where we eat, nothing more. I sit now, leaning up against the inside of this door. When my breathing starts to settle, though, I lean forward on my elbows to see.

Ma gets a glass down and runs the faucet, moving the handle to cold and testing the water with two fingers.

"Sit down with me, please," he says. "Come on—you waited on the dishes until we got back just so you could give me the silent treatment?"

She turns toward the eating room to drink the water, and I wonder if she knows I'm here. If maybe she's glad for the company. She drinks her water. All of it. Letting the faucet run in a way she never would allow us to do. Her face is tight, her lips small. She's back at the water, running her fingers through back and forth, now filling the glass to the very rim and drinking again without spilling. She leans against the counter with her eyes shut, gulping quietly. She finishes the glass and sets it down.

Daddy goes to stand with her or the plates stacked in the sink. "That looks good," he says. "Can I get one?"

"You could have been home by now."

He picks up her glass, says, "I don't want you to have to wash one more thing—especially tonight." He runs his other hand over the edge of each dish in the tallest stack, his lips moving like maybe to count.

Ma swats at his hand. "It's fine," she says. She takes her glass from him, sets it down, and gets down a fresh one. She moves the faucet handle to the middle and fills his glass.

"Can I just say something? I'm not trying to go against your wishes, but I need to tell you—"

"There," she says, "now you're all set." She places the glass on the counter and he picks it right up.

He takes a sip. He sets it back down.

She picks up the glass, runs a sponge over that spot of the counter. She pours out the glass, watching the water go down the drain.

"Francie."

"Tate."

He touches her on the arm and says her name again. She gets to the other doorway, her toes on the dining room carpet.

"I'm sorry," he says. "I'm fucking sorry!" His hands come down *bang, bang* on the counter. *Bang*, and the plates jump.

"Go right ahead." She smiles. "Feel better? Go again?"

She does not move.

He looks at her.

Something touches me from behind and I scream and almost fall on the floor. Vivvy covers my mouth and dangles my sandal in front of me. I don't take it so she puts it in my hand.

She goes right in the kitchen and I reach out to yank her back—Ma will *kill* us for listening this long!—so now I'm in the kitchen right along with her. Ma just goes back to the sink and the dirty dishes, slips on her rubber gloves, and doesn't even turn around.

Vivvy hugs Ma's side, twirls a finger in the dishwater. Even as small as she is, she looks too old to do such a thing.

"I wanted to give them something nice. Make a family. It's summer, for god's sake," he says. "I should have told you but, Francie, you make that difficult . . . never being around . . . never saying yes." He looks only at Ma. "Francie," he says and puts his chin out.

"Girls, upstairs!" she says and we go.

I'm on my bunk and Vivvy's over my head on hers. She leans down to see me, her hair one long horse's tail hanging smooth and shiny.

"She's not being fair to him," I say.

"Is she ever?"

•

I creep downstairs when I see the glow of his headlights finally light our ceiling, hear the gravel popping out from his tires. That sound sets me on edge.

Ma still stands at the sink. She sweeps shattered glass from the counter down into the sink, the palm of her rubber glove stuttering across the counter. Pieces clatter and chink as they touch and hit one another falling to the water. She pulls out the stopper and shakes her arms twice over the draining sink. The yellow gloves are still on.

"Where's your sister?" Her voice startles me.

"Sleeping?" I say, like I'm asking her.

There is a plate of lemon bars on the counter. Ma looks at it. I can smell the XXX sugar she sprinkles overtop and it tickles my nose. I've been smelling it all night, even upstairs, my mouth so wet it feels pickled.

"One," she tells me.

I press my tongue to the roof of my mouth, making a slick of crumbly crust, lemon goop, and sugar there, melting.

I go hug her back, wrap my arms around her and press like she's the cookie and I'm the tongue. She turns to look at me, her face long but peachy, bits of hair come out of the hair combs hang down over her ears.

•

I had a brother once. Older than me. Older than Vivvy. He was six when I was middle-two. Always, just six. With lots of yellow hair like me and fat cheeks like if Daddy's eating a handful of peanuts. He used to carry me around, drag me sort of. He ate rocks out front in the driveway when he was a baby, and sometimes after; there are pictures from when they still thought it was funny—now Ma won't show them to you.

There was something wrong with him. The older he got, the more was wrong. He lived in the hospital for a whole year. Ma's milk was bad or he didn't know he needed it. Daddy says I can ask him anything but all he can say is it wasn't her fault. Shelly just never wanted to eat at first.

That's what makes none of the rest of him make any sense, because even I remember that all he ever wanted was food.

When he came home, he wanted to eat more than anyone. Ma baked cookies and muffins and cakes, Daddy said, until he was big, with a belly, and his wrists creased and his thighs bubbled like a baby's. And the doctors said they had to tell him no.

So one day, Ma said, "Go outside," because Shelly wanted cereal and she said no, and he had to have cereal and so he put his face in Floey's dish and ate the canned stew balls the dog was leaving for later and even the little stewy peas she always nudges into a pile in the corner of her dish, and Ma said, "I hate you," and that's when we went outside.

That day, lots of days, Shelly whined at the back door like a cat but then we went to the driveway. He plopped me down and put chunks of gravel in our hands.

I don't remember this. I only know because of Vivvy who had flu and was looking out the window on that day. She saw everything.

Me in a blue plaid bubble suit so my thighs are mashing right into the rocks. But he is here, wants me here with him. There's a look that comes over his face: some big idea, he'll put the rocks in my hands and just see if he can get me to do anything he wants. And he can. Sun is behind me and lights him up. All goldy. I picture it as almost fall—oak leaf clumps nibbled off the trees down in the yard for all the squirrels out hunting. But I know truly it was March.

"Smell that?" Shelly asks, putting his nose up in the air like a cartoon after some great wafty cloud. He wants it. Doesn't come out with saying so, but says he smells Ma's brownies starting to cool on the countertop. "Uh uh uh uh uh uh uh," he goes and I say no but he starts rocking and he says, "You go," and picks at his knotted shoelaces but they won't come undone so he bends in half and the gray frazzled laces are in his teeth and he's chewing. They don't come back out.

Vivvy's still watching, still watching. I'll have flu next week and Daddy will take me from my crib in the middle of the night to Dr. Gibson.

"Uh uh uh uh uh uh uh," he says, so I wander back inside to load as many brownies as will fit into the gathered sides of my bubble suit. Vivvy says there's no way I can remember but I do.

I go for the brownies and they're here on the metal rack cooling. But I'm too little and spend some time hoisting myself on the stool and grabbing hold of them with my little hands. The door shuts. I feel it in my belly. I turn around to see who is here, who has caught me. But it was someone going not coming.

The rest I know from Vivvy before we stopped talking about it. I do have the memory of sitting on the stool eating two brownies. That I was a piggy and wasn't even there.

Ma was only moving the car down to the street. Not even going somewhere, though she had a satchel and her racket, Vivvy said. Daddy was reading downstairs and ran past me when the sound—which wasn't much of a sound at all—made it into the house. But it wasn't him. Vivvy fell out of the bunk. That was it. There wasn't any screaming. There was no smashing of the car.

No crying out. Nothing. Just the dull *thwunk* upstairs of Vivvy dropping to the floor.

Daddy carried him in, I think, because I do know Ma stayed in her car all morning. All afternoon. Until Dr. Gibson came and put her into bed. Daddy had Shelly wrapped in his sports coat, the sleeves crossed over his front, keeping him warm or maybe just covered. But everyone knew he was gone, and that meant dead. Everyone knew, though the only change was a slim trickle of blood out his left ear. Daddy sat on the living room sofa with Shelly in his arms, and Floey and the cat we had back then came to put their noses in his lap and then lay at his feet. Vivvy rubbed at the purple swelling on her forehead and I rubbed at the nicks and grooves from the gravel where it had pressed into the backs of my legs.

And then Shelly was gone from our house. There was Daddy and Floey and the cat, and Vivvy and me, and even Ma upstairs. And he was gone just like that, like the cat curled on your lap and you don't notice the moment she jumps down but only come to look and see your own legs instead of her fluffy fur. The day blurred.

Ma slept for a couple of days. I remember that. Daddy made sloppy Bisquick pancakes for lunch and supper. We smiled even though it didn't seem right. Vivvy told elephant toenail jokes:

"Why did the elephant hide in the strawberry patch? Because she painted her toenails red today."

I told my one and only joke: "Why was the hippopotamus on the ceiling? Because there was popcorn in the chandelier."

Vivvy's came from a book. Mine came from my head. Daddy laughed hard for hers; on mine, he laughed until there was water coming out of his eyes and he had to blow his nose in his handkerchief.

Once she came out of her bedroom, Ma spent the next few days tearing apart the house and putting it back together. She said it was time for spring-cleaning. When I told her my joke she didn't laugh. Vivvy didn't bother. We pulled all the canned beans and tomatoes off the pantry shelves and Ma decided we'd give away nearly all of them. I begged to keep the mashed potato flakes and butter rice and she said, "Choose."

I put the flakes back on the shelf but that night snuck the butter rice out of the trash sack and slid the box deep down between my bunk and the wall. For years, whenever Vivvy was out and Ma'd been stern with me, I lay in bed and fingered the grains of rice in the box, listening to their rummaging as I tipped it end to end and took out one grain after another to suck on.

Once she finished cleaning, she went through our clothing, sorting for size and wear. She took my favorite blue T-shirt and wouldn't give it back. When I found it in her closet in the sack on its way to the thrift store, I hid it away inside my pillowcase but it was gone again the next day. And so was the sack.

Ma wouldn't look at us. Not at me and Vivvy. Not at Daddy. Not even at the cat or Floey, whom she'd shoo if one or the other came near her lap for a pat.

Then Daddy made her stew recipe in the Crock-Pot along with buttermilk biscuits from mix. She cleared the table after dinner and set the dishes in the sink to get started washing them. He came up behind her. He set his chin on her right shoulder and had his cheek to hers, his hands around her front, his thick fingers moving over her hip bones.

She screamed. Just like the cat some nights chasing neighbor cats through the trees and fences.

So he let go.

Francie

This was my boy. These are my girls. He, that man, is my something.

These are my earlobes. This is my nose. Here are my shoulders. This is my elbow, my ulna, my basilic vein, my round thumb knuckle, my spinning gold ring.

These are my toes, my ankles, my shins. Flip me around for my calves like Thoroughbreds after the derby—I am granite. My knees with their dimples: bone-sucking skin. Here is my waist. My hand. My fingers nearly touch, if I wrap both around my middle. And I do.

Sternum, little-girl breasts with spring pinecone nipples. Here are my hip bones, two fists beneath the covers. When I stand, my thighs leave a triangle, rectangle of light, of air.

Put me in my kitchen. My cupboards. My fridge shelves lined full. Labels straightened, boxes squared. The milk always in half gallons. The eggs always brown. Red-needled scale set back from the counter's edge so little fingers, little careless people, grabby and insatiable, won't disturb its tare. A silver dish atop, removable, washable. Notepad and pen. Pocket calculator, blue keys.

Enid

Today the forsythia bush is moving. Floey is on the other side of the yard, in the blackberries. So is Basey. They're both rooting around over there: Floey taking a few steps and Basey coming up behind to sniff her parts.

I climb our tree and from up high I can see people in the hollow center of the bush. They move sort of herky-jerky. I'd know that blond ponytail anywhere. And I know the other one is Clint. What I don't know is why in the world.

Vivvy's the first to stand up and high-step out of the center of the bush. Her face is as pink as Ma's lipstick. Her hair is hanging down from the rubber band in streaks around her cheeks. She looks right up at me, makes sure I'm paying attention, says, "You're dead, Enid."

I pretend I'm only swinging in the tree. I let my knees take the limb and let my hair fall. I watch Clint come out of the bush, grabbing hold the zipper to his olive-green Scouts shorts with the clip and patch pockets all over them. Dorkus Welby, MD, was what we were calling him last night in our bunks. There'd been a light on in his upstairs and Vivvy could see it through a bare place in the sycamore. I started to climb up into her bunk to see but she pounded my fingers off the rim of the bed.

"Get off," she said. "You're too young." But then she said, "Close your eyes and I'll tell you like you're blind."

I made silent kisses on my knuckles. I wouldn't shut my eyes for her.

"He's reading in the window seat. Lying back on a pillow."

"What's he reading?"

"Enid," she said.

I couldn't see him. Couldn't picture any of it so I did shut my eyes.

"Does he like the book? Can you tell?"

"I think so." She moved closer to the glass full of night. The bed creaked over my head. "He's getting up."

"What's he doing?"

"He went out of the room."

"I bet he went to pee," I said and we laughed but I pulled the sheet up and turned on my side, thinking of Clint and what he reads and what makes him smile.

"He's back!" she said. "Walking around with a toothbrush hanging out of his mouth."

"How uncouth," I said.

"Who do you think you are, Mom?"

"Shut up."

"He's combing his hair," she said. "Setting his part just so."

"No mirror?"

She didn't answer. She was quiet a very long time.

"Now what?" I asked. I opened my eyes.

After a bit she said, "He's gone to bed."

"In his clothes?" I said, because it didn't make sense. "That's it?"

"He already undressed," said Vivvy, and we left it at that last night.

•

Sometimes Shelly is pushing through the porch door or calling after Floey. I can smell him near me—when my eyes are shut and I'm in the sun, swinging in our tree or pushing my bare toes into the mess of dropped crab apples the brown-tailed thrashers turn over for grubs. He smells like sand and like dirt and leaves sitting over roots for more than a year.

•

"What's wrong with you?" Vivvy says tonight, brushing her teeth. She stands behind me so all there is of her in the mirror is her head looking around my shoulder. "Enid," she says, spitting out my name along with the paste suds.

"What do you want?" I say and go to our room because I'm through getting ready for bed.

Vivvy comes in after me and I see her look for Clint's light on, even though she knows he has Scouts campout starting today. So she looks back at me because me is what there is.

"You're a wreck," she says and we've heard that in our house before and we know who's who and we know where it leads. Her hand is on her hip and my fist is over my heart.

"What's there?" she asks and pulls my hand to her, pries open my fist. Inside, she finds one smooth, perfectly triangular drive-way stone.

Tate

Holly took my phenomenology seminar last quarter. How could I not notice her? In the beginning she stopped in before class and after class. She used to ask for help.

"Explain phenomenology to me again, Dr. Sobel?"

Again and again.

"Pull up a chair," I'd say.

One day, she dragged it behind my desk.

3

Enid

Daddy isn't allowed to take us anywhere now so he comes over for dinner.

"I'll clear if you want, Enid."

It's my turn to clear and Vivvy's to wash so she's trying to trick me.

"Nuh-uh," I tell her and start stacking up dishes and silverware. Daddy's and my plates look licked clean like they've already been set down for Floey, who knows not to even fool with begging from either of us; she goes straight to Vivvy's elbow and lies there throughout the entire meal, then trots behind her into the kitchen.

I hear Vivvy sloshing and clanging in the kitchen sink and Floey's tongue pushing her plate around on the linoleum floor, hard up under the lip of the stove drawer, where she always winds up, in the corner.

Tate

I am lying on our bed. Above the covers, of course that goes without saying, and Francie beneath. The brass bed, just a headboard we bought at an auction near her dad's place in Boone—the one I told her was ostentatious, the one she said she loved.

The list of what I would like to ask her is endless but I know better. She has gone to bed in her green tennis skirt and white Izod shirt. She doesn't even play tennis; she runs on the old campus courts—sprints square laps around the base- and sidelines because she thinks runners are fanatics, which is what she wants to be.

Francie lies stiffly on her back now, maybe sleeping.

"I don't know how to find you," I say.

Her eyes flash open once, then shut and open again.

I don't move, like to pretend it was somebody else waking her. She turns her head, looks straight at me. "Stop trying."

I shift my head from its nook here between her arm and the layers of fabric covering her tiny breast, the string of rib bones pushing up through the cobbly cloth of her shirt.

This is not the first time we get exactly nowhere doing this.

"Please go," she says, but I cannot move.

Not from her.

•

I wake alone in the bed so I leave it. On the landing outside our, or rather Francie's, bedroom door, Enid's body is like a puddle. I scoop her up as best I can.

"Sweet," I tell her and she turns in her sleep to suck a little at my shirt. "Love." I kiss her face, which is hot like mine. I put her into her bunk and drag the covers around her. The girls are never more opposite than when sleeping: Vivvy lies as if thrown into bed and tosses about with absolute knowledge of her right to the world; Enid curls into herself like a plateless armadillo.

•

Francie is in the living room reading. The night air is muggy but she has a blanket draped over her lap. She has changed for bed and I wonder if she shut herself in the bathroom or risked undressing in front of me.

"Thursday still okay?"

"Fine," she says. "I'll put something in the oven."

I feel foolish standing in my own living room, a room that now isn't *mine*. But it is: there's the Staiger landscape I got signed for Francie's birthday, and the little glass-and-chrome tables we picked up in Philadelphia at a design festival, and Floey on her side like she's been shot dead.

•

I drive to the apartment, drop my satchel and keys at the door, and head for the kitchen. I open the fridge door and pull a tube of biscuit dough from the shelf. I warm it in my hands. I twist it to pop the side seam and it splits open. I pull the doughy rounds free of one another, layer by layer, and they are gone. In my mouth, just gone.

"Stop this," she says into the phone. And I nearly object, thinking she has called me; but no, I remember my fingers pressed the square buttons.

I just want some quiet on the other end. Not the way she lets out all her air at once in accusation. "Please."

"What do you want from me?"

"Could we just sit here?"

"What is it you want, Tate?" She is walking, pacing.

"You've taken away every last thing," I say. "You stopped my fucking heart."

Vivvy

I have the only photograph. In it, Sheldon looks like the neighbor boy. Like Clint, and I like that. Shell had hair so yellow Mom called him butterhead and butterball and Dad pretended to lick him. In the picture, Shell is in the yard at Grandpa Raymond's, running around tearing at long grass shoots that smell of onions. He gave us this picture when Mom took Enid and me once, down to her dad's house in Boone.

At home I have always had the top bunk and nobody is allowed up here. Mom makes us make our own beds so I slip the picture beneath my pillow when I sleep and beneath the mattress when I am gone.

He was sick. He always needed something more to eat and ate like a dog. Whenever he spoke it was a question: "Juice? Mama, juice? Juice?" And if he found a bit of cracker or dried-up cube of cheese, he hid himself in a corner with it. She watched him constantly, keeping a list of each bite he had in a day. There could be only so many, and she ticked them off on her scratch pad until they were all gone and she turned the dials on the cupboard locks.

He and Enid were always together. I was in the middle. I was so close to him in age—just a year away—but it was always Enid whose hand he held.

And I am the only one who saw it happen. Not even Mom did—because that is just it: she *didn't* see him.

I saw her in the car, before she turned the key and was just sitting there as if waiting for one of us to come get in the car with her. The engine pinged. The taillights turned his hair orange. She looked straight ahead and the car rolled back until it stopped. He fell backward, his legs still folded Indian style.

Sometimes I look at squirrels that are roadkill and put their legs just so and loll their heads over to their right shoulders.

She hit him, waited and then hit him.

Enid

I remember he was strange. Sometimes he couldn't get the spoon to his mouth without leaving a trail of Cheerios from his bowl to his lap.

Ma'd clean closets at the start of a new school year and anything he'd outgrown she boxed for the thrift store. But he screamed and shook and threw books at her when all she wanted was a pair of holey socks and a blue T-shirt that had gone white around the collar from him wearing it all the time. Vivvy and I hid, watching.

"No!" he hollered and slammed his door but the latch never properly closed without locking, so he used to slump against the wall behind the door and kick it shut each time it worked its way back open. *Click, creak, kick.*

"Sheldon," said Ma, calmer than made sense because she'd just been through Vivvy's and my clothes. "I won't have this behavior in my house," she told him. "You hear? This is *my* house. Give me back the shirt."

He kept on with the door. *Click, creak, kick. Click, creak, kick.*

"I won't have this. I won't entertain your notions. I will most certainly not."

Click, creak, kick.

Then she barreled into his door and I could hear it bang into his right knee, but he didn't say a word. She picked him up by one arm and dragged him to the bed.

"Find it," she said. "Give it to me."

He'd hidden it. He was always hiding things.

She left after that. Got in her car and drove somewhere and Daddy made soft spaghetti and we stayed up late asking him to read over and over from the fairy-tale book that was big and broken-spined; but really we were waiting for her.

4

Vivvy

If he likes me, Enid will shove off today.

If he likes me, Mom will take us to the pool.

If he loves me—that is not what I meant. If he likes me, then . . .

These are too hard. Okay: if he likes me, I will find a penny today. And Mom will smile.

Fat chance.

Enid

"Waffles or pancakes?" Ma asks, pulling the Bisquick off her tidy shelf.

Vivvy and I answer at the same time: "Pancakes," she says, to my "Waffles." We look to see what Ma will do, if this'll make her set the box back down and snatch out the Quaker Cream of Wheat.

But she's sort of dancing in her stepping, crossing the floor like she's good and happy and will be awhile. "Both it is," she says and Vivvy and I laugh. She lugs the waffle iron out, the big skillet too, and starts measuring up the batter into two different bowls. "Eggs, girls!" she says. "Mother needs eggs."

I hop to it and grab the milk too, because I know that'll be next.

"Good girl," she tells me.

Vivvy gathers the butter plate and our silverware for the table.

I get syrup and napkins, ask, "Could I have a banana on mine?"

She turns around to face me, touches the bits of my bangs going every whichaway, picking strands off my forehead. She's about to tell me to wash my hair.

"Enid," she says, "I love you," and out the door she goes.

"Why do you have to be so stupid all of the time? Couldn't it just be some of the time?" Vivvy runs the spoon through the eggs, breaking the yolks but not really mixing them. She lifts the spoon and the gloppy strands of egg white hang heavy then drop. She lets the spoon clang back down in the bowl and turns to see me. She smiles.

We can finish the recipe. We've done it a hundred times. I move closer.

"Couldn't it, Enie-Weenie? Couldn't it just be some of the time?" Vivvy hits me fast in the belly.

Vivvy goes straight for the back door without even a word. *Good*, is all I can think. I look on top of the fridge. I let myself read the names on the bags, look for the chips and then pull out the stool to get that bag down. Tostitos. Not as good as potato chips, but we're only allowed potato chips at Daddy's. I'm the only one left but I still take the bag downstairs to eat in the basement where crunching can't be heard—the entire bag. Salt rubs between my wet fingertips. When there is nothing left but the bottom of the bag, I will roll up the sack and take it out to the trash can under the carport and bury it under the bathroom trash, all wadded Kleenex and smashed paper cups.

Vivvy

No one is around so I walk the perimeters of Clint's yard, our side and the two other sides. The air is thickly quiet like being underwater. I head back to our yard but when I get to the pine trees, I stop moving. I stand in their shade, think I will climb one, but still I don't. I simply stand here, one hand on a tree trunk, fingernails caught in the bark where I try to skin the tree.

I go back inside to read but look, instead, out my window and I can't help but think I have seen Clint moving around up there. His trip has been over for four days, five if you count the night he got back—it was not even dark yet—and I haven't seen him or talked to him. Enid said Basey was around here chasing Floey yesterday, but that is it.

Stupid boy.

Even though she smiled today. Even though I have four pennies in my pocket.

Stupid, stupid boy.

Enid

Upstairs, the door slams. I freeze except that I'm holding the Tostitos bag and it's nearly empty but not quite so I roll down the top and stuff the bag under the sofa cushion. But that's no good, she'll sit and hear the crunching. I grab it back out and rush to slip it behind the TV.

Footsteps cross the floor overhead. I stand still in the middle of the room and unroll the bag, slip my hand in, and eat and eat until the chips are all in me. The footsteps don't come back so she's either upstairs or in the living room.

I press the bag slowly against me and roll it up, making the crinkles as soft as I can. I slip it inside my shirt and creep upstairs and out to the trash. There is nighttime garbage instead of bathroom. I lift a bloody Styrofoam meat tray and set the chip bag beneath it.

What if Ma needs me and I'm here in the carport with chip crumbs down my shirt?

I go back in. The house is so quiet. I start pulling everything out on the counters. The muffin mix. More eggs, milk, the grater and hunk of colby. The strips of bacon and pack of sausage links. The jam. Honey. And cinnamon sugar. Lemon curd and chocolate sauce, too. I grab the bowl Ma had for the waffles and her swirly spring whisk, I crack a carton of eggs, being sure to scoop out any bits of shell, and start beating up the batter with one hand and sprinkling salt and pepper in the other bowl of so many broken yolks all smearing together. I grate the cheese over the eggs, careful of my knuckles and thumbnail. I pour in some milk. I beat the eggs. I beat the corn mix, love that scrapey sound of the metal whisk against the clumps of corn and the side of the bowl, love sounding like Ma.

I pour the mix into the muffin tray and know I've forgotten something: the paper cups. So I dump it back into the bowl, wash the tray, and put in the little pink and blue and yellow papers, make an orderly design of alternating colors, and then rescoop the batter. My skillet's hot so in goes a wad of butter and then the eggs. The frying pan's hot too, so in goes a wad of butter and then sausage and bacon that instantly start disappearing like baking up Shrinky Dinks. I pour orange juice and I pour milk. I get fork, knife, and spoon and start loading up the sick tray.

The eggs are going too fast, turning brown on the bottoms though I scrape through them to make fluffs as quick as I can. The bacon's charred solid and the sausage is all foamy where it sits in the black butter. I turn off all the burners because the cornbread's only near done. I go to the pantry shelf, get Ma one of her maroon vitamins, and put that on the tray. Sometimes she likes things underdone so I chance it with the muffins and take them out, put three on her plate where I've made little puddles of jam, honey, lemon curd, and chocolate syrup.

All this I balance on the sick tray. I check the living room but she isn't there, and now I make it up the stairs without spilling. Even though Floey starts out following but pushes through my legs to be first up. Then she sits at the top step, yawping her mouth and giving one big wagging yawn as if she's about to get it all.

I knock and push in the door.

"Good Lord, Enid," she says, unfolding herself on the bed. "What have you done?"

"Made you breakfast," I tell her but I can't look right at her.

"Baby," she says, "what's wrong with you? Don't you know me at all?"

Tate

"Please take her somewhere. Knock some sense into that girl, Tate." This is Francie's call to me Tuesday morning, early. "She absolutely refuses to go to the camp. She has got to get out of this house. And it's prepaid. A commitment's a commitment."

There are times I still think it could be about me, the phone ringing. That she has suddenly remembered what I am to her and she to me.

"What can I do?"

"At the very least get her out of my sight."

"You don't mean that," I say.

"I know it's wrong. I get sick when I look at her. I just get sick."

"Francie."

"I'll think I've got leftover meatloaf and can heat it up the next night," she says. "Then I open the fridge: it's gone! Licked clean, with the foil back over the rim of the loaf pan. Like she thinks I'll believe I wrapped up an empty container."

"I cannot talk to you about this, Francie," I say. "It won't go well for either of us."

She says something, whispers it, but I am not meant to hear and I do not.

"I'm coming to get her," I say.

•

"Come on, chickadee!" I call up to her.

Enid is in her tree. She pretends not to hear me.

I touch the trunk of the tree. "You sad, baby bird?" I ask her but she is silent, lips pursed into a beak. I reach for her, both arms up to catch her like when we are at the pool and she won't jump off the diving board unless I am treading water in the deep end, waiting for her beneath it.

She falls, tumbles into me with squatting bird legs and tucked wings, like a little bird shot down.

•

"There's something wrong with me."

These are the first words Enid says on the ride to my place. She clutches one hand in the other. It's like hiccups or a sneeze or even choking when she cries. A messy, runny-nosed, heaving-ribs cry. I don't know what to do for her, so I sing and whistle and make any kind of noise to distract her from what it feels like not to measure up.

Enid

Daddy gives me his blue nightgown top with the white placket and cuffs. It's long on me. It falls off the shoulders. I like to walk around in it, and feel the sleeves way over my knuckles.

We can't have Floey here at Daddy's. No pets allowed. Once he snuck her in, wapsed up in a sheet like she was big, heavy laundry. But she wriggled and woofed and then there was her tail and a neighbor saw and we smiled but had to turn right back around and take her home.

So I'm in his blue nightgown and thinking of Floey and wondering does she know where I am.

Vivvy

Enid is back home just for the day. We are in the kitchen, the three of us. And Floey, who takes in a deep breath and sighs it out with a moan, stretching all four paws.

"That dog's getting fat," says Mom.

Enid picks up the colored map puzzle she knows by shape not country. Fitting in the pieces, she presses each one into the wooden backing and against the edges of the other pieces.

"She just lies around all day," says Mom.

"She goes under Enid's covers," I say. "She claws at the sheet then turns in a circle like five times before curling up in a ball."

"Good Lord," says Mom, turning from the chopping board and her bell pepper. She turns back and starts chopping again.

Enid dumps the puzzle pieces out onto the kitchen table. "Come on, Floey," she says. Enid pulls up the dog by her collar and heads outside.

"I wonder if she's pregnant," says Mom. "Floey, that is."

"She's just fat," I say.

I go outside too but I don't look up to see if she is there. Instead I walk beneath where her feet are probably dangling down.

There are boxwoods all around the stone path to the back of his house. I like to pull off the leaves and let the cupped form of them cling to the tips of my fingers. Whenever Enid follows me out exploring, that is what I do. We walk the backyards that face into ours. We touch the tree trunks and she picks up speckled leaves from the grass. If there's an overturned potted plant, she turns it right side up.

I go to camp today for two weeks. Horse camp in Harrisonburg and Enid is supposed to come, too, but I know why she won't. In April we went for a weekend trial and she cried on the drive home. Mom came to get us and Enid didn't speak for days. She didn't eat either and that's saying something. First we stopped for tacos. Then at a Waffle House. When Enid didn't want anything there, Ma tried to drag us into a Howard Johnson's for grilled cheeses at the counter. Enid wouldn't even get out of the car. Just sat there holding her sides, sniffling little gobs of snot all over her face, and refusing everything.

She went straight to bed. She stared at the wall, holding herself tightly. "They said I was too big. In my class, my horse sat down when I got on and they said I was too big to ride."

I pressed my face to hers, a sort of kiss. "You are," I said and kept her face there in front of mine even when she pulled hard to get free.

Francie

Before Vivvy and I leave for Harrisonburg, I find myself in his room. There's a desk in here now. My mother's old sewing table and spools of thread, too. I have tried to make plans, make these ridiculous costumes.

I still smell him.

There is a way a boy smells different from the baked sugar of Enid's and even Vivvy's hands and faces. A boy is slightly sour; a boy is like wet sand, like warm rocks.

•

When I was a girl in North Carolina, I used to lie in the field beyond our house in Boone and wish on stars. My daddy called out to me sometimes, and sometimes I pretended not to be there on my back in the long grasses, feeling tufts of clover flowers tucking up into the soft backs of my knees. This was when I was younger—maybe ten, even twelve. Those summers, those springs and falls too, I lay amid the weeds with the crickets and hoppy June bugs, forcing myself to keep still though all I wanted was to scratch.

Mother left because she couldn't make up her mind. That's what Daddy told us, and I never for a minute failed to see that his explanation didn't make sense, given that she never came back.

Tate

I arrive to collect Enid, again, off her mother's stoop just in time to load Vivvy's camp duffel into Francie's car. I hug Vivvy but feel her body twist away. She will be thirteen soon and practices hating everyone and everything.

Enid and I don't talk in the car. We go pick up a flimsy pizza box that sags and slides open under the weight of *large extra cheese, pepperoni, and ground beef.* We considered double extra cheese. Seriously considered it, but I let Francie's voice tell me to act as an example. To make up for the extra stringy pulls of cheese we are scraping off the box lid while driving this pie home, I'll insist on silverware and napkins, and Enid's Coke drunk from a Muppets glass instead of the can.

"Can we have leftovers for breakfast, Daddy?"

She thinks two meals ahead at least. But we finish the entire thing tonight on the sofa, watching *The Dukes of Hazzard,* eating straight from the box, holding over paper towels, slugging back swigs of Coke and Bud straight from the cans.

Vivvy

"In the car, Vivvy," says Mom. "Now."

I somersault off the high branch to make her head explode. The mulch jams up into my sandals and I shake out each shoe, then drop them back onto the ground. Mom pulls a bra strap back onto her shoulder, shaking her head. I don't look behind me, through the pines, but I want to touch everything here. Every bush and every little stone at the edge of her garden. I drag my fingers through the forsythia and take a pinch of leaves with me.

"Vivian," says Mom, "quit being so destructive."

I open up my hand and let the leaves fall. She gets in the car and waits with her eyes shut like it's the end of the world. I walk slower. One foot in front of the other, delicately crushing each one of her border portulaca plants.

5

Enid

Today Daddy and I hit the doughnut shop. The one with the street window that looks in on the squirty dough shooting into rings on a conveyor belt and then flipping into dark, goldy oil. I get chocolate-frosted with peanuts on top. He asks for one filled with Boston cream.

The girl at the counter smiles at me. "You can heat yours up over there," she says.

"I know," I say. "I always heat it up."

"Throw a dozen surprises in a box for us to take home, would you please? For the girls," he says low to her, like I shouldn't hear him, "and some friends. For later."

"Later, huh?" she says, smiling.

It's just us and it's just going to be us, and I want to tell him it's okay by me, because sometimes people don't understand and we both know what's a lot of doughnuts and what's way too many doughnuts.

They're all in the case between us, perfectly ordered in rows of each kind on its own huge yellow tray, labeled: CAKE, SOUR

CREAM, CHOCOLATE-FILLED, BLUEBERRY, GLAZED, and so on. She reaches for a crinkle-paper and selects our doughnuts, taking her time considering the trays and picking the biggest, best ones from each.

"She's in my class, is all," says Daddy to me.

"Okay."

I put my doughnut in the sugar-crusted microwave, turn the timer dial, and flip the toggle switch. It comes alive in a great buzz of light and melts the chocolate right down the sides of my doughnut. The peanuts go sliding, too. I think of all the things I could melt into sticky goo if we had our own microwave oven. Seven seconds, six seconds, five seconds. I spin around and see Daddy talking to her at the counter. His right hand's on the counter between them, he holds the pink box under his left arm. The bell dings and I get my doughnut back out and take it to the window stools where we always sit.

He comes over and sits how he always does. Because his legs are so tall he leans his back against the counter and sticks his legs out into the shop. "What do you want to do today?" he says, picking a flake of glaze off his shirt and popping it onto his tongue.

I shrug my shoulders.

"It's hot for outdoors." We rode our bikes here, because we can. But we're like swamp creatures covered in slime. Even his shirt is wet across his back. He takes a big bite and licks at the middle goop of his doughnut, pops the last bite in his mouth.

"Could we paint something? Could we paint the kitchen?" I've always wanted a red kitchen and in the last few days his kitchen almost seems like mine.

"You think you might like to head up to see those horses?"

He turns sideways to look at me, then looks away again. He laughs so I look, too. He's facing her—that girl behind the counter—and that's what he's been doing all this time. She's watching him so that she doesn't even notice me looking at her. She has red hair and I've always wanted red hair, teeth Ma would call *braces-straight*, tight jeans, and an inch or two, or three, to pinch. She's *curvy*, which is what Ma calls ladies with breasts, and has a long pretty braid that sweeps over her shoulder—thick like rope on a boat. Pretty, too, and she's watching Daddy.

"You ready yet?" he says again, crossing his legs and spinning to face me, like he's trying to hurry me along.

"What's her name?" I ask.

"Who?" He sucks yellow filling from his thumb but looks at the counter. She stands up, turns her back to fiddle with something on the coffee machine. "Holly Lyman."

"I don't like her," I say.

"Clear your mess."

"No."

"What do you mean, 'no'? Clear your trash. I didn't raise you to be lazy and rude."

"I'm not lazy!" I say. I cross my arms and step away from my milk carton and napkins.

"Take your trash *now*, Enid, or I will make you." Daddy goes to the door and dumps his trash there. He stands waiting for me.

I pick up mine and walk to the far THANK YOU trash can. My back is to him. I stand there as long as I can and then I throw away my milk carton and walk back across to the door. "I want to go home," I tell him.

He can be smiley again so fast. "And paint the kitchen?"

"*Home* home."

Vivvy

Mom is too skinny, if I am. Her hip bones jut out of her jeans just above the front pockets. She never eats in front of us. Carrots, okay, and when she chops iceberg lettuce for our sandwiches or tuna fish salad, she snitches leaves and stuffs them in her mouth as if she's Enid with a butter wrapper. She draws a smiley face on the pad of paper next to her food scale where she records the calories: *42 + 17 + 6 = 65*.

•

Here at camp, there is a girl from Missouri who says everyone there is big into floating, which she claims is the Ozarkian name for sitting around in an inner tube. She says the one here in Harrisonburg, the New River, is lame compared to their Salt Fork. She has to be reminded we will not leave shore until her life vest is on and buckled. She rolls her eyes.

Her name is Agatha and her bunk is over mine. "I'm just here because my grandparents live in Lynchburg," she tells me. "I have to come for summers."

"My sister refused," I tell her.

"How old is she?"

"Ten."

"My brother's almost that," says Agatha.

I don't tell her about Sheldon.

In the morning we are back in the stables. I'm assigned Danwick and Agatha is next door with the palomino. I don't like palominos but she says they are the prettiest so she doesn't seem to mind or complain when the horse balks at a jump, and he always does. I curry-comb Danwick, who is a white-and-brown paint. The dried mud clouds up into the air and through the window bars that connect this stall and the next. I comb in deeper, faster circles. Danwick's hide tics around my hands. Agatha does not cough so I keep going until he shifts his weight enough that I'm pushed and held against the wall. I don't know if I can't breathe because of his size or because of his strength.

My eyes sting and shut. But I can't breathe so finally I cough and squeak and push on Danwick's flank. He allows two inches and I breathe again and move out in front of him. I wipe my eyes on my sleeves, catch my breath and heartbeat.

I peek in the palomino's stall. Agatha is bent over at the horse's left front shoulder, with his leg curled and coming through her knees. She cups the hoof in her left hand and holds the tool in her right, and is gingerly picking at the packed dirt in his hoof.

"I can't stand doing this!" she says.

"Why?"

"You have to be so careful around the frogs," she says, pointing the tip of the pick at the center of the hoof even though I was there, too, when the counselors went over grooming. "I'm afraid I'll jab one with the pick and my horse'll bleed to death. It can happen; I saw my aunt's horse go crazy and get shot after having its frog picked."

"Was there blood?" I ask.

"The sawdust clumped like cat litter there was so much," she says.

I lead Danwick more to the middle of his stall, place the saddle pad and saddle. I buckle the girth, wait until he lets out his bloated belly of air, and I cinch it up even tighter. And from the grooming box, I take the hoof pick and slip it in my pocket for no good reason.

I touch my horse's muzzle and know he would never hurt me. That is the kind of horses they have here. I bridle him, click my tongue twice, and lead him out into the sunshine and air.

Francie

With Vivvy at sleepaway horse camp and Enid at Camp Indulgence, I dress for tennis. Breakfast can wait. I walk deep into the yard, all the way to the back property line. To walk along Sheldon's low stone wall there. Deep, to where the grass is left alone and vines bully the weeds. I imagine I'm at the little plot at the back of my daddy's yard.

All this house and yard and wall is mine.

I watch the sun break through the stand of poplars and pine beyond the low stone wall and the netting of kudzu.

It's funny we buried Sheldon back home in Boone. Not we, really. Me.

Tate kept saying, "Forgive yourself," like something he'd read in a book.

Vivvy

"Leave me alone," I tell her, Agatha, the girl from Missouri who wants something.

"We could catch frogs down at the lake. Think we could catch a turtle?"

"That's stupid."

"Beth says there's a snake she saw and it's as long as a fireman's hose."

"Triple stupid."

I am sitting on my bunk, propped against my pillow, which I've folded in half to be able to write a letter. All I have down so far is *Dear* and I don't even know who I'm writing. She is next to me, though I did not move over to make her any room. And I don't know why. It isn't that she is nasty or smells; all the girls like her.

"We could see if Beth's right," says Agatha, picking up one of my braids and twisting it in the air. "Come on, Viv."

I take it back from her.

"She can't be right!"

"I'm writing my sister," I tell her and start drawing in the name with pretty squiggles and curls and buttons. *Dear Enid*, it goes. And then stops.

Some girls ask Agatha to go with them to the lake; Aggie, they call her. No, she says, she has things to do. She hoists herself up into her own bunk and I feel a little bit queasy every time the springs shift over my head.

> Dear ~~Enid~~ Enie-Weenie,
>
> Did you know you can kill a horse just by poking its hoof in the wrong place?
>
> Becky, Corrine, and Tina asked about you. They say "hi."
>
> We put baby powder on their pillowcases and they had dandruff BAD the next morning.

The kitchen ladies tried to pawn off slop as grits again this week. Mom would have thrown it back in their faces. I "dropped" mine on the floor by the corner trash and when they came out they called all of us spoiled brats.

Anyhow.

Has Clint come by? I don't think I mentioned to him that I was going away to camp, so it would make sense if he came around looking for me—anyhow, I just wondered.

Love,

Vivvy

Enid

I'm sitting on the front steps when she pulls up in the Datsun. My bike leans against my feet so I prop it and rock it back and forth because the kickstand snapped off once when I leaned too hard getting on. It's nine in the morning and I don't know where she's been. I rode the entire way from downtown and I can see it in Ma's face that she just can't believe it. I'm sticky-wet and stinky and she'll tell me I need a good bath, that I smell like Floey.

I follow her in.

"Don't talk to me right now, please," she says, crystal calm.

I start to say "okay" but wonder if that counts as talking.

She walks to the back of the house, to the kitchen. I follow but keep my distance, lean a shoulder against the doorway and watch as she starts pulling things from the fridge: jellies and dinner rolls, a plate of pieces of fried chicken, some cheese, the cold butter bin. Floey begins circling. Ma sets two buttered-and-jellied rolls on a plate, a few slices of colby, and two big crunchy drumsticks.

"Here," she says and holds out the plate to me.

I don't want to take it. I want to cry. "Thank you."

Cold fried chicken smells of salt and paprika and crispy, oiled flour. The rolls are just right: spread to their little corners, every bit of them covered in butter so soft it's smeared right into the jelly, one big marbled goo binding the lids to their bottoms. And colby's my favorite, has a little bit of tang to it.

I sit down with my plate and Ma's gone. I stare out the eating room window, at the feeder, the squirrels scampering up and down its post, falling off the domed lid again and again.

She's moving around upstairs. Her room, I think at first. Putting away the wash or something, but then it's shifted to the front of the house, the front corner. His room. Maybe our costumes. She's only finished Floey's wings and cape, not my pirate pants or Vivvy's leg spots or tail. But there's no churning of the sewing machine, no *clip-snip* of the pinking shears. Instead, it's just her footsteps: step, step, step, hold; step, step, step, hold. Back and forth. Once Vivvy said I loved brownies more than Sheldon.

I eat my squishy rolls, pull the crunchy knobs off the chicken, feel cold slabs of cheese begin to melt on my tongue.

Francie

I think of tornado skies. If I'm driving, I imagine the car being swept aside, the passenger door scraping until it catches and then rips against the highway railing. If I'm washing dishes, I think of the plates flying about my head, cracking into my skull—knocking me out. I think of the girls and want them to be carried off into another county, maybe as far as Pulaski, and cradled in a treetop.

I think of him and wonder what it would be like to lose a baby to the wind instead.

Tate

Three weeks into the July class, all is quiet. Vivvy is still at camp. And Enid called earlier to brag that she's sleeping over at the funny young neighbor couple's house on the other side of us. They have a hammer dulcimer and the man lets her pull his full red beard. They want kids, he once said to me—just out of the blue while dragging a sheet of dirty leaves to the curb: "We want kids." And then back he went to his rake and the pile of leaves.

Francie calls me tonight. "I could use a drink," she says. I picture her mouth, her sweet bow lips.

We meet at Ruth's, the only bar in town that is not a college hangout. It's veloured and smells of rotten apples. She is Francie to the hilt: black V-neck sweater tight enough to show that small circle of concavity above her sternum, black skirt and strappy black sandals that twist and fasten around the ankle. She is perched on a stool at the bar and has started without me.

She is smiling. God damn, if that isn't rich.

"I never touch the bottle of Tomatin you left in the basement with the others." She sips Kahlúa and I can smell it on her, am suddenly aware that I have not seen her drink for years. "Where did that come from again?"

"Came with the house."

"Oh right."

"Your sweet tooth is back," I say.

She cuts her eyes at me.

"My class is going all right. There might be one or two in there who can actually get Kant." I motion to the bartender for a draft.

"That's good," she says. "Real good." She touches a finger to the outer corner of her eye. Just a thin finger with her usual short, clean fingernail—nothing particularly alluring about it and, in fact, a bit peculiar because she does not seem to be doing anything with the eye. Just sort of parking her finger there. "Your dog is pregnant."

"How?"

She rests her elbows on the bar now and cradles her chin on the tops of her hands. "When a boy loves a girl . . ."

"Story of your life."

"Hmm," she says.

I smile and sip my beer.

Pieces of hair hang down along her temple and I wonder, given the peachy pink of her cheeks, how long she has been here. Maybe she called from the pay phone in the back.

"So what happened?" I ask.

"When? Oh, this? Well, I don't know. Sometimes I just . . ." She stops here and takes the last centimeter of Kahlúa in her mouth. Then she does something strange: she touches me. My arm. She is facing me and props herself up a bit by taking hold of my wrist.

I forgot the electricity. It's been eons.

She lets go. "I'm making too much of this," she says. "It's nothing. I only wanted to get out of the house."

"Is it Enid?"

"No," she says. "Yes and no, but no."

"There is so much order in that little head of hers."

"*Compunction*," says Francie, correcting me. She replaces her hand, lets it slide down to my knee.

I take a sip. "She's a good girl," I say. "Sometimes I look at the two of them, though, and say to myself, 'There's a whole lot more going on in one than the other.'"

Francie sits up straight on her stool, teeters a second, then gains a stiffness to her spine. "Did you actually just call Vivvy *shallow*?"

I want my arm to reach out to her in the same careless falling way of her hand onto mine. She remains rigid so I feel more like I'm trying to shake her hand. I tell her, "Vivvy is better able to cope. Enid needs extra care. You know that."

"You love her more."

"Maybe I understand her more."

"You *baby* her!" says Francie, her eyes narrowed. "Admit that you do." But she turns away, looking for another drink, perhaps, or someone else to talk to.

She has the right idea, I suppose.

"Well," I say.

Francie spins back around, one hand holding the edge of the bar tight but her eyes sharply sober. "You *indulge* her. Same as you indulge yourself. You give her everything she wants. You feed her—doesn't matter with what—you're constantly feeding her."

"She's hungry," I say.

"I don't mean always with food, though there's certainly more than her share of that."

"I'm not talking about food either," I say.

"She's never met a french fry she didn't need with every bit of her heart," says Francie. "You and she both."

"I mean *love*," I say.

"Oh please!" She waves her arm through the space between us. "I walked here," she says. "Take me home."

I drape my sports coat over her shoulders because even in July Francie gets a chill. She takes my arm. She steps fast then slow. I put her in the car and get her in the front door. The neighbors' lights are out next door where our daughter sleeps. I slip Francie out of her shoes and into the sheets.

"Slide up here by me," she whispers. "Baby." Her eyes are shut. She is in and out of sleep. She rolls onto her back and opens her eyes.

"Darling," she says. Her hands run down her thighs, start hiking up her skirt. She lifts her hips off the mattress to roll down her panties.

I kiss her syrupy mouth. There is not one thing I would rather do, but I move back from the bed, out of reach.

"Pleeease," she moans, lifting up her sweater. "Please."

"I love you, Francie."

"Don't *need* that."

"I love you, so I'm going." I move to the door.

The whole house is pitch black and I stand in its darkness.

"I thought maybe we could try . . ."

"This isn't the way."

She wraps her arm around her side, grabs hold of herself and lets one finger lie in the gully between each rib. "It's like he's caught in my throat," she says. "I'm trying to swallow but I can't get him down. I can't."

"Oh, Francie." My eyes are wet, my face is. I'm afraid to spook this wild horse, but I sit at the edge of the bed and stroke her hair. "Maybe you don't need to," I say.

"You know nothing about me, Tate. Not one thing. Don't start thinking you're on to me." She reaches for the sheets, pulls them up around her hips. "I've gone seven and a half years with this—" She stops and runs her fingers back over her bones, taking an inventory.

I leave, go downstairs. I slam the front door. I start the Plymouth then turn it off and sit a minute. I am sweaty, stuck to the seat, the backs of my knees dripping.

I go back in. Floey sits waiting just inside the door. I stroke her head then run a hand along her side. Her belly is hot, swollen. Her eyes are all pupil. Somewhere in that dog brain she knows what will happen soon and accepts the inevitability of it so much better than we ever will.

I stand still now at the foot of the stairs and listen until I can make out Francie's breathing. I go up and Floey follows. We sleep on the landing just outside the doorway to be sure.

6

Enid

Daddy's here. Ma's here. Vivvy's with the horses. I come in and they're having breakfast together. Sitting there, looking at their bowls—one full and one empty—and then each other. Daddy's left arm is long across the table in her direction. Ma's arms are folded like wings. They're both very still. Even Floey's sacked out on the floor and just sweeps her head upwards to see me standing here, dumb.

Francie

Fat girl. I'm a fat girl today. I count up last night's drinks. I lose track after the third. First it was champagne—just 24 calories in an ounce (she poured me more than an ounce, but I only sipped). Then Tate showed and it was Kahlúa because champagne would have been all wrong. I sipped slower. Then Mother's voice came through, talking to Daddy years ago: "Just have a night sometimes. When you want it, just have it. Quit fussing and give in,

Raymond. Get up and dance!" I believe her, sometimes, and then I am weak.

So I sipped and drank and nodded for another. Another.

Today: nothing. No calories in, just out. Lots and lots of out.

Enid

I go to the forsythia because Vivvy's not here to claim it. From lying on my back, the way the whips shoot out from the center looks like they're stuck in somebody's vase and won't last but a week. Ma says Vivvy's always killing things so I think of this as another one of Vivvy's jelly jars stuffed with pigweed and blueberry blooms—the ones that make Ma's eyes roll because she'd rather sprinkle the wild berries over her yogurt than have Vivvy walk around the house sniffing the tiny flowers for a single afternoon. Sometimes Vivvy sleeps with fireflies nearby her pillow and I can hear their bitsy feet go climbing the glass walls. She says, "Don't be stupid, Enid. That's your head making it up. They're too little to hear—besides, they're all sleeping."

Clint is here. His red sneakers near my hand. He peers into the bush at me. He brushes the whips away from his face, crawls in, and I sit up.

"Where is she?"

"Camp."

"Still?"

"Still."

"I thought she'd be back by now."

"No."

"You got chocolate on your cheek."

I grab at my face, cover it. "I don't have chocolate on me. I *do not.*"

"There," he says, "ha," and swats at my chin.

"Stop it," I say, but my skin is already so hot.

"You're in fifth, right?"

"Yeah, will be."

"I'm gonna kiss you."

"Are not."

But he does, where his finger smeared the chocolate chip meltings.

Vivvy

Camp is nearly through: three more days and two nights. I want to stay. We trade horses every day. Sometimes we double up because the school ponies are too tired for morning ride. All the other girls have labels sewn into their clothes: their names in curly letters and a ballerina or smiley in blue ink so we can keep track of what is ours. Mom forgot so I hide my green T-shirt, the yellow shorts with a flower on each back pocket. I hide them deep in the ends of my duffel, with the hoof pick and a peach ribbon from Agatha's hair.

Tate

I sit near Francie in the eating room and pretend we are ten-years-ago happy, or maybe fifteen.

We hear Enid coming down the stairs. Then we see her.

"You're walking funnily," says Francie. She lays down the style section beside her cereal bowl, which is really just her mother's old sugar bowl—nothing sentimental there; she loves it for its diminutive capacity alone.

Enid stops before us. She tugs at the edge of her shorts.

"Walk," says Francie.

Enid just stares at her.

"Walk," she says again.

Enid looks to me and I'm a coward with a crossword puzzle to figure. She starts moving. Quick scuffle-steps.

"Enid," says Francie.

She keeps moving.

"Enid! You do this deliberately with shoes and I won't have it."

I look up at Francie.

"No," says Enid. "They're fine."

"Show me." Francie scoots her chair back from the table and takes hold of the foot Enid timidly offers up. She tugs at the bit of leather trying to cross Enid's plump ankle. "You really jammed that in there, didn't you? So how many's that since March? Two pairs, three?" She pushes Enid's foot away.

"They're okay," she says.

"Fine then, wear them. Good. I'm glad they're so fine." She takes up her paper again.

Enid comes to sit on my lap and I tuck her beneath my chin. She is a baby. Francie reads the paper, shakes it out at both of us.

"I don't feel good," says Enid, tipping up her face to me. I press my hand around her ear, hold her too tight.

"You need air," says Francie. "*I* need air."

Enid's eyes are doleful; she is working me.

"Not a bad idea," I tell her, gentle but letting her know.

She slips off my lap, walks to the back door—her near-snapping sandals slap her swollen pink feet the whole way. She touches the doorknob but walks by, on to the front of the house instead. Her slow steps move upstairs.

Francie will not look up. She pulls her leg up onto the seat with her, folds it in half alongside her thigh. She rubs the top of her own foot, the skin there as thinly translucent as her water-and-egg-white crêpes.

"You terrify her," I say.

Enid

I'm outside Clint's door, making fake fingernails of the boxwood leaves, seeing can I get a whole hand's worth to stick-put on my fingertips long enough to fan my hand through the air making pretend I'm rich and glamorous with a tiara and rings.

Ma has a ring she'll give me when she dies. I've asked; she's agreed.

I'm about to leave when out comes Clint.

"Isn't she back yet?" he says.

I press the leaf curls to my fingertips, replace the ones that just won't hold with new ones I yank from his bush. Then I'm sorry and set these back into the bush, hoping—though I know it isn't so—that they'll somehow live.

"Come on," he says, and I follow him to the forsythia.

Tate

"I'm her father," I say, my voice restrained, reasonable. Still, I get up and shut my office door. "I should go with you to pick her up from camp."

Francie's nails brush the edges of her telephone, making the call sound like long-distance.

"I'm back in the house, am I not? We are, I mean, we're . . ."

Again, she is silent.

"Is this about her shoes this morning?" I ask.

"Enid asked me just last night."

"Asked what?"

"If we're a 'family.'"

"Like that?"

"Like *that*," she says, the opposite of how I would say it.

"What did you tell her?"

The fingernails stop. There is nothing for a beat, then: "No."

I hang up the goddamned phone.

•

I think of the first time it happened, run it through my mind again and again to see where I could have been firmer and actually stopped Holly. Other times, I run through it for the more obvious reasons.

This was in early April or end of March. She had followed me back to my office after class, and was picking up the picture of the girls and Shell with Francie at Busch Gardens. I didn't like it, them face-to-face, like they were meeting.

"You have a boy, too," she said. "Why haven't we ever talked about him?"

My cheeks flushed. I touched my hairline and pretended not to blot my brow.

"You should go," I said. "Another time, okay?"

"Okay," she said but first she came to me, placed her head against my chest. She tipped her head back and her eyes were shut. I kissed her then. Her fingers slid up my neck, behind my ear. Her lips were soft, full. My hand found her braid, ran the length of it then came up her front to her full breasts, slipped beneath the red camisole and between them.

"Go," I told her. "You have to go."

She pulled her shirt down. Pushed a few stray hairs up into her braid and backed out of my office.

Vivvy

Agatha is sleeping, snoring with her mouth open wide. Enid wrote a postcard: *Please come back. And don't kill a horse.*

Tomorrow is the last day of camp. I wake Agatha by touching her arm. I just lay a hand on it. I hand up her shoes. We go creeping through the bunks, out the door, around the trail up into the woods. I head for the stables but she turns off, pulls me to the lake. She says there will be boys there. She says Jonathan Berry will be there. Okay, we go.

"Nobody is here," I say. "Why is nobody here?"

She plops down on the bank. "We'll wait." There has been no rain the entire two weeks we've been here and a long time before that, too, so the ground is pleated in sharp ridges. "They'll come."

"I have a boyfriend," I tell her.

"Do not."

"Do so."

"How come it's the first you've mentioned him?" she asks.

"You never asked."

"What's his name?"

"Clint."

"You're making it up, Viv." She slaps her calf. Mosquitos have chewed us alive all two weeks. Every time I see her shoo or slap, I scratch at one of my own.

"We kiss," I say.

"French?"

"What else is there, Agatha?" I say. There are scrawny willow roots that run aground beneath us. I yank one up, tear it bit by bit from the ground.

"I had a boyfriend," says Agatha.

"What happened?"

"It was at skating camp last February when I went to Colorado Springs to stay with my other grandparents."

"Did you love him?"

"I don't know. No." She removes the rubber band from my hair, pushes her fingers through my braid to unkink it. "Are you in love, Viv?"

"I might be." I stretch my nightgown over my knees and hug them to my chest. "Maybe."

"You are. You love him."

"Probably," I say. "He definitely loves me."

She hugs me around the middle: arms, knees, and all. Squeezes me. The tip of her nose is cold against my neck. Then wet. Then strange. It is her mouth. Kissing at me. I face her, and then it's like Clint, only this time I am doing it, too.

She pulls me up and we go back the short way past the stables and I go to the stall of the horse I rode today, Singapore. I cup my hand beneath her velveteen muzzle and feel the whiskers poking through such silkiness, the in-out of her wet breathing, the big nostrils and such big, soft eyes.

Agatha comes back from checking on Houdini, seeing if he has made it out again despite the seventh lock bolted onto his stall door.

"He's gonna be gone any minute," she says. "Can't keep *him* in."

I stroke Singapore's neck and feel my hand linger on her short hairs, slide my fingers over the length of muscle that runs shoulder to jaw. Up and down and I watch her ears swivel back my way.

"Tell the truth," says Agatha, standing in the doorway. "You've never kissed before, have you?"

I keep stroking the horse's neck, that muscle up and down.

She laughs and walks out of her stall.

That muscle up and down, up and down, up and down until my fingers come together in a pinch of horsehair and skin and she whinnies and nips the sleeve of my nightgown. I let go and slip back into the bunk beneath Agatha.

Enid

Saturday morning, we get up early to drive to horse camp and be there in time for family breakfast.

"We've got a surprise for her, don't we?" I say to Daddy, taking his hand.

Ma doesn't smile. "Quit running; you'll trip."

She's been a grouse all day. I don't care. Doesn't matter because here we are and I'll be the one to find Vivvy.

"Vivvy!" I call and run to her, hug her, put my face on hers like we do, but she's stiff.

"Enie-Weenie," she says.

"What did I miss? Was it good? Are the horses all here? Any babies? Did they give you real grits? Cheddar and butter and hot milk?"

She sits on her duffel and I plop on down beside her, mess with the new woven floss bracelets going up and down her left wrist.

"Who gave you these?" I ask.

"Nobody."

"Can I have one?" I say. "Can I have this one?" I separate out the best one: green and pink and khaki tan. The one Ma will like the best.

"No," she says and pulls her arm to the side so I can't reach them anymore.

"Can I have any?"

"No."

"Will you make one for me?"

She's looking off to the left at her wrist, then at the empty cars.

"Will you show me how to make one?"

"Don't touch it, Enid," she says.

"Ma let Daddy come," I tell her.

She looks at me. "She did?"

I nod and we go off to find them and get some grits.

•

On the way home, Daddy points Ma into a place off the highway that we don't know, Carolina's Kitchen.

"Will there be french fries?" I ask him.

"Hush," he says.

"It's like your show in here," says Ma. "Like Mel's Diner, isn't it, girls?"

"It's called *Alice*," says Vivvy.

"Don't knee-sit, Enid," Ma says and goes back to looking cross with her menu.

She's not watching so I don't climb down.

"Enid," says Daddy, and so now I sit flat.

Ma breathes in deep once, then lets out all her air.

Daddy gets a pitcher of beer, fried chicken with gravy and mashed potatoes. Vivvy chooses a mushroom-and-cheddar omelet. I have trouble choosing from the cheeseburger and fries, the chicken-fried steak, and the spaghetti and meatballs, so the lady taking the order says she'll come back to me. Then I'm ready: chicken-fried steak, but Ma's got questions: "What cereals do you have?"

"Oatmeal. The oatmeal's real good. Creamy."

"No," says Ma.

"We have granola, too."

"If I order an egg-white omelet with onions and green peppers and a snip of tomato, would that be grilled in something?"

"In a pan, you mean? No, it's done on the grill back there."

"Fat, I mean. Would it be cooked in butter or lard or oil?"

The lady scratches her face right by her ear. "Yes?"

"The water will be fine," says Ma and the lady leaves without remembering to take my order.

The four of us sit here silent. Looking at the car. Ma smooths the pleats in her pants. Daddy pats each pocket for his keys. His face is turned under, long bangs hanging over his eyes. Vivvy yawns and flexes her neck back and forth to each shoulder. Ma starts flexing, too, and before I know it Daddy yawns his big open mouth without excusing himself. He jingles the keys, then slips them back into his front shirt pocket.

"Baby," says the lady, who's come back for me, "you decide yet?"

"Egg-white omelet, onions, mushrooms, tomato," I say.

She glances at Ma, then writes it down and is gone to the kitchen window.

Beneath the table, Vivvy pushes her knuckled fist into my thigh.

7

Tate

I stop by the house midmorning and Francie and I sit on the porch with coffee, the newspaper, and the dog flopped at our feet. The girls are outside, running. Enid chases after Vivvy the best she can, their new sandals slapping the mulch chips beneath the pines. Vivvy stops short and twists Enid's braid until she collapses in the sapped, dry needles.

"Enid's got a sticky butt," says Vivvy, singing it at her sister who still, somehow, smiles. "Enie-Weenie's a big fat sticky butt."

Francie looks up at me. "Well she is," she says.

Francie

When Tate leaves, I wash our cups and set them on the drainer, and I stand in the center of the kitchen, surveying. My count card and calculator are neatly stacked on the scale. I touch them, square up the corners a bit more, this-way, that-way. On the wall above is the calendar, which Enid could have turned to August today if she had remembered today is the first. So I lift the new page and retack them all to the wall.

It's nearly lunchtime but I prolong the feeling of air slowly leaving a balloon, prolong my hunger. I put away the rest of the morning's clean dishes, tidy the glasses in the cupboard, and go back to the calendar. I lift the new page and tack it to the wall. I check the clock again. I do 30 squats at the counter. I look at the clock again.

It's 12:01 PM and so I begin.

Turkey bologna because I feel like splurging today. 70 calories. Light bread, 90 calories; crusts removed, 72 calories. Yellow mustard, 0 calories. Lots of iceberg lettuce, 3 calories. Onion slice, 6 calories. Omit the tomato slice today, save 9 calories. Three rice crackers, 12 calories. Two tablespoons fat-free lemon yogurt, 45 calories. Carrot sticks and hard-boiled egg white with salt and pepper and dill weed sprinkled, 16 and 17 calories, respectively. Dried apple rings, 47 calories. One prune, 12 calories. Half a peanut butter granola bar, 90 calories.

The scale falters. It flashes, blinks off, then jumps back on. I must start over. Take apart the sandwich, scrape off the mustard to get a fair reading on the bread slices.

Everything checks out. The scale's fine. All is accurate, all is well.

Total: 390.

Skinny girl today. Skinny girl.

Vivvy

Mom is always doing this sort of thing to us.

Enid and I are in the basement painting at the double-sided easel and today Mom wants a garden: sunflowers the size of dinner plates, all shades of yellow. I paint mine big and round, tall on its stem, so tall and reaching. More in the background, by the neighboring trees. So much yellow and orange with shiny black centers, all dripping to the grass beneath so that my flowers look planted in their own petals. I step back on my side of the easel, step away and to the side, admiring.

Down the steps she comes, passing me with a tray of red Kool-Aids and graham crackers—just glasses and plates for two, of course. She sets them down on the rusted-out TV tray we never get to use because dinners watching TV are uncouth.

"Oh, Enid!" she says and pats her own cheeks like she is too happy to live. "What a smart-looking table you've painted."

I go around to Enid's side and the painting is hot dogs and frothed pink shakes and buttered eggs. A ham, pineapple-studded, shiny with currant jelly. A tote of biscuits and a bowl of orange beans. "What are those?" I say.

Enid turns around to me, beaming. "Tater Tots."

"Baby," says Mom, pushing fingers through Enid's dirty hair, "well we certainly don't need any of this now, do we?" She turns to replace the glasses and plates and the tray and lifts it all back up to rest against one hip's bone.

Enid forgets to wipe at her smock. She grabs a pleat of Mom's tennis skirt as she starts up the stairs. Now there is a blue fist print on Mom's skirt.

"Look what you've done!" Mom's face is red and flat as my painted sun.

Enid tries to stuff her hands in the smock pockets.

Mom looks at her. "Take it, then! Eat it all," she says and drops the plate of graham crackers to the floor. "We mustn't pretend you aren't a pig!"

Tate

Today begins the final week of class. All last week, I hurried straight to my car afterward and drove to the house. Today, though, I go back to the apartment, where the telephone rings a handful of times. I have been dodging her, she says, bolting at the end of class and not even keeping office hours. She called and called last week and I never picked up.

"I'm sorry," I say. "I've been in and out. We must have missed each other."

"Have we?"

"Of course," I say. "I'm sorry."

The line is quiet.

"No," I say. "That's not it. I'm sorry, Holly. I just, *it* feels—it's as though you were making my girls disappear."

"What?" she says. "I did what?"

"I haven't seen them in a week—or I hadn't. You were here so much, is all. I'm sorry."

"I haven't even seen you for a week."

"The week prior, I mean."

"Are you fucking kidding me, Tate? If there's something else you need or want to do, just say so. Is that it?"

I picture her painted toenails, her thick legs stretched out before her on her bed or folded up beneath her at her window. She is unbraiding her hair for the night.

"Tate?" she says.

"You are so young."

She says nothing.

"I know, I'm a broken record. But think of it from my perspective: you're far closer in age to Vivvy than to me."

"Nineteen is a legal adult. I can vote and—"

"You're my student."

She sighs. "I know."

"I want to see you . . ."

"*But?*"

"No buts," I say. "I want to see you. I just need you to wait."

Vivvy

"Strive to be a better person," Mom tells Enid.

My sister just looks at her, not getting it.

"Don't knee-sit, Enid," she says, even though she has moved on and is looking at me and pointing in the yard. "Get the stone, baby. That one, get it for me."

"So can I go to the birthday party?" I ask.

"Don't *knee*-sit, Enid."

I get her the rock she wants. It is blue like an old car. Flat, heavy blue. Ice-pop blue since Enid mixed the colors. We painted each rock a different color and Mom spread them out in a design for a new front walk like crazy bath tiles winding their way across the lawn. She still has not finished our Halloween costumes, even though she's had a month, and Floey's wings are chewed up because Enid tied them onto Floey and then forgot; Floey slept in the grass beneath the crab apple, mushing up her hair and the wings in the pulpy mess below.

"Enid, *knees.*"

"Get off your knees, Enie-Weenie!" I tell her because I just can't take it one more time. And she does. "Mom?"

Now she can suck in all the good air and let out all the bad. "Tell me again what it is," Mom asks. "Clint's sister's bowling party. What could be wrong with that?" She fits a pink stone—a tiny one—to the blue one. "Pretty, isn't it," she says to herself.

Enid chips and scrapes green paint from one of the rocks. Mom doesn't notice and I won't tell her. "So I can go?"

"Fine, yes. *If* we finish this today."

"Okay," I tell her. "Which one next? This one? That pretty red one? How about the purple?" I think of what to wear.

"Oh, yes!" she says, rubbing her palms together. "This will be a beaut."

Enid is back up on her knees.

"Enid, can't you see how you spread your thighs doing that," says Mom, "making them even wider? You'll train them to flatten out like that forever."

Enid squishes over to the side, until she is flat on the ground.

Mom turns back to the stones and says, "We could make a walkway all the way around the house, for getting to the side faucet and compost." She sucks in her face, hoisting up another stone. Her cheeks tuck inside her mouth.

"That would be so pretty," I say.

"What do you say, Enid?"

"You'll never really do it," she says.

Mom turns to see her. "What a horrible, wicked-girl thing to say to me."

Enid looks up. She does not look scared.

Mom stands and brushes the imprint of grass from her knees. "You can be such a rotten, ugly child, Enid Elspeth." She lets the screen door hit softly behind her, which is far worse than when she lets it slam.

Enid sits up. She chips away more flakes of green. "It's true," she says.

"But why do you have to go and say it?"

"I hate her."

"Now? Finally?"

"I hate you, too."

"You are so stupid," I say and shove her. She flops right over onto her back and I hold up the purple rock over her head. "Want me to do it?"

Enid turns her head away, one ear in the grass, and she is looking at the neighbors' house. I'm not even sitting on her holding down her arms or anything.

"Raaahh!" I yell and throw the stone aside.

"I'm not stupid," she says.

"Original."

"*Kiss my grits.*"

"Oh my god."

"Why can't *I* go?" she whines from the ground.

I look at her. Her limp pigtail braids and fat cheeks. The stretch of lilac shirt across her fat stomach.

"You are so gross, why would anyone want you there?"

"He kissed me."

"Shut up."

Enid gets to one knee and pushes up to her feet. She looks at me hard. "If I'm so gross," she says, "why'd he do that?"

"Who?"

She will not answer me.

"Who?" I say.

Her big cheeks redden. Under her fingernails, rolled green paint swells and festers.

"In the bush."

I shove her hard this time, both hands on her shoulders, and she topples right over. The screen bangs behind me.

8

Enid

At breakfast a few days later, Ma yells, "No more playing house!"
She runs upstairs and slams the door to Shelly's room.

Daddy stands up with his toast plate, though he isn't done.
"She just needs some peace and quiet to work on your costumes."
He sets the plate into the sink.

I listen for if the toast sloshes in water or if it's fine and just
sitting there unharmed.

"How about a sleepover at the apartment tonight?" Daddy
stands in the big doorway between the kitchen and the eating
room. He's dressed for teaching in a plaid short-sleeve collar shirt
and tan pants.

"Whatever," says Vivvy.

I nod and smile enough for both of us but he scratches the
side of his head, fluffing the curls over his ear. He goes home.

Vivvy heads upstairs. I take Daddy's toast and go stand in the
eating room behind the wall. Floey watches me from under the

table. I finish it and lay the plate back down in the sink. I open the bread box and touch the sacks of the English muffins, the sandwich bread, and the oatmeal bread. No one is coming. I could have more.

I go upstairs, step slow and quiet in front of Shelly's door and lean my ear against it.

"Whatever she's doing," calls Vivvy from our room, "it is not sewing costumes."

I leave his doorway. Floey's tags jingle up the stairs and we both get in my bunk. Vivvy is in hers reading.

By late afternoon, none of us has moved—except maybe Daddy because we can't see him. I hear Vivvy turn her pages every few minutes. I whisper things to Floey and rub her ears.

A car door shuts. Floey rolls up to her elbows. Through the space between the wall and bed above me, I see Vivvy cup her hand around her eyes against the window.

"Mom's ready," says Vivvy.

We don't move, though.

She honks the Datsun's horn. *Toot-toot, toot-toot.*

•

At Daddy's apartment, he is in the kitchen washing up. Tonight was flank steak and baked potatoes, green beans too, so Vivvy won't tell Ma about the coconut cake. He made it all. Before she even dropped us off—up-down, up-down, lurching over the parking lot speed bumps—and the cake was fluffed up, like someone's fat kitty. There's half left and all I can do is think of it for breakfast—*please, please, please!*

"Which color do you want?" Vivvy asks me.

She's got three bottles of nail polish she leaves over here at Daddy's and we've been through them a million times—mixing up colors in tiny bowls. There's Field of Poppies, Babydoll Pink, and Orange Dreamsicle.

"Which one are you?" I ask, picking out the lint between my pinkie and fourth toes, getting ready.

Vivvy makes a face, but I've seen her do the very same so I don't quit. She plops down beside me on our turned-out hide-a-bed. "I'm Poppies," she says. "Let me guess. You want to be a Creamsicle?"

"Babydoll," I tell her.

She rolls her eyes.

We sit with our toes in each other's laps and start slicking on the paint. Mine are always smooth and end up looking like magical pixie toes; Vivvy's are like Vienna sausages dunked in raspberry jelly.

"You girls ready for me?" Daddy tickles our knees, so up we fold like a drawbridge and he slides his bare feet right in between us at the head of our bed. His feet are nearly square for being so wide. His toes are thick, their big knuckle-waists curly and blond. The skin across his feet alternates peach and full-out orange in tanned sandal stripes.

"Which color?" she asks him.

"Orange Dreamsicle," I say.

He nods. He smiles big.

Vivvy starts brushing orange on his right foot. I paint on the orange.

The door knocker taps against his door and it spooks us. We've never heard it at Daddy's, except for when we're the ones tapping it. We all get up, hear the hide-a-bed moaning, creaking as Daddy rolls over on his side to the edge. We walk tilted back on our heels to keep the polish from gumming up the rug, or the rug from gumming up our polish.

He checks the peephole, unflexes his toes. He stands with his hand to the shut door, his back to us. "Vivvy, you two go finish. I'll be in soon," he says.

She takes my hand and I'm to go, I understand. But I hear the door and turn back just as someone is poking in her head. And I've seen her before. It's Holly.

They talk on the front step, with the door shut.

Vivvy pulls out the Narnia book we're on, *The Voyage of the Dawn Treader*, the one where Edmund and Lucy venture to the edge of the world, but first to the land where dreams come true. She reads but she keeps looking up to the window behind us— though the blinds are shut and she doesn't dare poke a finger in between to give her a view—and out into the hall where we can see only the slimmest bit of framing to the front door.

"Let's play cards," she says and tosses the book over the side of our bed.

"Spit," I say, because it's the only thing I've half a chance of winning.

She starts divvying out the deck. We make our five piles, our hands, we start and already I'm beating her. But something's off. I look at her smudged toenails.

I touch her big toe, her legs folded in front of her, Indian style. "Sorry I'm no good at it," I say. "You're mad."

"Unh-uh," she says, shaking her head. She looks down at her toes. "Well yeah, but no."

We go on and I win this round, too. Vivvy keeps looking up.

"You're not even playing," I whine.

"I don't want to play," she says and flops down on her back, one knee crossed over the other one so she can pick the extra nail polish off her skin.

I gather the cards, shuffle a bunch, then lay them out before me for solitaire.

"I know that girl," says Vivvy. "I've seen her."

"At Carol Lee's," I tell her. "Holly." I move the cards fast.

"Now who's not really playing?"

I start to gather up the cards but I smear them all around on the blanket.

Vivvy's quiet again, lying on her back, studying the bits of rolled-up polish she's pressing between her fingertips.

"Daddy lied to her," I say. "He bought doughnuts and he said they were for all of us even though you were at camp."

Vivvy pats my head and leaves her hand there, weighing down my bangs. "You're such a baby, Enid."

I kick her once, hard, in the side, and she grabs my foot and twists my ankle.

"Uncle!"

I curl up on my side, don't mean to face the view into the hallway but there's no other way to keep my back to her. I watch that edge of the front door.

If Vivvy wants to go to sleep, she can get up and turn out the lights herself. I'll wait for him.

Tate

"You can't come here." I shut the apartment door behind us.

"I wanted to see you." Her fingers touch the buttons of my shirt.

"You're making this even more difficult."

"For you," she says.

"For me, yes."

She lets go of my shirtfront, takes up her braid instead, playing with the end tuft.

"I don't know what I can say to you," I tell her. "I don't intend to be mean, but my life is already spoken for. I owe a lot of people a lot of things. And not one of those people is you."

"But we've got something; you see that, I know you do. There's a way I get you that she doesn't. I mean, you're here and she's, well, not here. And there's a way you get me—I've never been so . . . known."

I grip her by the shoulders. "What do you want me to do here? Do you want me to have to say things that will make it ugly? You don't know a thing about me. I don't care to know a thing about you. As far as I am concerned there's nothing to know. You're nineteen, right?"

"You shouldn't tell a person she doesn't love you. And you shouldn't say there's nothing in her to love. I didn't think you were like that, Dr. Sobel. I still don't." She sizes me up, toe to head, then, "I think something's happened and you're keeping it from me. You're trying to protect me is what it is."

She grabs me above the elbow and reaches up to kiss my cheek. "It's okay, Tate. I understand."

She walks off. She is capable of a great number of moods. I watch her get in her car, the taillights dimly red behind her.

The girls are asleep and I stand in their doorway trying to get my breathing back under control. Vivvy lies flat on her back.

Enid is curled in a ball, facing me. I kiss her first and she shifts, gripping her knees tightly. But I feel so clumsy here with them, almost drunk against gravity, so I leave the room without saying good night to Vivvy.

I find myself in the kitchen. Standing there like I have come for a specific chore but cannot recall what it is. I open the fridge. Shut it. The freezer. I take out a Breyers half gallon of Neapolitan. Peel back the thin plastic sheet sucked into a couple of quick gullies made in the last few nights, squirt in Hershey's syrup, grab the peanuts and shake them in. There won't be enough left in the jar for another serving so I dump in the rest, too, almost obscuring the ice cream entirely. Drop Cool Whip on top. Three cherries dripping, cutting gruesome paths through the white fluff.

I get a tiny spoon to make me go slower. This was the kids' baby spoon. I take the carton to bed. Turn out the light and peek out the bottom of the curtain to see if any of it was real.

I lay the carton on my stomach for the chill, but it's at a severe disadvantage against my internal furnace: the box goes soft, the contents turn to slurry. I scoop faster. I swallow it all.

Francie

"Cat got your tongues?" The girls are strange this morning. Both of them, and that's unusual. "You didn't have fun?"

Vivvy looks over at me; Enid stares straight ahead at the road.

"Did Daddy say something?"

"I'm sleepy, Mom," says Vivvy and she looks it. Her cheeks dark. Her eyelids heavy. I reach over Enid to stroke Vivvy's hair.

Enid says, "I'm hungry."

"What did you do last night?"

"Nothing," says Vivvy. "Cards and Narnia."

Enid looks at her. "Spit and Narnia."

"Did Daddy play with you?"

"Painted our nails, too," says Enid, moving her feet off the hump in between the footwells, right onto the dashboard for us all to see her pink-nailed glory.

"Gorgeous," I say.

"Daddy's are orange," she says.

Vivvy looks out the window. I make out her left hand grabbing a twist of Enid's thigh and pinching it slowly.

Vivvy

Right after breakfast today, we go out to the tree. Enid straddles the main branch, I hang by my knees. Upside down to me, she looks less lumpy. I touch her ankle. She pulls it away from me. I hold on to her ankle and she relaxes the leg and lets it dangle again.

Clint's dad walks the mower back and forth in long lines that stripe the grass, depending on which direction he has walked. Sometimes he stops to move a stick out of the way or, like now, when Basey sniffs at something right in front of him and won't move out of the way. He picks up the dog and carries him to the tie-out wire they strung across their yard between two trees. He sets down the dog and clips him to it.

Mom walks out the door and Floey comes with her, the dog's belly swinging side to side. Mom waves, calls out something we can't hear but is surely "Tennis," and gets in the car.

I somersault out of the tree.

Enid turns this way. I brush off the backs of my knees and motion to her to come on.

Inside, I get the scale, a stack of note cards, and Mom's blue marker and calculator. Enid comes in as I'm setting up the pass-through window. "Sit anywhere you like, hon," I say. I smack my jaw as if chewing gum.

Enid claps her hands together twice. "*Alice!*" she screams.

"No, hon, name's Flo."

She straightens up her posture, tugs her T-shirt down, and takes a seat at the eating table. I tie on Mom's special hostess apron around my waist. From the pantry, I get a bag clip and twist my hair up on top of my head. I stick Mom's marker into my hair, slip a handful of her calorie-tallying cards into the apron's pocket, and go to Enid.

"Have you decided?"

Enid holds her hands out in front of her like she is reading a menu. "Yes, please. I'll have the tuna melt on rye."

I pluck the marker from my hair and start writing. "Tuna melt on rye, okay. What would you like to drink?"

"A tuna melt," says Enid, "but hold the tuna."

"Hold the tuna?" I ask. "So you want a melt on rye."

"Yes, that's right. A melt on rye, with fries and a Coke."

"All righty."

I go back to the pass-through window and lean on the counter. "Mel, you're gonna love this one." I smack my invisible gum two times. "I've got a tuna melt on rye—hold the tuna—with fries."

Enid runs over to the kitchen side of the window. She lowers her voice to be Mel. "You what?" she says. "What's a melt on rye? What is that? I'm supposed to know what that is? I'll tell you what that is, it's air! The hot air between two pieces of bread. Here," she says, taking a plate down from the cupboard, "you give her that hot air right here on this plate." She uses a spatula to pretend to slide hot air on the plate, then shoves the plate across the counter through the pass-through at me.

"What about the fries?" I say.

Enid tries not to giggle.

I lift the plate up above my shoulder like waiters do and give Enid a chance to get back to the table.

"Here you go," I say. "Tuna melt on rye, hold the tuna."

"My turn now," she says, standing up.

I sit down. Enid goes back to the kitchen to compose herself and get her supplies.

"Miss?" I say. "Miss, I'm ready. I would like to order."

Enid looks at me, eyes big with worry.

I cover my mouth to be Mel's voice coming from the grill, where he's flipping burgers or frying eggs. "Hey Dinghy, are you going to take her order or do you need me to dock your pay until you remember how to do your job again?"

"Don't do 'Dinghy,' Vivvy. You know that."

I give a little shrug, pretend to study the invisible menu in my hands.

"Yes? What'll it be?" Enid turns over an old tally card in her hand.

"Oh hello!" I say, pressing a flat hand where it goes for Pledge of Allegiance. "You snuck up on me."

"Sorry."

"Do you have any specials?"

"Oh my god, Vivvy! Don't keep asking that every time you're the diner."

"She wants to know. She's very meticulous."

Enid looks at the pad and doodles something that, at first, looks like cursive writing but is really just nonsense. She keeps going and doesn't lift the pen from the card until she is done. She smiles to herself.

"You don't even know what *meticulous* means, do you?"

"We have Philly steak sandwich. We have french fries or onion rings. We have pie."

"What kind of pie?"

"Strawberry," Enid says.

"I cannot have pie."

"Then why did you ask?"

"Today, I will order a salad, no dressing, does that come with cheese? Oh god no, no cheese. What else is on there?"

"Um," says Enid, "lettuce, tomatoes, nuts, dressing, and croutons."

"I don't want any of that," I say. "Just the lettuce. In a bowl. A water. And do these shorts make my butt look big?"

"Vivvy! Play right."

"Vera!" I yell as gruffly as I can.

"I'm Alice, Vivvy! I'm not Vera!" Enid drops her order cards on the table and shakes her head like Floey after being out in the rain. One barrette dangles from her hair.

I reach out fast and grab it.

"Ow!" She holds her ear, pressing against it. "Why did you do that?"

"It was going to fall. Geez, calm down."

A few cards went on the floor so Enid bends over to get them. On the insides of her thighs, her skin is puffy and pink with red scratches from the tree.

"You can be Alice," I tell her. "Or you know what? You can even be Flo."

She lays Mom's calorie counts on the table in front of me as if they are the salad I ordered. "Vivvy," she says, "*kiss my grits.*"

9

Tate

She slips in and shuts the door.

Holly is seething. She is actually spitting. "Lay it on me, Dr. Sobel. Tell me I am irrational!"

She picks up a stack of the summer class's blue books, their covers turned back beneath. She begins to go through them. She shuffles. She drops some. "Here, here we go," she says and throws down the rest while reading random marginalia back to me. "No justifying argument provided . . . Where are your counterarguments? . . . Multiple tautologies!"

She looks up, those bottle-glass eyes piercing. "No, Dr. Sobel, I don't think I'm quite swift enough. Please explain to dumb little me how it is that the existence of a girl who is me isn't proof enough of your cock and your heart wanting the same thing."

Holly bends to the floor, straightens the exam books she scattered, and stands again. I cannot move from this spot of rug. She gives a slow and pained smile. She opens my office door and turns back. "I'm sorry," she says, and is gone.

•

I get a call the next day. It's Francie. I start to say it has only ever been her, but she, too, has a speech.

"I need you to come stay with the girls. Or take them to your place, but it's really better if they're in their real home. And there's the dog, too. School starts in two days and the girls will want their own—"

"Is everything all right? Where are you going?"

"Can you do this? Yes or no."

"Francie, where are you going?"

I can hear her mouth purse. Her lips push side to side; she's not so much deciding whether to answer as waiting a beat. "Please just say yes or no."

"Francine."

Nothing.

So I say it: "Yes."

"Anytime this afternoon. They'll be at Clint's playing. Or in the yard. They'll be in the vicinity."

"Okay," I say. "How long do you have to go?"

"Long enough."

"I really think, Francie, I really think we should try again. One family."

"For god's sake."

Vivvy

Holly. The girl who came to Dad's, Enid called her Holly. Mom is gone, has been gone all day. Off to tennis, no doubt, which is not real tennis at all, just a satchel and short Kelly green skirt, the pink balls bouncing from the backs of her ankle socks and no racket.

She always calls, "Tennis, tennis, I'm off to tennis," and pulls the Datsun down the driveway every single day. All I can think is that if she were ever truly sorry about Shell, she would have stopped parking in the driveway a long time ago.

We are in our tree.

Because it has a view and Clint's light is on.

After breakfast, Mom was asking too many questions. So up we shimmied, Enid first swiping a square of baking chocolate off the counter and refusing to spit it out when Mom told her it was bitter. But, out of her sight, Enid keeps clearing her throat and scraping her finger across her tongue.

"Do you know how disgusting that is?" I say.

"I can't help it," she says, coughing up more thick brown mess, all juicy-wet.

"How stupid are you?"

"I thought it was chocolate," she says. "Why would anyone make a thing so awful look like chocolate?" She still holds on to a corner of that square. She looks at it. I can see she is actually considering trying another taste.

Finally, she drops the hunk, lets it fall to the needles below. Floey in the spotty shade of the big sycamore will not be bothered.

We are both quiet. Enid watches our house and I look next door. His light's out.

"What I want to know," says Enid, swinging sideways from her knees but refusing to let go with her right arm—she looks like a stiff flag, a pennant at a Hokies game. In goes a deep breath, in goes air and more air. Her belly filling big, bigger against her waistband. So much air. "I want to know how come it is they think we don't understand exactly what's going on here."

"You are so weird, Enid." I pull her upside-down braid until she looks scared enough to fall.

Enid

The big Plymouth Fury pulls up. Daddy sits in the sunshine a second, then swings out the big door and hoists to his feet.

We stay still because we're not speaking to each other. We're up so high he can't see us and he's got an armful of papers and his satchel but he reaches back into the car and comes out with a duffel bag and goes right in.

"This means something," says Vivvy, so maybe we are talking again.

Yes, yes it does: today will be good.

•

Tomorrow will be the last day before school, so Vivvy and I dig out our leotards from dance classes last January to practice being magicians.

"I bet yours won't even fit," she says. "Better try it on first."

"You're just jealous," I say. "You want my pretty turquoise one."

"Anything but a black leotard is for babies," she says.

"You are."

"Good one, dummy."

She steps out of her shorts, drags her blue T-shirt overhead. I start undressing. Gather up my ballet tights that are the color of Pepto-Bismol. I turn my back to her, step into the scratchy turquoise suit and pull it up slowly. Ma doesn't believe in underwear beneath tights and when Vivvy turns away from the mirror on the back of our door to pick up her own seashell-pink tights, I see it: the start of sunshine hairs coming in between her legs in a V.

Vivvy's taller than when we went to Mrs. Cavallo's every Tuesday and Thursday for lessons after school. Her leotard pulls up her bum, stretches in tent draping from the center of her cheeks up to each shoulder. Her sleeves are the same, though: still too long for her. I am bigger. Bigger than last winter. Bigger than the spring. I am bulging out everywhere, but the leotard is on; I'm in it.

My undies bunch and I work hard at stuffing them and smoothing them up into the leg-hole puckers of my leotard. I can't stand the girls who don't notice their undies are lumping out. Vivvy unfolds a pink wrap skirt with a velvet tie, holds it out behind her and then pulls it this way, then that. She smooths it against her flat stomach and nothing hips and looks like all the older girls who line up along the practice barre outside the dance studio, stretching and waiting their turn.

I sit on the edge of my bunk watching Vivvy. She's practically grown, a college girl or something, the way she pulls her hair back into a ponytail then twists it up into a bun and pins it once, twice, again. Her neck is pretty. She flattens her palm on the bun and when it springs back secure, she takes a skinny black ribbon and ties it around in a little bow at the top.

My belly aches. The sides of my face twitch. I want to wear my ballet slippers but Vivvy laughs at me. I do even though the elastics cut into the tops of my feet. And then she wears hers anyway.

We walk through the pines into Clint's yard.

"You are the assistant," she says.

"You too," I point out.

"You're the assistant's assistant."

Vivvy pushes in the front door and we go up the stairs to the playroom, where he's got a desk draped in yellow and red bath towels.

Clint arranges cups of water and little bottles of powder and bright colored liquids in neat rows. I smile because he's setting all their labels in one direction, nice and straight. He stands back to check on them and then adjusts one that's a hair off. I saw it too; *glaring*, Ma would say. I reach for Vivvy's hand. She shakes me off.

"What took you so long?" he says to her.

"I'm not late," she tells him, like I'm not even here.

He holds up his hands, checking one last time. Now he looks up. "That's what you're wearing?"

"Enid wanted to; it was her idea." My sister is a liar.

"Well here's the thing. I'll do the tricks and you just hand me stuff," he says, then looks over to me. "The both of you."

"We know," she says.

"You can count, right?" he says to me, poking a finger into my arm.

"What do you think, I wear diapers?" I check for a bruise.

"Wear diapers," he repeats, folding in half like he's laughing but not really. "Good one. Now count up all these playing cards." He must have three or four decks on the red half of the desk. "It's crucial—*crucial!*—that they're all there."

"Okay," I say, happy for a job but looking up to see if he gives Vivvy something better to do.

Clint walks off to the bathroom and turns around to make sure I'm counting and Vivvy follows after him. The door shuts. I count. I lose track thinking about Floey, who followed us over, and Basey out in the yard. She barks and then he howls. Then it's quiet until a few minutes more when she barks and he howls. I start over. I make piles of ten once it's clear that's about all my head can hold before I lose concentration and start thinking about what they're doing in the bathroom. I've got my tens in perfect rows upward and sideways and just have a few more to go when out comes Clint.

"You aren't even done yet?"

Vivvy comes out. Her cheeks are pink.

"Come on," he says, "we've got tricks to do."

Clint practices his card tricks on us and they don't come out right. He accuses me of miscounting the decks and then moves on to the cups of water. He slips a tablet into one of the cups, then drops red food dye into the water. One glass turns the water red, the other turns it purple. "Magic!" he says and waves his arm like he's selling a car. Vivvy practices fanning one hand through the air and wiggling her hips for the imaginary crowd. Like Ma, sometimes. I stand on the other side of the desk and shift my weight side to side but don't guess it looks like Vivvy's wiggle-waggles.

He has a few more tricks. One of the card tricks does come out right but that's with Vivvy choosing her card and when he asks was hers the nine of clubs she says, "How did you know?"

Vivvy and I go down the steps and out the back door, through the pines and up into our tree. She still has on her wrap skirt and

I'm worrying about it getting sappy or snagged because maybe soon she'll hand-me-down it and I can try wrapping it around me, like an apron is all.

"That wasn't your card, was it?"

"Shut up," she says.

"Knew it." I stuff a bit of undies back inside my leotard. I rub around on our branch just to let the bark grip hold of my seat and thighs, to show Ma and make my needing new ballet clothes about something other than her rolling her eyes and saying *Jesus, Enid.*

"You wanna play dress-up?" I ask.

"No." She sits on our branch, lets go, then just slips to hang from her knees.

"We could play wild bears," I say. We're already in the tree.

She doesn't answer. I look back over to the window into Clint's playroom. The sun's too bright to see inside but I stare at it anyway, picturing him swishing his arm back and forth again, though the tricks were all duds.

"What were you doing in the bathroom?" I say. "Before."

"Leave me alone." Vivvy drops from the tree, lands right on her pointy-pink ballerina tippy-toes. She doesn't leave though, just squats in the dirt like she's lost something.

Vivvy

"How about pizza tonight?" says Dad at the foot of the pine.

Enid hoots and hollers.

He puts his hand on my head where I kneel, picking through the mulch, looking for pink quartz pebbles. So far just one. I slip it in my shorts pocket and I don't know why but I think Enid is watching me too closely, so I face the neighbor's shed that stands next to our carport.

"Real crust or *pita* pizza?" says Enid.

He cocks his head. "Do you mean to tell me you don't sit up at night dreaming of my delectable creations? My delicious, crispy, yummy, perfectly good pita pizzas? Is that what you're saying, you Looney Tune?"

"I sit up nights for Tater Tots," says Enid.

"You sit up nights for a whole lot more than Tater Tots," I call up into the tree.

•

"Sugarbell," he says to me.

Enid is getting cleaned up upstairs and Dad is weird. He will look at me but if I look back at him he starts fussing with the pizza box. He lifts the lid and shuts it, lifts it and shuts it, letting out puffs of steam.

"Did your ma say anything to you?"

He looks like Clint asking can he touch this, can he touch that. Scared of me. Scared I might say yes.

"About where she headed."

"Tennis," I say. I take a fork and knife from the drawer for me—Dad and Enid will use their hands. I walk away to the table.

"Anything else?"

"No."

"Well," he says. He picks up the box and their extra cheese has the bottom of it so greased and heavy that he can get it to the table in one piece only by burning his palms to support the underneath. "Everything is fine, you know. We will have a fine time."

"Yeah," I say.

"Nothing to it."

"Quit being weird," I tell him.

"Right-o, Captain."

"You better not be eating my extra cheese!" hollers Enid, running down the stairs. She is in regular clothes now, too, but when she sits down next to me her shorts ride up. Red grooves the leotard elastics made circle her thighs.

"Don't knee-sit," I tell her because someone should.

Tate

I rinse the dishes and load them into the dishwasher, wipe down the table, and leave Floey in charge of the floor. I open the fridge to see what there is for tomorrow's breakfast and supper if she's not back by then. Surely she will be.

I go out to the trash can and bury the pizza box beneath layers of unopened newspapers. Upstairs, I wash up at the mirror where Francie used to stand and ask me, "Do I look different?" What she wanted me to say always was, *Yes, very different*, but I only ever said, "In what way?" I wash my face, hang the cloth on the bar next to hers. I hold it to my nose and smell the sour dankness of her cleanser. Unpleasant but warmly familiar.

Without Francie in the bed to preoccupy my brain, I realize the mattress is all wrong. Or I'm all wrong in this bed anymore. I smell her pillow, pass my leg across her side of the bed.

The lights are out and I'm halfway asleep.

The door pushes in.

A little hand to mine.

"Daddy," Enid says, and I tug her up into the bed, open the covers for her to crawl in.

Enid

Today is the day, but we don't do the magic show. We don't sell the tickets Vivvy and I markered on the back of Ma's basting tape. Today is the last day of our summer and we are sulking instead.

I put Floey in her fairy wings and she and I begin running bush to tree.

Vivvy's inside, upstairs, listening to *Grease*, the slow ones where Danny and Sandy sing alone into the night. She said, "Go play, Enid," when I asked her again about the bathroom at Clint's. "You wouldn't understand," she said and just shook her head like I'm dumb on purpose.

I lie on my back in the grass, look up into the white sycamore, and when Floey comes over to sniff my face and stick her wet nose in my ear, I tug her down on me. She smells good. Like skin and fur and forsythia blooms.

Francie

I am here. I'm in the grass. I don't speak to him. But I lie here just the same.

I'm back in my old yard in Boone. The back corner where the grass should be a different green, a sort of patch over the hole.

But no, it's the same and I worry the next time I come, I won't know the exact perimeter; I won't know where Sheldon is at all.

My hands touch the grass that has become him. Sheldon had a rabbit die of frost once because we didn't know any better and thought two wool thermals draped over the outdoor hutch should be enough in winter. He walked in the house that morning cradling a bloody-nosed thing in his arms; frozen stiff as it was, I first thought he'd covered one of Vivvy's baby dolls in dryer lint. Tate wanted to bury it for him but Sheldon refused and walked around the house, dressed, and ate his allotted lunch, all with the animal thawing out and going damp, the fur sticking to his skin's moist heat in the crook of his elbow.

I screamed at him. I hollered: "Get that thing out of the house!" I even threw something at Sheldon when he appeared at the table for supper still holding it.

I lie on my side here, I lie on my belly. The grass is full of heat. Daddy doesn't mow as often as he should so it's long enough to swallow my ankles and wrists, even come up to my ears. How can I shepherd Sheldon through the world when I'm not even certain where he is? He's invisible. He's gone. He was a fussy, obstinate, compulsive boy. And now he's just gone and I can't even walk around with him in the crook of my arm, drag his body to the table for supper, dangle his legs over my lap while I read the paper.

I cannot pretend at all.

He gave up his rabbit at bedtime. Tate said, "I'll make you a double-scoop ice cream cone," and then snuck it to him upstairs. That was as deep as Sheldon's love ever went. Tate held Sheldon and told him, "Bunny knows you loved him." Sheldon was tired, his left arm must have been numb through the elbow. He slipped into sleep and finally let go.

Tate

I knock on Vivvy's door and hear her stop the record by dragging the needle up. "Sweet?" I say.

She does not answer. Instead she comes to the door, opens it into her body, and stands there keeping me out.

"Whatcha doing?"

"Nothing," she says, then points her chin back over her shoulder toward the record player.

"Can I ask you something?"

She nods.

"Do you know why that girl came to see me, came to the apartment?"

"Holly?"

I nod.

"I don't know." She shrugs.

"She'll be in one of my classes this fall. You see? She had a question about a paper she'll have to write."

Vivvy looks up at me. Her eyes squint and her forehead creases.

"There's so much about being a grown-up. There's just so much."

"Okay," she says and that is that.

"You ready for school tomorrow?"

"She bought us stuff."

"Good. That's good," I say. "Have you been missing your friends?"

"Sure. I don't know. Not really," she says, then, "Her name is Holly, right?"

"Did your mom tell you that?"

"Enid."

"Right. Of course."

10

Enid

By the time the bus picks us up at the corner of Preston and Eakin, there's only one more stop. Just one to get through and then we're on our way. Clint and Vivvy sit on the wisteria vine that's there.

"Who do you have this year?" Clint asks her. "I got Ramsey."

"Nelson," says Vivvy.

I have Mrs. Moss.

"Ha-ha," says Clint to Vivvy.

"I know. Everyone cool got Miss Ramsey." Vivvy cinches her backpack's strap. She has it on her left shoulder and Clint has his on his right. She releases the buckle and makes the strap go loose and long again.

I loosen my strap, too.

When we see the yellow edge of the bus swing around its turn, Clint does a weirdo voice, saying, "And away we go!"

"Who says that?" asks Vivvy.

"My dad. It's from some old-time show."

The rest of the bus grows in the distance. I move a step closer to the vine. Vivvy and Clint haven't budged and they don't. Not yet. Not until Mrs. Healey pulls up to us. All the side windows are dewy on the inside because the school got some new buses with AC and we got lucky. The brakes *whoosh*, the door folds in. Already I see the blurry bus boys moving around in back.

Clint gets on first. Vivvy hops up next. Now I tug myself up the big steps. I follow their backpacks down the aisle. Mrs. Healey shuts the door and doesn't wait for us to sit but Clint goes all the way back now and so does Vivvy. I hear their names over and over again in happy greetings. They sit on opposite sides of the aisle in the second-to-last seats.

I'm looking for where to sit. I need to sit. I'm not allowed back there but too far up front and they'll see me as still a baby even though I'm in fifth grade now. But too far back and they will see *me*.

The bus takes a big turn. I start to fall on someone I don't recognize. She looks up at me, like to see if she needs to move over. She doesn't move but the seat opposite is empty so I sit here. Smack-dab in the middle of nowhere.

"E-N-I-D, E-N-I-D I-S F-A-T!" chant two boys in the back.

One second the bus is full of chatter, laughter, and the *whoosh* and *rhunge* of stopping and starting the engine. The next, there is nothing but the Mickey Mouse song set to new words sung out loud and clear by the bus boys.

"Give it a rest, Rob." It's Vivvy.

I peek around the seat to see Vivvy flicking one of the bus boys' hands away from her chest.

"Give it a rest," she says again.

They keep on singing.

Vivvy laughs like a twittery bird. The song is over.

We pull up to Margaret Beeks Elementary and I'm off the bus fast as can be. I walk the big kids' hall now, fifth and sixth.

"Enie!" calls Vivvy from so far behind me. "Enid, your lunch!"

My hand still holds my side, the other keeps my backpack in place on my shoulder. I forgot my lunch. And it's so far behind me now, way too far to even look or go back. I keep on going down the hall.

Tate

Francie wanted to be a chef. She wore the white shirt with all the buttons. Even at home. Even in her apartment, without even a kitchen—well, maybe two burners and a toaster oven. I have seen one picture.

The shirt was pristine. If any meal got made, its production was immaculate. Literally. The shirt's pressing and starch, both original. She pinned her hair over her ears back then, too, but different. Austerely.

Once in the middle of the night, or maybe early morning, she twisted inside my arms, the skin of her bare breasts tugging against mine, her forehead tucked beneath my chin.

"You don't know this about me," she said. "I'm not to be trusted."

I was in and out of sleep. We were engaged then, not yet married. I woke myself up.

"I can't be trusted," she said again.

"Baby," I said, like it was anything of comfort.

"On the pastry unit. There was so much butter left. I was pickup one night. I and another girl, but she had a boyfriend who waited in the lot and I told her the most wicked thing that night. I said that I'd seen him flirting with some of the women working cheese when they went out front to smoke. So she left me alone. It never would have happened in day class, you know. They're more serious, more committed."

I think maybe I laughed here and she stopped a moment, deciding whether to go on.

"Well," she said, "plus I'm better in the day. Stronger."

I ran my palm up underneath her breasts. Felt the entire width of her rib cage in the span of my hand.

"Nighttime comes around me and I don't quite own myself," she whispered. "I couldn't stop. And all our profiteroles were in the school café's walk-in freezer. You don't know me, Tate Sobel."

She could be dramatic. I did know that already so I kissed her cheek.

I did not understand what she was saying. That she was telling me everything.

"I was alone with the pastries and sticks of butter," said Francie. "And then they were gone."

Vivvy

I am being kissed. Behind the cafeteria, where the extra teachers—subs and coaches and volunteer library mothers—park their cars. His chin is pointy and poking my jawbone. His lips mush against me. He smells of pizza sauce.

It is not Clint.

I'm not sure how I got here. It was lunch and I was sitting with my friend Sarah. Someone tossed a folded-up bit of green paper onto my lunch tray and I thought it was just trash and wouldn't have even touched it but then the boys said it was a love letter and hooted at me. So I uncrimped it, pressed it smooth against the table, and Sarah and I shielded it from them and we read: *Meet me at the dumpsters.*

No name. No time. They oohed and aahed not even knowing one word of it, so Sarah and I cleared our trays and went outside to jump rope.

"You have to go," she told me. "Don't you want to know who sent it?"

I shrugged. I've never seen Clint's handwriting. I looked for him, studied all the boys outside to spot his friends and they were alone. I went.

•

"Turn your head."

That's all this boy says now. We are standing and I do turn it just a little for him, which makes me think of being at the dentist when he wants a better angle to get at some new cavity way at the back.

He is just my height, which means short. I know who he is, though we've never been in the same class. He is in Mrs. Rider's sixth grade and so there's music together and lunch, of course. Evan Greeley. A popular boy. Best friends with Travis and Andy.

"What do you think of Travis?" he asks me, stuffing his hands where they've been this whole time—deeper in the pockets of his tan corduroys.

"Travis?" I say, not understanding.

"He says you're kind of cute."

"I don't know. I guess he's kind of cute, too."

"Want me to tell him?"

"Okay."

"Bye." And he's gone. Back around the corner of the building.

Sarah comes to find me. "Evan Greeley?" she says. "We don't even know him."

"I guess that doesn't matter."

"What did he want? You're all red."

"I am?"

"Did you do it?" she asks.

"What?"

"Whatever—did you?"

"My neck's sore."

She grabs my hands and pulls us both down to sit on the curb. "What was it like?" She leans so far forward my cheeks go hot.

"Sort of gross."

"Oh," she says, and sits back, looking off to the mom cars.

We go back to the jump ropes and take both from the younger girls. Enid is here and I give her a little smile anyhow. "Come on," I say to her. "Jump."

Sarah and I swing the ropes double Dutch as slow as we can and Enid jumps facing me, then turns to face Sarah, then back again. She is silent and I like knowing she is not going to talk because she is a little bit afraid I'll remember who she is and throw down the ropes. Sarah watches the boys off to the side on the monkey bars and underneath the basketball net. She watches

Travis in particular. And beautiful Dawn, who goes with Andy, watches me. I feel taller. I know things.

Enid

I watch Mindy, the biggest girl at school, walk to one of the lunch tables. I watch the way she walks—like a girl in an animal suit. She eats out in the open, for all of us to see.

When my class first came out from lunch, Vivvy was jumping rope with the older girls. I'm not supposed to talk to her but she'll let me sit on the blacktop Indian style and pretend I'm nobody. I want to sit near her now, promise myself not to even look at her. But she's gone. The girls are still jumping rope but she's missing. I sit down on the corner of the blacktop and retie my shoelaces, tug up my ankle socks, tug them again wanting to be sure no little bump will pop up beneath the tongue and the top of my foot.

Francie

Sheldon's grass is the stillest spot of earth. I don't have to think. I don't have to move or eat or refrain from eating. I don't have to drive by the doughnut shop and not look at that girl and imagine what it's like to press a glazed doughnut against one's lips and then kiss my husband.

Daddy calls from the porch: "Francine. Francine!" Soon he'll go upstairs to look down on me from the back bedroom's window. He's always done so. "Francine!"

Vivvy

We are sleeping in the basement tonight to watch *Grease* being shown for the special late-night movie. Sandy got her perm eons ago and we are still up messing around with the bottles down here. Dad is snoring in Mom's bed and she still has not come home so it doesn't matter.

Enid likes the smell of Dry Sack sherry—"like soy sauce," she says. She likes it for the saltiness. She holds the lip of the bottle to her snout and breathes deep. "Yummy," she says.

I take Kahlúa and we sip straight from the bottles.

"Oh," she says, making that face. "Oh, no! Awful!" She is about to spit, or try to spit.

"No, don't do it," I say and put my hand over her mouth. She shuts her lips and squeezes tight to keep it down, to prove she is as big as me. I take another swig, thick as syrup, prickly at my throat like the shocks I get from scuffing around carpet in socks.

There is bourbon here for Mom's whiskey cake. And ouzo, which only Dad likes.

"Now," she says, heaving a big sigh. "Now I'm a wreck." That's Enid pretending she is Mom, down to the hip bone, only Enid doesn't have hip bones. Enid falls asleep mashing her face to the flat cushion of the couch.

Tate

"Your hair smells nice."

"It does?"

"Mmm." I bury my nose in Holly's neck.

•

Before I ever saw Francie, I heard her voice. She was in a different room. A party at Jaquess and she had come up to Pennsylvania to visit a girlfriend who'd run off from home. So Francie was just this sound, this sweet glass of champagne with bubbles coming to the top to break open in giggles and a smile. I turned the corner, tripped on someone's shoes—I remember that distinctly, that there was a pair of loafers there in the doorway. So when I looked up finally and saw her, I about died.

She was this beauty—not in the classical sense, I guess. Deep brown hair, nearly black. Like coffee beans. It went to the middle of her back, held tight against her temples with a thin band of ribbon or something. A black dress when such things were strange, were a little dangerous. Low, flat sandals with straps that wound up her ankles to buckle, like she used to wear. Slick red toenails. Red lipstick to match, and nothing more or less to her face.

"You don't go here, do you?"

"I'm at Hollins," she said. "For art. Art history."

"That's all girls, isn't it?"

"Why do you think I'm *here*?"

Francie

I first heard his voice from another room. Booming. Hollering. "This is important, dammit," he said. "This is fucking *meaning*."

I stood in the doorway of the bedroom where I'd been sitting all night talking my friend through the best decision of her life, leaving Boone just because she was pregnant—though, at the time, I was trying to bring her back. When I heard him, I went to the doorway and waited there. He was standing, as if already delivering lectures. And that was attractive to me, I know, seeing somebody who didn't have to think at all, somebody who simply was. He wore a corduroy jacket, no suede elbow patches but there was a hole in the cording of the right elbow and I recall picturing myself on a sofa whipstitching on a single minky patch.

He made his way to me. The room picked up again. Pouring drinks, fussing about the music, saying good night. He was such a big guy that kids standing between us had to take several steps out of his path before he could get through to me.

I spoke first.

11

Tate

Enid tiptoes into the bedroom too early today. Barely any light slips beneath the curtains and the air is still cool. Francie has been gone eight days.

"Daddy," says Enid, rubbing at her eyes and flapping the sheet around my middle.

I must have carried her back to her own bed in the night. Or she made her own way, I don't know.

"Daddy," she says again, tugging the buttons of my nightshirt. "The dog is falling apart."

We go look, her taking my hand to lead me. Her bed is a lump of twisted sheet and light blanket. Enid pulls up on the covers and there lies Floey, panting and pushing out the first pink, gelatinous puppy.

"I had a feeling," I say.

Vivvy peeks out over the edge of her upper bunk, bleary. "So Mom was right."

"Ma knew?" says Enid.

"Nobody told you?" I say. "We didn't know for sure but—"

"*You* knew?" Enid says to me.

"I thought she would have said something."

Enid drops the covers again and looks at me.

Vivvy jumps down and uncovers Floey all the way to the head. Her eyes are dilated black and she looks particularly beast-like. There is something very undomesticated, something down-right savage yet trance-quiet, about this dog in labor. I pick up the first one, rub it around in Enid's sheet to work it free of the membrane holding its tiny legs to its belly. This thing is all head. Slit-shut eyes and a snuffing nose. Floey licks at it now and it rasps a few squawks. Enid turns around, her face in contortion.

"Totally normal," I say.

She sniffles and turns back to watch the dog.

Vivvy stands beside me. She gives a little shake of the head.

The dog makes quick work of the next but it is only sac and thin veins, not a puppy. I lean into the bunk to take it but Floey wants it more and snatches it up in her mouth and swallows. She lowers her head again. She pants. We have to wait for whatever will come next. I go down for coffee. Enid stays right there soaking it all in, rubbing Floey's head and belly. Vivvy comes down for milk and OJ.

When I go back maybe an hour later, Enid still sits with Floey and the only pup suckles while Floey licks it clean.

Francie

When I was young, Mother left me a note. She preferred writing down her thoughts and left them around the house for me to find. *This isn't for you,* she'd tape to a tin of cookies and date it *March 7, 1952.* She always dated them, in place of her name or a single arrow-stricken heart. Hanging along with the coral hand towel in the hall bath: *Do be careful when wiping your hands that you leave this as nicely folded (in thirds) and straightly draped as when you found it. October 22, 1951.* And laid on top of the row of Mary Janes and tennies and sandals on the floor of my closet was, *Please learn the beauty of right angles. July 2, 1952.*

Vivvy

I find a box in Mom's sewing closet where there are old shoe boxes—some empty, some not—labeled for what they used to hold: *White Slingback, Navy Crossover Pump, Dress Black Sandal, Patent Leather Open-Toe.* Enid and I used to beg her to pull these down off the shelf and let us hobble around in them. And sometimes, when the mood was just right, she would hand us each a box and let us play.

Then I take another one down, the sandals, only it's not empty. The box is heavier than shoes and is solid and unwieldy. There is so much weight to it, I almost lose my grip.

I open the box, tuck the lid beneath my chin. There are photographs. On top of rocks. His gravel rocks. A blue Margaret Beeks T-shirt from first grade.

"She hides things," says Dad real quiet from the doorway. He comes in to stand right beside me. "She has always hidden things."

He puts his hand in the box, down into the rocks. He spreads his fingers and it's more than I can do to support the push of his hand diving in beneath the stones.

"Dad," I say, "Dad," because he is not taking back his hand and I know I'll drop the box. "Daddy."

"Go on to Enid," he says, taking the box in his arms.

I stay. There is nothing we can do, not even if we all loved him.

12

Tate

I decided to make flank steak for dinner, so I am in the kitchen to turn it in the marinade. The underside is brown with soy and honey. Nibs of garlic have wedged themselves in the scorings. I have scrubbed the russets, snapped the beans.

I hear the girls at the foot of the stairs, down in the basement with plastic horses, Barbies, and paper dolls playing on the wooden steps. First it is just the sound of stories coming to life in low voices, of the slight embarrassment that accompanies make-believe when you are ten and twelve.

I seek out the meat fork. Drawer after neat drawer. Francie began moving everything years ago; she continues to re-organize regularly. Dinners have gone cold while I try to find silverware.

Downstairs, the big dolls tell the littler dolls to clean their rooms or eat their limas or how much one hates the other for being gone all week long on a trip. There is nothing subtle about my girls. No mysteries here.

Enid's voice separates out of the neighing of their horses, the *clip-clop* of hooves when they seesaw the stiff-legged horses back and forth to simulate a slow canter. "Ma said he was lucky," she says, "because he was so sick."

Vivvy's horse hooves keep moving.

And for a split second, I don't know it's Shell they're talking about. The splittest of seconds.

"But it hurts."

"That's what grown-ups say when they don't know what else to say."

"It hurts, Vivvy."

"There has to be blood for it to hurt."

"I'm the one that held him," says Enid. "Nobody but me."

"What is wrong with you?" Vivvy's mouth pinches each word. "It's like you're retarded. Like you go around the house making everything up. You didn't hold him or even touch him. Dad had him and there was red blood in the blanket. He made Mom crazy and you just stood there eating all those brownies."

They both fall quiet for a moment, the horses' hooves, too.

"Pinch me so it goes away," says Enid now, and I can almost see her hand on Vivvy's forearm, her eyes big, asking *please*. "Pinch me so you can stop hating me."

Vivvy screams, all her air coming out at once, and there is a soft thud of her sister tumbling from being knocked over. Vivvy storms up the steps. She comes through and when she sees me in the hall she blows out her cheeks. "I hate you!" she says and runs upstairs.

"I know," I say, but she is gone.

Enid

It's late but I can't get back to sleep. Daddy presliced the leftovers so I'll just go down and snitch a few. A few wiggly strips. And I'll dip my fingertip in the juice and suck at it but then I'll come back up so there'll still be enough for him and me later and we can butter our bread and lay down the slices and then squash the meat inside, letting the white bread turn plum with so much of the juices.

There's a light on. Ma is home and she's sewing our costumes. I put my hand to the shut door first. Just put my cheek to it because she doesn't like to be bothered when she's in Shelly's room. No sewing machine whirring. No hard snipping of the pinking shears. No tossing a bolt away after cutting her yards. Instead it's like Floey with a rawhide she wants to hide but can't decide on where. It's the sound of touching things, to see are they good enough and then deciding no.

I hear boxes sliding. Drawer fronts pulling. Closet door squeaking on its hinge. But all of this quietly. All of it delicate, gentle. Calm.

I change my mind. It's not her. It must not be her.

•

I wake again, look out the window and see sacks at the foot of the driveway. Two big trash sacks stuffed like on raking days. So I stand on my bunk to see Vivvy and put my forehead to her narrow rib cage. I twist up my fingers in her hair. I think I sleep.

In the morning, there are no black garbage sacks at the end of the driveway. Vivvy is reading to herself in her bunk. The door to Shelly's room is open. Daddy and I splurge with edge pieces of steak on our English muffins with scrambled eggs and colby cheese. My eyes are doing that thing where they look at my plate and then at him and then at my plate and then up at him. And it's not safe either place so they just keep moving.

Francie

The time is blotted out into one afternoon of sunlight so strong off slanted glass, it makes the world a solid white blink.

We slept with Sheldon in between us in bed. When he was first born. For the first weeks he was weak. The doctor said, "Make sure he gets enough milk." He'd cry the moment I touched his lips with my nipple. Then they took him, made him stay in the hospital where they could force-feed him. When he came home months later, his appetite was endless. Just as soon as he finished eating he cried, so I began sleeping on my side to be able to fall back asleep while he nursed. There were even nights I woke to find Sheldon had made his way to my nipple. Like a kitten and cat, we lay at right angles: me eventually sleeping, him suckling even as he dreamed.

It's the only time his face approached a smile. The pressing together of lips tight around my breast was instant delight. But his constant night-feeding did not fill him. He grew even more insatiable.

I had every intention of loving Sheldon but he was this little machine. Not a person. He wanted pieces of me. And once he was old enough for Cheerios and mashed-up baked potato, I was as good as an oven to him. A handle on a cup. A fetch-it.

Sheldon was not normal. Nobody understood. Dr. Gibson said, "Feed him more. Babies know when they're hungry."

Enid

"Does skin have a smell?"

"Yours does," says Vivvy, pinching up her nose. "P. U.!"

She tosses down a peeled carrot onto the pile we've made. Daddy's got a secret plan and we are helping. He left instructions and a mess of carrots and we're to peel them and grate them as soon as we're home from school. He thought I should be the one peeling so my knuckles and thumb tips stay clear of the eyes of the grater, but Vivvy rolled her eyes reading that part of his note so I said I could do it just fine and went to get the wax paper for underneath.

"Well does it?"

"What is wrong with you?" she says, looking right at me. There are plenty of carrots so I go back to shredding them up on the grater.

It's just the sound of us in here—the slick clipping sound of the peeler combing the rough skin away, the swiveling of its blade, and the *voot vroot* of the grater's holes stripping their bits of carrot.

"What's he got up his sleeve?" I ask.

"Who knows," she says. She's on her last carrot and glances over to the big pile in front of me.

"Is there a PTA meeting? Maybe Ma signed up to bring something."

"No."

"Maybe he's getting us a rabbit."

"He is not getting us a rabbit, Enid."

"He could be."

She gives me her look, Ma's look: hand on hip, elbow flung out, head leaning over almost to her shoulder, lips tight like tasting lemons.

"Fine," I say. "No rabbit."

"Where're my girls?" It's Daddy and I didn't even hear the car. Floey didn't get up either. Now she just lies on her side, her tail *thwunk*ing the floor. Lazy dog. The puppy jumps on Daddy's feet, though. His teeth tug at Daddy's hands so when Daddy stands back up, his fingers are wet and pricked cherry with tooth tracks.

"Did you get us a rabbit?" I ask, jumping high to hug around his neck. Then I feel the mushy carrot on my hands and let go but don't tell him it'll be in his hair. "To eat all these carrots?"

"We did what you said," says Vivvy. "Enid's not done yet, though."

I pick up my carrot hunk, grate it while I talk. "I'm nearly done," I say. "Only three more."

"Perfect," he says. "Perfect." He sets down his satchel in the doorway and slips out of his blazer. He goes to the pantry and comes back tying Ma's apron around his waist, only the ties won't reach so he stuffs them in his pocket and lets the apron hang from his neck.

"What're we doing?" I ask.

"We," he says, making a big to-do and leaning over a recipe book, "are making—"

"Carrot cake," glums Vivvy, spoiling his announcement.

"Yes, indeedy," he says. "A lot of carrot cakes. Vivvy, get the eggs. Enid, move it along with those carrots. We need flour and sugar. Pull that cream cheese out to soften." He points inside the refrigerator door's cubby.

Now it's the sounds of all of us: my *voot vroot vroot*, faster this time; the slapping of Vivvy's bare feet to-ing and fro-ing across the linoleum, from fridge to countertop to pantry to cupboard; Daddy reading over the recipe to himself. He gets the mixer bowl ready, Ma's favorite wooden mixing spoon—the one so slick and tall, dyed red up to five inches from the top from us making Kool-Aid with it when we knew we weren't supposed to; she cried in her room and never uses it now on account of it's *ruined beyond repair*. The oven's warming up and Vivvy's swabbing butter into the pans—cupcakes we're making, tons and tons, he says, of cupcakes: "As many as it takes." Daddy starts up with "a bluebird on my shoulder," and then we sing, Daddy and me.

•

"What's wrong with her?" Daddy asks.

"Don't know."

Vivvy has gone upstairs. We're waiting on the cupcake tins to cool. Staking them out, Daddy and me—you couldn't pay us to leave this kitchen.

"Watch your finger," he tells me because I keep sponging into the tops of the little cakes to see do they spring back. And they do. And I can hardly stand it. I need one, hot and squishy, so bad.

"Does she have homework, maybe?" he says, wiping down the countertop, making a thick line of flour he then scrapes into the trash can.

"Don't know," I say.

He sticks his fingers on a cupcake top, presses down.

"Daddy!"

"What? Just checking." His arm comes back from the pan.

"Are they ready?"

"I think they might just be."

I start grabbing at the pot holders to dump them out on the cooling racks and then into my mouth.

"Eh eh eh," he says, stopping me. "Got to frost them first."

"Just one?" I tug at his loose apron tie.

"No, fish stick."

I go to the book, looking for the frosting recipe to help speed us along. He's already holding the cream cheese wrapper over the mixing bowl, letting the soft hunk fall down in. Then there's powdered sugar and egg whites he lets me separate even though Vivvy's the one who's good at it. I scoop the yolk back and forth, shell to shell, dangling the gloppity white until finally the yolk lets it loose and it falls plop into the bowl. I swipe my finger through the smooth creaminess up around the collar of the mixing bowl.

"Enough of that, you hear?"

We used to snitch together.

"Go see if Vivvy wants to help frost."

I go upstairs, wishing it would be just him and me doing it. She's on her stomach in bed, her feet up in the air, ankles locked. She's looking out the window. Looking to the tree, the yard, to

Clint's house. I step up on the side rail. "He says we're frosting now, if you want to come."

She's quiet. She rubs at one cheek, then at the inside of her knee like she's got an itch on the move. "She might not come back," she says.

Tate

"Can I?" Enid puts her hand over the capped end of my pen as I'm writing her mother's name.

"Go on outside and play," I tell her.

Enid looks at the card. She looks at it. Then she looks up at me. Her face puzzled, trying to get to whatever it is I'm doing here.

"Go find a friend," I tell her.

She starts out the door.

"This is sort of private, that's all," I say and still she shuts the back door behind her.

Vivvy

Shell is not a secret. But that doesn't mean anybody talks about him. A whole year can go by, maybe more, without a single word or name or glimpse inside the room that was his. Mom keeps his door shut and only she can go in. Then I start to think maybe my splintered memory of that day—with him living just as pieces of sounds, bloody knuckles, me holding Enid's crinkly face, saying, "Shh, shh"—means he was not real. Or not as I remember him. But if so, then what are those two blurs that smear across us in all the holiday pictures of Dad, Enid, and me, where we are staring straight ahead and even Floey is there, lying in front of our knees, her head up and facing the camera, too? When I look really close with the magnifying glass from the downstairs bookshelf, I'm certain her eyes are looking straight out of the room, looking, about to be following, where those two white flashes have gone.

Tate

"Puppies!" says Enid, out of habit—it was her first word, her favorite. She used it on anything she loved. Right now it's for beef cattle. Her hand presses to the side window in back; her face is quick to follow.

"Such a retard," whispers Vivvy.

"Girls."

Clover comes in through the vents, tangy and sweet.

Enid touches her sister's kneecap. She waits, maybe for a laugh, then touches the glass with both hands. "The hillsides are like mas' tummies. Like there are babies inside."

"They're called mountains," says Vivvy.

We travel I-81 south, sidling the Blue Ridge for a bit. A stand of silver birch trees lines the base of the blue hills in the distance, white as fence pickets. Now there are silos and a dairy farm that must have sold off too much land to the Christmas tree growers; their angular cows push right up to the highway railing.

"P. U.," says Vivvy, holding her nose shut.

Enid takes a deep breath. Breathes it out steady. "I love it."

"You're so disgusting."

"I know you are but what am I?"

I roll down the window and the wind is all I hear as we move through this cut in the mountains, down I-77 now. The farms are few but Enid is right: each square of farmland seems upholstered to the hillside, plumped and soft; these rounded, corner-tucked pillows are just like a woman fat with love.

Francie

Each and every day Daddy brings me another. He says it smells good, he says if I won't eat them he will—but it's a hollow threat. He opens each new box, and there, taped in place for the preservation of messy white swoops of cream cheese frosting, is the most divine little carrot cake I have ever met. He sets the boxes in the grass around me and I watch them. Watch to see how long it takes the ants to find folds and seams, to make their way in. A few climb all the way to the top and fall gleefully from the stiff box flaps into the white frosting.

The trees are shifty today. Lots of breeze. They can't decide on a single direction, so the branches weave together then apart, like the dance around a maypole. The leaves are beginning to dry so they do not *shush* and whisper but make sounds like an old radio Tate used to like to leave on at night for the way the dial glowed orange, his face wide and strangely pink to me in its light. A private kind of crackling came through its cloth speaker, now comes from the great canopy of poplars above me.

I pee in the cool bathroom at the front of the house. Outside the window, the corner of the house is shaded in a cluster of yew trees so close to the wooden siding that behind them the house is the same bright shade of yellow Mother painted it way back when.

I climb the stairs feeling it in my head, the dizzy stars of fasting. I step down two, three, then step up again just to feel that surge of gravity and weakness collide, just to make my vision go split-white momentarily. The cuts in my lips sting. I smell.

I go back where I belong. Feel the pain of lying flat again. I turn away from the house, on my side. Looking into the grass, I pluck a blade and study the many greens of it.

"You want it or not?" Daddy says, appearing over me with another box already open.

I reach for it out of reflex, take the box from his palm, and Daddy shuffles back across the yard, dragging his slower left leg.

I rest my cheek right back into the ground, the hard, hot earth. Tips of grass tickle my lips. I nibble at one, swallow the color green wet and warm, its tang down my throat. I lift the box on the tips of my fingers and set it down.

I bite the grass again, clearing a spot around my chin and nose. I swallow. Wonder what it is to be a cow with so many stomachs and food coming up and going back down as a matter of course.

The smell sneaks up on me. Cinnamon and nutmeg. It creeps from every box around me, slips over my shoulders, and climbs within me.

Today, there is a note.

I know you're scared.
You are not alone.

XO,
Tate

I cannot help that my face is wet. I eat the cupcake. And the next.

Tate

It's only late August but Francie's dad's yard, what is left of his wizened vegetable patch, is already starting to fade. Francie has been in Boone eleven days. The girls do not know why, that she lies with Shelly here. All they know is that we are here together and they mustn't stare at Francie's condition.

They camp out beside her and pretend to sunbathe. Enid starts to pull off her T-shirt but Francie slits one eye open at her: *inappropriate*, it says without need for sound, so our girl lies back, her arms restlessly folded beneath her head.

"Dolphins' bodies are designed like a torpedo," she says to Francie, playing with the snarled straw of her mother's hair. "They have a melon in their head, but it's not a *melon*; it's full of tissue—it's brain."

"Where did you learn that?" says Francie, her eyes still shut.

"I told her," says Vivvy, who rolls to her side.

"So they're melon-heads," I say to Enid.

"Daddy!"

"What? You said it."

She comes over and straddles my belly. This is good, I think; it's going well.

"You shouldn't have brought them," Francie tells me later when the girls are inside with their granddad.

"They want you."

"You shouldn't have come at all," she says. "I wish you hadn't brought them here."

"Here is where you are. You're in trouble so you came here. You know that, right?"

"I'm just taking some time to myself. I'm fine."

"I can understand that. Sort of," I say. "But how much time? It's not like it was a month ago. We haven't had him seven, seven and a half years."

"I refuse to feel guilty for this."

"No one is talking about guilt."

"I mean for *this*. Now," she says. "You blaming the girls on me."

"That doesn't even make sense."

"Sometimes I think I might not love you anymore," she says. "But then I realize it's that I don't like you. That's the change."

"Go to hell," I tell her.

•

"Girls, you clear the table," I say.

Raymond and I sit a minute while they collect from around us the chipped plates and battered silver service Francie grew up scooping and cutting and skewering with. Francie must look like her mother because there's nothing refined or particular about Raymond. His head is oval. His eyes somewhere in between tan and gray. His cheeks always clean-shaven and his skin pocked with old scars—chicken pox and bad acne. His wife ran away from him and now his daughter runs to him. There's no way he would turn her away.

"It's none of my business ordinarily, Tate. But her coming here, well that makes it my business."

I nod.

"This is serious."

"I'm taking her back."

"I don't think she wants you back."

"Back home. I'm taking her back home."

"Right," he says. He lays his napkin on the table. He reaches both arms around to his back and clutches at his shoulder blades, stretching.

"I need to be careful," I tell him. "She's in a delicate state."

"Mind you don't step so lightly she doesn't even know you're here." He stands up from the table, walks through the kitchen, and touches each girl's head where they stand side by side at the sink, washing and drying.

•

"It's late," I say, squatting before her. "The girls are in bed."

"I'm going to stay a bit longer," she says. She puts her hand in the grass, lets her fingers comb through.

I sit. I watch her hand and she watches it, too. Like it is a dragonfly blowing off and then lowering to the same shore reed over and over.

"You won't tell them, will you?"

"Tell them what?"

Her hand goes suddenly quiet, but she still does not look at me. "Maybe you already have."

"Francie, I have not the slightest idea what to say to them."

She picks up again, the business with her hand.

"Hey," I say, touching her, trying to keep hold of that hand, those searching fingers. "Hey, stop a minute. Talk to me. Come out of this."

She shakes me off.

•

In the morning, we load her in the car, I guess. Into the back, sandwiched by the girls.

Francie's face is orange from twelve days of sun. A band of dark freckles has surfaced across her nose. Her lips are white like a mountain climber's, layers of skin sloughing off. Her hair is greasy black and knotted at the base of her neck. Her fingernails are transparent and when she stumbled getting into the car, and put her hand out to catch herself on my arm, two nails soft as sticks of gum folded against my skin rather than scratching me.

It occurs to me that she is dying.

Raymond said she didn't eat. Only water from the tap.

"She's your daughter," I said. "Aren't you scared?"

"I've had Francie longer than anyone. I know her. She came *here*, to me."

"This hardly has anything to do with you. She's in the yard, Ray. She's lying on our son's grave."

He stood up from the table, pushed in his chair, and walked out, saying, "Seems to me it matters a whole lot less what she's running to than who she's running from."

Francie

He drives. They swish their legs and hum. I finger-count my ribs, onetwothreefourfivesixseveneightnineteneleventwelve. Each side.

Tate

I leave the girls with explicit instructions to retrieve the dog and pup from the childless neighbors, then stay in the house with their mother so I can go to the apartment to pick up more clothes and books. "I'll be fast," I tell them. Francie is sleeping or resting.

Not two minutes in my place and I'm like a robber, indiscriminately fisting balled sweat socks into a bigger duffel bag. I grab shorts and T-shirts, and a few fancies from the closet. I stuff the duffel, sling it over my shoulder. Into the backseat of the car, I load all of my blankets. I start the engine and shift into reverse but think of one more thing I can't leave without, so I shut it off and head back inside, feeling sweat in the folds of my eyelids. From a drawer of letters, I take one of Francie's yellow hair combs and slip it inside my pocket.

13

Tate

I walk Francie from bed to the toilet. I answer for her, say "no" when Vivvy asks can she please read *Watership Down* to Francie and say "yes" when Enid wants to cook her eggs.

Francie's cheeks fill with distaste for the idea. Enid brings a plate of scrambled eggs and juice, then disappears somewhere. With the new dog maybe.

Vivvy peeks around the door.

"Check on your sister," I say and shoo her from our bedroom.

Vivvy comes back, says, "Enid's quiet."

"Okay," I say. "Go read something *happy* to her, goose. Will you do that for me?"

She backs out of the room, watching her mother and the plate of eggs I have pushed onto her lap, the single yellow bit on a fork that she refuses to take in her hand.

"Francie," I say, "you have to do this. You simply have to and that's all there is to it."

I sit back. The fork is already loaded up with two little knobs of egg because I was feeling optimistic after the first bite. I hold it back from her, then set it down on the plate. I wipe at her face with the napkin Enid rolled the fork inside, clean her cheeks and chin like breast milk off a baby. "I'll call the place in Roanoke tomorrow morning."

"I want to be good," she says. "I know this isn't it."

"I'm going to call in the morning."

She is so dehydrated that her eyes are laced red and her breaths are heavy and fast, they click at the back of her throat just like those of a dog who has panted too long. She pinches her eyes shut but there are no tears and no sound. Her body is shutting down.

I tug her up for the bathroom and push her toothbrush around in her mouth. I let her sit on the toilet for this because too long standing she begins to weave. Next I gather up the material of her flannel gown—winter weight because she's so cold even with all of my blankets, the thermals pulled from the linen closet, and the girls' extra sheet sets draped over the bed, too. Long pink cracks score her knees for how tight and dry the skin pulls, the same as her elbows. So I hoist the gown up around her hips and I look away.

When the faint trickle stops, I wipe between her legs, feel only bone above the wadded tissue. What's in the toilet bowl is clear water.

•

"What are you making tonight?" I asked her.

"Sausage rigatoni, garlic bread, a yummy salad."

"Sounds divine."

"There's tiramisu, too, just in case you don't get your fill."

We had just moved together into grad housing in the town of Shippensburg in the summer of '68. We were still a little nervous and always sweet.

I was in graduate school then at Jaquess and Francie was trying to paint in the mornings and get her master's in art history in the afternoons, but she could not paint. Not at all well. So she gave it up. This was well after she dropped out of cooking school. The meals were elaborate and became even more so: crown roast, sausage-and-broccoli orecchiette, lamb moussaka, chicken biryani, Korean barbecue. She was a nut planning each supper. She highlighted recipes and stuck scraps of paper at every page she intended to try. Once she'd made the dish, she jotted notes—*He loves this*; *Go light on the sage*; *Not so much*; *Yes, yes, yes (me too)*— and folded down the corner of its page.

Francie

He's picked out a skirt and blouse, referring to the two as a dress. He tugs the sash of the wraparound skirt until it's around me two and two-thirds times and a great lump of extra unsmoothed fabric covers my backside. He slips the blouse over my arms and back, pulls the placket to him to fasten.

It hadn't occurred to me we were going somewhere.

"If they don't think you belong in the clinic, one look at this getup and they'll take you upstairs to the loonies." He looks up from his place at my feet.

In Boone, there were whole days I spent thinking about a spot

143

behind his right ear where I'd have liked to be kissing him.

I make my mouth work, push through the stiff dryness, feel the cuts reopen all across my lower lip. "It's okay," I tell him.

His torso comes forward. He presses his mouth to the sting in my knees, makes it hurt so much more. His hair is soft. His cheeks bristly with not having shaved these couple of days.

"I'll eat," I say.

"Yes."

"Not in Roanoke. Here."

"You won't."

"I will."

"Baby, I love you. You won't."

"Please," I say. "Please don't take me away."

"You are strong, Francie. You are strong but you took it so far. I don't know if you can undo this yourself now. It's past that point."

"It's no use if someone else runs my food," I say. "That's a temporary fix."

"But if you aren't doing it yourself—"

"I'm not criticizing. I just need to be in charge of it. I'll eat."

I touch his face. He shuts his eyes and I press at the bit of smooth skin between his eyebrows. Outline his eye socket with my thumb. He used to love me rubbing him here.

"Is this a mistake?" he asks me, worry stiff in his voice. "You've hit bottom."

He holds me and I watch the clock, our appointment time at the hospital passing by.

14

Enid

Vivvy rides home with Dawn today. Clint wasn't in school. I consider walking the footpath but it's still hot out so I climb into the bus and take my usual seat. I slip lower, brace my knees on the seat in front, where the little kid section begins. I look out the window, let the sun blaze out in my eyeballs so all I see is white and the green of trees as we go by.

"Hi there, Enid." A bus boy sits down beside me. He puts his hand on my leg, just above my knee, and squeezes it.

I can't talk or move. My face goes hot, my teeth feel like they swell too big to fit inside my lips. Now he's gone. Just like that!

I try to think *what joke is starting now?* but all I can really think is *was that real?* and *please come back.*

Francie

The girls are strange. Vivvy talks to me but won't look. Enid ignores me but I find her staring, fascinated. They come in from playing out back and are quiet these days.

Vivvy looks out the back window, saying, "The teachers read a new book today after lunch."

"What was it?" asks Tate. He's spooning up onto my plate what he swears is plain rice though it glistens yellow. Too much. Too much.

"Something *Farm. Farm on the* something *Hill* . . . I forget."

"Can we get a goat, Daddy?" says Enid.

"I'd really like more salad," I say, trying to speak just to him, to not interrupt the entire table. "I bet I can eat a lot of salad."

He looks up from the plate he's created for me. He's not dumb. He holds it out to me. And I take it. What else can I do?

Roll: 90; half serving rice: 80; probable butter: 60, knowing Tate more like 75, let's say 85 just to be sure. 255.

Enid swings her legs up to knee-sit. I can't recall exactly why I ever wanted her to stop. Vivvy notices her sister, looks at me, then at my plate.

Asparagus and carrots: 45; chicken: 125; salad: 18.

188.

"Don't knee-sit," she whispers and Enid purses her lips while scooting flat in her chair.

I've lost track.

Roll: 90; half serving rice: 80; butter: 85. Up to 255. Jesus. Asparagus and carrots: 45 = 300; plus chicken at 125 = 425; salad at 18 = 443. And the garlic and Pam: he goes heavy on garlic, three cloves per: 21 = 464. And spray on the vegetables and the chicken, two squirts each a second long: 14 = 478.

"Francie." He touches my arm.

478.

"Yes?" I say.

146

478.

"Vivvy is asking you about Halloween."

"What?" I say and see I startle him by the way he sits back in his chair.

"Vivvy wants to know about Halloween. About the costumes. Ask her, Vivvy."

"Never mind," she says.

I work at my plate, slowly. He watches. Seems each grain of rice goes down separately.

"I'm not an—" I mouth the word to him: *anorexic.*

"You're not?"

"I wasn't. Before."

"I know."

"And I'm not in denial about it."

"You're far too complex for that."

"I know you don't mean that kindly," I say, "but you should."

"Eat."

15

Tate

School begins. Holly takes my feminist philosophy course because it will not be offered again before she graduates. To request an independent study requires cause, which requires an explanation. She has left a ton of messages at the apartment and a sheaf of pink While You Were Outs here in my department mailbox, saying only semi-cryptic things like:

> *Lacan's driving me nuts.*
> *Are you okay?*
> *I don't know when the paper's due—call me.*
> *Where are you?*

Today, in Holly walks and she is gorgeous, so wide through the hips, so cream-cheeked. Her hair, unbraided, hangs in loose waves over her shoulders. "You're back to keeping office hours, huh?"

"It's complicated," I say.

She chews at her lower lip.

"Are we all right then?" I ask. "Do you want to sit down or something? Talk about Lacan?"

"Um, no," she says, and starts to leave.

"I'm sorry," I tell her.

She looks back over her shoulder. "But for all the wrong reasons."

I shut the door behind her. Lock it and pick up the phone.

"Hello?" says Francie after letting it ring four times.

"Were you sleeping?"

"Thinking."

"What about?"

"Things. What do you need?"

"I just wanted to hear you."

"You're checking up on me."

"No."

"Tate, don't treat me like a baby and then lie about it."

"Did you eat the rest of the sandwich?"

"Not yet." She is defiant, tapping a pen on the countertop or something.

"Francie."

"I'm not hungry yet. I'll eat it," she says. "Lay off."

"Are the girls home from school yet?"

"It's only quarter to three."

"Right."

"Anything else?" she says, as if she has appointments all lined up for her day and wants to keep on schedule. "Tate, anything else?"

"I love you."

"Thank you. G'bye."

•

At home tonight Francie is calmer. She looks good. Her skin is pink again. Smooth. The cords that pull vertically alongside her mouth are beginning to soften into the start of what may become cheeks. She eats what I give her and listens well enough to the girls to fool us.

"I think I'll get back to work on the costumes tomorrow," she says.

Enid's head swoops around and she smiles big.

"Floey's wings are wrecked," says Vivvy. "Enid lets her sleep in them."

"So?" says Enid. She tugs off a nib of cornbread and sets it delicately in her mouth.

"I'll just start over on those," says Francie. "Besides which, doesn't the baby need matching wings now, too?"

"Don't wear yourself out," I say.

"What if you don't get to ours?" says Enid. "You should finish ours first. To be sure." She lowers her voice, says, "Or let us have store-boughts."

Vivvy flicks her finger hard against Enid's elbow.

"Dad!"

"Girls," I say.

"May I please be excused?" says Enid, already standing with her plate in her hands.

I nod and she escapes into the kitchen with her dish.

"Come here," I say and she comes back slowly to stand before me. "Right here," I say to make her squeeze in between Francie and me.

I give this girl a hug around the middle. "These pants seem kind of big," I say, giving a tug. The waistband is a finger's width away from her belly. "Are they new?"

"Good girl," says Francie and now Enid wheels around to Francie, bright as a parade. Her mother's hand strokes her hair back behind her ears. "Good, good girl."

"Francie! That's a horrible thing to say." I hug Enid tighter to me. "Are you eating enough, sweet?"

She nods to me a slow up, down.

"Dad," says Vivvy. "She's *ten* years old. I can't stand this anymore!"

"I'm with you, kiddo," says Francie. "No more glutton gestapo, Tate."

I give Enid raspberries on both cheeks. I tickle her sides. I send her off upstairs without making her do the washing or drying. Vivvy leaves too, without asking, and Francie and I let that go.

"You're mad at me," says Francie, bringing a bread plate, then a cup from the table—just single items, like that.

"I'm speechless."

"If it weren't for me, you'd think it's a good thing, too," she says.

"Everything those girls do, they filter through you."

"And you."

"Right, sure—but when it comes to food and little girls' bodies, your whole life sends a pretty strong message. I just don't think we should be doing a single thing that affirms it."

"What about you and food? What about *your* message: *eat, eat, eat!*" she squeals.

"I don't know," I say. "But I guess that's better than thinking I am such a worthless piece of shit that I deny myself anything I want. To the point of—"

"Fuck you!" she yells, spinning around, her fists in the air pounding at me. "Fuck you to hell!"

I walk away. I go upstairs and the girls' door shuts quickly. I start to walk to their room, to tell them something that will make it make sense. That she has been better today. And yesterday was good, too. She is eating. That is clear.

16

Francie

In the mornings, Tate stays in the house, monitoring me, until the last possible moment he can make it to his classroom on time. 11:18. He keeps my car keys on his own key ring now. His pocket bulges with the extra metal. But I've a secret set hidden away: the beauty of the homemaker, the key box of extras for house sitters and family come to town, for emergencies. So I could leave again; I could go anywhere.

But when he isn't watching me, the girls are on strict orders to do so as soon as they're home. In between wardens, though, there are a few hours to myself.

I go to the kitchen now and retrieve from the fridge the lunch plate he makes for me every day. I spoon some of the yogurt out, scrape at the peanut butter on the bread. He has no idea how caloric peanut butter is. I remove three carrot sticks, and slice up the apple so that I can give half of it away without them knowing. Floey loves me now. If anything does, she'll give me away, her nose always tucked to my side, the pup trailing fast behind.

I stand in the bathroom in front of the full-length mirror. I listen to the house: utter silence. I start. Feel my muscles coming back. Feel the space between my vertebrae extend, decompress. Three hundred jumping jacks and the tired oak floorboards count with me. I cycle through again. I watch myself. I smile.

I go back upstairs. I try to read. I try the sewing room but can't make myself turn the doorknob.

Tate

We talked sometimes, after, about whether he was autistic and maybe he was. We did not know. And what if he was on the road to living a life even more impossible than his mother's?

Once, when Shell was three, he wouldn't get into the car. Vivvy was in my arms, where she mostly lived those years because Francie insisted on making Shell mind her. Which never worked. The two of them were just a wrong match. I strapped Vivvy in the car seat. I got in to drive. Francie couldn't persuade him in any way. So she dragged him and he bit her fingers until there was blood on his lips.

Enid

I'm in the forsythia, in its lines of shade. Slid beneath the low branches, into the hollowed center. I'm on my back watching the sun, seeing can I make myself go blind. Sometimes I have to blink or it's like onions.

Floey noses around my edges. "Go on," I tell her. "Get out of here." She picks up her head and looks at me. Her baby is fat and nearly as tall as Basey now. He tumbles around in the dirt by the sycamore. Squawking and needle-teething sticks. "Go on!" I tell Floey. "And take your baby dog with you." But she just stares.

I shut my eyes and let the heat cover me and I almost can taste the thick orange.

"Hey."

My eyes are starry white when they open. I blink and think maybe I have gone blind. But then it comes back. Clint stands outside the bush, looking in at me. I try to sit up but there's no way really to do that in here. And now he's coming in. He peels back the branches, stoops low, and slips in between them, scratching his bare shins and near-poking his eye.

"What do you think you're doing?" I ask.

"Why do you have to be such a creep?"

"I'm not a creep. Who asked you?"

"So let me come in."

"Fine. Suit yourself."

He wedges himself between me and the thick stems shooting up out of the ground. He's on his side, facing me.

"Quit it," I say.

"What?"

"Looking at me."

"Who says I'm looking at you?"

"Quit it."

"Shows what you know," he says, making a *harrumph* noise like Daddy when he's grading. "Your dog's getting on mine. Your dog's a perv."

"Is not!"

"Look right there," he tells me and points over my head.

I prop myself up on my elbows. She is. She's nosing his bum and then jumping up on his hind end while the new dog rolls in something stinky. Clint laughs.

Then he's on me. On top of me. He's pushing his mouth at mine and it's wet and soft and then there's his tongue poking at my lips and I give a little breath like maybe I'll know what to say if I can get some air. And his hand, his right hand is on my shoulder gripping me hard.

He leans back. He looks at me. This boy with hair the color of fuzz on a peach, and black eyes. With tan freckles and white, white skin.

"Wanna do it again?" he asks.

I shut my eyes and pucker.

This time he doesn't mash me so much. I start with my mouth open and his tongue moves around on mine slow and squishily.

"You're built, Enid."

I think maybe it's a joke and want to punch him but he smiles and so I let him go on, his hand smoothing around on my skin.

Vivvy

Today's mail is: pretty catalogues, a magazine addressed to Dad, which is odd, bills to Mom, and a blue envelope for me. A letter. With a Ziggy sticker on the back and a Hello Kitty sticker right by my full name: Vivian Scilla Sobel. I go for Mom's letter opener and carefully slice the top of the envelope.

Dear Viv,

How are you? I'm fine. School's boring. But I like my teacher this year all right. He's a man. And he has a moustache. He's kind of hairy—you know, down the front of his neck. The boys in class are retarded, though. They want to hold hands and they give me quarters if I'll sit by them on the bus.

I could come see you. On a train. I'm not sure how much a ticket to Virginia costs but I'm pretty sure I'll have to sit with a whole bunch more boys.

Do you miss me?

I miss you.

I told my friend Larissa about how you jumped three in a row—and not trotting poles, either—and she didn't believe me. (She's not a very good friend, so don't worry.) Anyhow, I didn't tell anyone about the pond.

Keep in touch.

Write back soon.

Love,

Agatha

I take it to my room. I read it again. Her handwriting is neat, even if it slants forward a bit too much. The ink is thickly blue. There is a purple tulip at the bottom of the page. I get out my box of stationery. I open the top drawer to my desk, select first a green pen, then a good lavender one. I lie on my bunk rereading her letter. I start: *Dear Agatha.* I cross it out and tear the page down the middle. Too messy.

I start again: *Dear Agatha*. Regular. Better. Neater, loopy, curvy. *I am fine. How are you?*

Then I am stuck. I stare at hers, at mine, back and forth, wondering if Mom will let me use her special green notepaper, and finally I remember.

I run downstairs. The dogs get up and look at me there.

The plate is in the refrigerator, still piled high with her lunch. "Mom?" I call out, knowing by how quiet the house is. "Mom," I say again, this time soft as a whisper.

Enid comes trundling up the basement steps, a bag of chips in her hand. "Ma?" she asks me and drops the bag as if, if she is not holding it, I will not think it ever belonged to her. I run out into the yard, not calling her, just going to the driveway and standing there, looking at her car.

Enid and the dogs follow me back inside. We run upstairs. To her room. The bed is empty; her stack of blankets hangs off the far side of the bed.

"Daddy?" I hear behind me.

"Enid, no!" I say but it's too late. She has called his office.

"Don't be mad."

I go to the bed. I look quickly to the bathroom but the door is wide open, no light or sound. I pick up a few of the blankets, lift them back up to the bed. Floey lies down in the rest. The littler dog gnaws at the satin fold-over edges.

"We don't know where she is," says Enid.

"Get off, Floey." I pull what I can out from under her.

She stands and shakes her neck so her tags come around to the front. At my feet, nearly covered by Floey's fur and the remaining four blankets, Mom is a circle on the rug: eyes closed, not moving.

"Enid!" I yell.

She stretches the cord, rounds the end of the bed to where she can see, and her hand squeezes mine. I let go and bend down to Mom.

"She's here, Daddy," says Enid. She has both hands on the mouthpiece, holding it so close to her lips her voice must be hissing on his end. "Yes, I'm certain . . . No, I don't think so."

I take Mom's pillow from the bed and try to wedge it under her head. Her eyes flash open.

I let go, take the phone from Enid. "You need to come," I tell him.

•

I don't know why we are parked in the Kroger lot. Dad leans into the car, kneeling on the seat to get her, and then slides her out—almost lifts her right into the air getting her to her feet. I slide out after her. I want to touch her hand. Or the hem of her shirt or something.

Enid takes my hand in her balled-up fist. "I'm scared," she whispers.

Dad helps Mom to the curb. I shake off Enid's clutchy fingers. I walk behind Mom, watching to see if she will fall. Dad takes her first to the rows of stacked fruits and veggies. He rips open a bag of carrots, wet and unpeeled so they're white and dull. Two old ladies stand staring.

"A good start," he says and puts a carrot to her mouth. Her lips are tight against it. Her whole body says *no*. He unwraps a head of cauliflower, twists off a tiny bit, and puts it to her cheek.

"This is nothing," he says. "Just crunchy air. Just chewing is all. Just chew."

Mom's eyes shut. Her neck bends to put her face more in his hand. Her peeling mouth breaks apart just enough that he can work in the bite.

"Yes," he says. "Like that. *Just* like that." He tries another but she clenches again. He picks up a head of iceberg lettuce and puts the leaves to her mouth. He rubs her temple and her mouth opens. She takes the bite.

"Crunching water, that's all," he says.

The faintest smile crosses her face. She's always loved iceberg. He gives her another and another bite. Then we are to fruit and he tries apples because he doesn't know any better. Bananas next, but they are even worse.

I pick over the oranges, hand him the smallest one. "Fewer calories," I say. "Don't let her see that it's a navel, though."

He takes it but then studies me. I'm not sure what he's thinking. I look at her and feel him turn away, back to her.

Mom steps back from the cool spray coming down on the plums. She begins to wander away slowly, leaning on the produce bins for support. She moves toward the end of the fruits, toward the sliding exit door. She is dressed like a mental patient: a skirt that sits hip-level and slides side to side, so the hem of it dangles down to the left or right, the front or the back, no matter what she does; a pink blouse buttoned all the way up yet still floppy around her neck and shoulders; and Keds that flop around on her feet like clown shoes with each step she takes. Dad turns back to her again and peels the rind of the orange. Juice dribbles all down his arms and in a stream down the belly of his shirt.

"Sweet," he says, offering her a segment.

Her tongue catches a drip. Maybe she lets herself taste it if only to keep tidy. Or maybe she can't resist. Her mouth takes the entire piece and I can see her work through the motions of chewing. Then something happens. Her face changes. She lets the pulp fall from her mouth. Dad catches it but quickly puts another wedge inside her before she shuts again.

"Okay," says Dad. "It's okay. You're getting something from the juice. A little sugar is all. That's good. See if you can't get that down." He puts his hand over her mouth, saying, "See? You're doing just fine. You're doing it. It's not so bad."

She gets that one down. It moves along her throat like a man's Adam's apple sliding down-up-down.

Next is grapes, then kiwis that Dad bites into to start them out of their fur. Then he leads her on to the milk case, one arm behind her waist, encircling her entirely, coming back around to grip her by the elbow. He picks up a tub of yogurt, peels back the foil, and scoops his fingers into it. I expect a real fight at this, but she is easy. She is willing. A few more scoops and he drops the near-empty cup to the floor. A tub of cottage cheese. A stack of American slab slices. And he is just dropping these as they go.

I turn back to see the trail behind us, take an inventory in case she asks me later. I am thinking: 2 for the cauliflower, 35 the kiwi, 7 cherry tomato, and 4 for the grapes. 75 in yogurt, two cheese slices at 60 apiece. I lose track and start over: $2 + 35 + 7 + 4 = 48 + 75 + 60 + 60 = 243 =$ five or six miles of quickwalk.

Enid has trailed us so slowly through the store we've gone through entire aisles without seeing her. Now here she is, trying to hold all the smeared containers, all the rinds and wrappers they have dropped. I look away.

We turn for the next aisle and we have a crowd following us. I check their faces. Make sure I don't know any of them and they don't know me. Ahead of me, Mom stumbles and Dad steadies her. We are in the crackers now. Ritz and Town House, Premium and Krispy. Every time he rips open another wax paper sack, he takes them by the handful and crumbles them into her mouth. Broken corners and smashed dust cover her sticky chin. His shirt is stained now with Mom's spit and some milk, salt, and sugar. His face is flushed and shiny, his eyes dark with pupil.

In the cereal aisle, he begins pouring Rice Krispies directly into her mouth. And she actually tips back her head to allow it. She crunches and crunches, now struggles to gulp. Her mouth smacks open. Dad pulls her along into the juice aisle.

She balks at the apple juice he twists open.

"She wants lemon or lime," I tell him, handing him a little squirt bottle like the ones she puts in her water as a suppertime treat.

He doesn't take it. He pours from the jug of White House and lets the juice drench her face and chest until she lifts her chin to it and starts to swallow.

A lady comes up behind us now in a blue smock and name tag. "I'm sorry," she says, "but what's going on here?"

Dad doesn't answer. He has looked at nothing but food and Mom, Mom and food since we got here.

"You can't," she says and tries to take some of the wrappers and box tops from Enid, who will not let go; she stomps and twists, keeping her grip like it's the one thing in the universe she can do for them, for her. "You'll have to pay for all of this," says the lady.

"We're not thieves," I say and keep going after Dad and Mom, who are on to the ice cream aisle. And she never goes in the ice cream aisle so I can't have any distractions now.

Enid comes up slow behind us, dropping things and stopping to rearrange them in her arms.

He has a spoon from somewhere, a pink plastic party spoon, and Mom is sitting on the tiles, leaning against the freezer case while he spoons something white with fudgy chunks into her. Surely she will need to know the numbers on this one. I try to see the nutrition table on another box still in the freezer, but only a couple are turned to face me and the door fogs up.

Dad gives her the spoon and so I watch her. She is really eating now. I watch her scrape the surface and put the ice cream to her tongue—upside down so she can suck at the spoon properly, something Enid does. The ice cream is softening; her scrapings get thicker and she keeps scooping even without Dad holding her hands.

Enid has caught up. So have a lady, a man with her, and a little boy and his mother.

Dad leans over her now. Squatting as well as he can, he starts kissing her forehead, her cheeks, her nose. His fingers wipe away the crust of cereal dust and cracker crumbs stuck to her chin with orange and apple juice. The wet chocolate at the side of her mouth. And she keeps eating, keeps spooning it in as he does this.

The boy is led away. The Kroger clerks surround Mom and Dad until they are out of view.

I see Dad and Mom standing below the manager's office tree house. The man leans on his half wall. He disappears and now he is standing with them. Dad hands him money; he looks at it first, some of it, then just hands it over to the man. We can't hear what they say. Dad shakes his head at the man and Mom stares on blankly. She is looking our way, mine and Enid's, but it doesn't look like she sees us. She is the biggest mess I have ever seen. Dad tries to smooth her hair and kiss her disgusting mouth. I take Enid's hand and we go out to the car and wait.

17

Enid

I'm in the tree. Hanging upside down, nearly. Two fingers—one, two—making sure.

The air's steamy-thick. The backs of my knees red because they're wet and pine bark is rougher than cats' tongues.

One finger—just one. Around a slimy branch but still enough to keep from falling.

No fingers. Hanging still.

Vivvy

I walk along the street looking at the peeled paint around door-frames, the cracks that vein the paint. I could head up the hill on Preston. But I walk right up to Clint's front door.

The house is dark brown; the wood trim cuts grids across the windows even darker, as if the whole house sits in shade.

His mother is out in the yard, pulling up ivy from the base of the house, gripping it and yanking down tendrils from the brick wall. "Lisa's at a friend's, honey," she says.

"Is Clint home?"

"Oh sure," she says. "You can go on up."

I stand in place, deciding.

"Are you all right?" she asks.

I nod.

"Sure?" She is pretty but big. Pretty in the face.

I go in. I look around because barging in doesn't feel right, even though she said to. The house is so quiet. I almost walk straight through to the back door and home.

"Mom?" he calls out.

"No."

He doesn't say anything.

"It's me," I say.

He gets to the top of the stairs. "Oh, hi."

"What are you doing?"

"Science. You done it yet?"

"No. Why weren't you at Lisa's party that day?"

"Why would I?" he says. "Come here."

I thought he would be there. "Okay," I say and I walk up the stairs to him.

We go into his room.

"When will your mom come in?" I ask him.

"I don't know."

"Oh."

Clint looks at me. I don't know where to look but finally do—right back at him. There are things he doesn't know about me and I like that. I have been kissed by another boy since the last time I was up here. A girl too, though that doesn't count.

"Come here," he says and heads into the bathroom, which is stupid. Nobody is in the house; it hardly seems necessary.

"What's wrong with here?" I ask.

When he finally reaches for my face and leans up to my mouth, my eyes shut because I can't help that but my mouth opens.

"I don't want to anymore," I say, from nowhere.

He rocks back on his heels, his hand shoved down into his pocket.

"What, you like Evan Greeley now?"

I shake my head. "I don't like anyone."

He picks up his science book and stands just looking at it. "Easy," he says, sliding in his chair with his book still in his hands. "That's what you are."

I go down the stairs, hearing the pull of his mom raking through the ivy. "Cow," I say through the open screen door. Then I run out the back. Enid's about to fall from our tree. I pretend not to see her, think: *let her fall, let her fall.*

●

I try to write Agatha but I fail again. I try to tell her things that matter, then things that don't, but nothing comes. I think of her hair, her loops of curls at night in the bunkhouse.

Enid

At home, Vivvy's on her bed, propped on her elbows with the box of pink notepaper. She presses her felty purple pen to the crisp sheet and drags her hand through the letters. Then she's unhappy and crumples it up, starts over.

"Who are you writing?" I ask, standing pulled up onto the side of the bunk.

She covers the page with her hand. "Get off."

I hang there on the side of our beds watching her, trying to see. But she just stares at me and won't start up again until I'm out of sight.

I crawl into my bed. Vivvy crumples another sheet above me.

I lay down my head on the pillow. All I know is that our sheets are weeks overdue for a wash and they smell like dogs. I hold my breath.

Tate

Holly did not come to class today but is waiting outside my office door. Paper in hand. Eyes red and arms crossed.

"I don't know why this is hitting me so hard," she says. "I used to be such a strong person."

"You're still strong."

She unfolds her body and holds out the typed pages. "Anyway, here's my paper." She wipes underneath her eyes, gets up, and goes.

I move to call to check on Francie, but know it will only make her angry.

Vivvy

Mom has shut herself into Shell's room again, saying she's working on our costumes. Dad worries Enid is getting too thin. He asks me if I've noticed and whether or not she is still eating.

"She snitches," I tell him. "She is always snitching."

"Does she go anywhere in particular when she's done eating?"

"No . . ."

"Are you all right?" he asks and puts his big hand over the top of my head.

"Sometimes outside, in the tree. Upstairs to bed . . ."

"And you?"

"Or to Mom's room sometimes."

"Vivvy, how are *you*?"

"I took one of Mom's blouses. The dot one with red buttons. I took it before she came back home from Grandpa's and I was going to put it back before then, too, but things were so weird; she wasn't even getting dressed most days. I forgot. Then yesterday she was in there in her closet, sliding the hangers back and forth. They were scraping on the bar and I knew, I just knew what it was she wanted. And when she asked me, I lied."

He looks at me.

"I'm sorry."

"You're good, then," he says. "You're just fine." And he walks away.

It was her favorite. I wore it to school. I was kissed behind the dumpsters and again by the bike trail woods in that blouse. When I came home her car was still gone. I walked up through the front door, up the steps, past her bedroom door, and right into our bathroom. I took the long, straight hair scissors from out of our sink drawer and snipped the dot blouse into inch-by-inch squares. Two handfuls in my pillowcase. And yesterday when she called out for it, I smiled.

Enid

It's lunchtime and I went through the line and gave in my quarters, and it's tacos in a paper boat, fries with nacho cheese squirted into a paper cup pleated in neat rows, a cool box of chocolate milk sweating on my tray, a big butterscotch cookie that's always chewy.

I don't eat any of it.

I'm striving to be a better person. I can smell the salt, the gooey melt of the cheese. The tiny grinds of meat in my taco shells, the tangy orange drips blotting the shells to their paper boat.

I shut my mouth and decide not to open it again all day. I go outside and stand in the sun.

Vivvy

> Dear Agatha,
>   I am fine. How are you? I don't love Clint after all. You were right. I don't know how much a train ticket is. I'll save my quarters, too.
>   I miss you. Write back soon.

> Love,
> Vivvy

I don't send it. Not yet, anyhow. I slip it in the envelope and lay it in the paper box. It's not what I want to say. But it's not what I don't want to say either.

I can see Enid outside. In the bush, thinking I don't know she stole my hiding spot. She is up on her side, her back to the house.

Floey mills about, the new dog trailing her with high-kicking front legs like a Tennessee walker. I have a book report due, but I watch Enid instead.

It is late afternoon so the sun is coming through the bush at a low angle behind her, no doubt why she has turned her back to the glare. Something in me feels tight. Enid sits up. Probably, too hot. She'll sneak a popsicle or pudding to cool her down—Dad does the shopping now. Her T-shirt is sucked flat to her side and back. Then I see Clint. He's beside her. Behind her. There he is and he is leaning up on his elbows. I pull closer to the window. She stands, comes toward the house, and then is out of sight. I listen for the door but before I hear it, Clint gets up. He yanks Basey out of a hole he's dug beneath the crab apple.

I hear her come in. She does not stop in the kitchen. She is quick up the stairs and I feel caught. I pull out my letter. Take it from its envelope. Read through it again. I take up my pen and try to start writing.

"Hi," she says, going straight to her bunk.

Still out back, Floey barks so the other dog yaps and growls. Basey must have gone in because he doesn't answer.

"Where were you?" I ask.

"Outside."

I redot my *i*'s on the page. "Duh. What were you doing outside?"

She pulls off her shirt—her back to me again—and takes a clean one out of her drawer. "Nothing. Thinking," she says.

I start over on a fresh sheet.

Dear Agatha,
  My sister is a liar. I miss you. I'll save lots of quarters.

I slip this page and a square of Mom's shirt into the envelope I already wrote. I lick the back and smooth it flat, press a Boynton sticker over the seal. I take it down to the mailbox and leave it there for the mailman.

18

Vivvy

"Just hold on," she says and puts a hand up to make me wait. "Here." She pulls the cap off a tube of Maybelline lipstick, finds a brown Cover Girl compact, the mirror dusty with powder.

"Watch in the mirror," she says, so I hold the compact out in front while Holly runs the color, a pink called Taffy, around my mouth.

Today is a teacher planning day at our school so Dad brought us to campus for student conferences. He asked me to watch Enid. He likes us with him nowadays.

So I was on the bench in the hall outside his office, trying to hear him tell a boy who came up the stairs like a sleepwalker that there was just no way he could pass the class after a test as *boneheaded* as his was. Then down sat Holly to go in next. Enid was here too and when Holly started coming down the hall to us, Enid grabbed her stomach and said real loud, "I'm gonna be sick." She looked at me. *Come on* said her face. But Holly is pretty and the first thing she did when she sat down was take the elastic off her braid. She put her fingers into it, untwisting the sections, fluffing out her long hair, kinked and the color of cayenne powder.

I couldn't look away.

So here I am and it's wrong. Enid is at the end of the hall, coughing, throwing a fit that she thinks is subtle. Finally she heads down the stairwell, which Dad wouldn't like.

"You're a real looker, Vivvy," Holly says.

Beneath the hazy residue of powder on Holly's mirror, my cheeks are bright pink. "I don't know," I tell her.

"What are you, thirteen?" she says.

"Yeah." No one ever guesses close to my age. "Almost."

Her face is round, her chin full. Her stomach pooches out a little when she leans forward to pick at frayed threads across the left knee of her blue jeans.

I pull my legs up Indian style on the bench so that we nudge knees.

The door opens; the boy comes out of Dad's office. Holly stands. From here, Dad is only hands on top of his desk. One flicks a blue felt pen. The other slides papers in and out of stacks, in and out, then back out and in. Holly picks up her purse and book bag. She reaches behind her head and pulls hand after hand to get all of her hair in front of one shoulder. She goes in. The door shuts and my hand is laid out across the wooden bench, across her seat, and the seat is warm.

Francie

The first time I left him was in 1969 and I had made lamb stew. He loved it: forked the cubes of browned meat, devoured three bowls full, sought out extra potatoes fishing his fork into the Crock-Pot, sucked at the ladling spoon, sopped the last of the roux with another crumbling scratch biscuit.

We sat moony-eyed.

I became optimistic in these moments of making another person so content; I began to believe love was possible.

"I have to tell you something," he said as he washed the dishes.

I rocked behind him, felt my hip bones against his soft backside.

"I hate stew."

My body went on swaying. I was sure this was the start of a joke.

"I didn't know how to tell you," he said.

I felt him twist to turn to me, to make this right face-to-face, but I kept my grip and he went on with the sponge and squirted more lemon Joy into the murky water.

"It's so . . . dry-tasting, so brown. I have never liked it—I never ate my mother's. You're mad now."

"No," I said and stood with him awhile more until he finished scrubbing everything but the ceramic pot, which he left to soak.

I did not plan to go. In bed he kissed my eyelids and pressed his cheek to my heart, saying how slowly it beat, that I should run marathons.

I don't think I spoke.

"Dream sweetly," he told me later and I had every intention.

There was a storm that night, terrible snow so unusual for October in Jaquess. I left him. Only for three days but I left.

Then I called him.

"I didn't know where you were," Tate said. He was crying. He coughed through loose phlegm.

"I'm so sorry. I'm coming back as soon as the roads clear."

"I didn't know where you were."

"I'm coming, love."

"How could I sleep not knowing that?"

"I'm coming now." It would have been wise to wait out the weather but as soon as we hung up, I took my bag and got back in the car and drove the six hours north all through bad storm. When I arrived, my knuckles were split across in red grooves for how tightly I'd gripped the steering wheel. I should not have driven; he should not have let me.

Tate was on the stoop of our building; the top of his head glistened, for now the snow was starting to melt, the air warming into morning. He opened my car door, smiled and kissed me when I stood. Reaching up into the wet flakes in his hair, I kissed his face where his mouth was lost in beard. We went up the stairs, inside our door, and we held to each other. His arms were soft, they were warm.

I hear him now downstairs talking with the girls but cannot make out their words.

Enid

I'm not a copycat, but I take Vivvy's box of pink notepaper to my bunk.

Dear Sheldon, I write because I call him Shelly but it doesn't sound serious enough. I go on:

You shouldn't have sat there. If you wanted brownies, you should of gone for them yourself.

Love,
Enid

P.S. I'm not mad.
P.P.S. Maybe a little.
P.P.P.S. I still love you.

•

Vivvy and I set the table around her, Vivvy singing and sliding on the linoleum in her sock feet. This morning it's scrambleds and french toast. Daddy sets kisses in Ma's hair each time he brings a plate to the table, squeezes Vivvy's shoulder, and pats my back. And Ma, Ma is eating.

After we clear plates, I'm out in the yard. I'm up the tree. I'm hanging. By my knees. Two hands. One hand. Other hand.

Sometimes when we used to hang like this and Ma saw us, she put her finger over her lips like a secret to me and snuck up behind Vivvy. She reached way up then and swatted her on the bum and Vivvy always nearly lost her grip and fell. She didn't, though. But almost.

"Hey!"

I snap my neck and scrape my palm twisting to see.

It's Clint. "Come here, want to?"

I pull myself upright on the branch. I sit there a second. "What do you want?" I say.

"Come here and find out."

"No way."

"Fine." Clint shoves his hands deep down in his front pockets, makes tight round fists within them. "I have something," he says. "You want it?"

"What is it?"

He looks up at me. Blond and freckled. His dark eyes squint up into the light breaking the treetop. "Just come here, Enid. God. It's for you."

I start down the tree. I don't worry he'll figure out how to climb it. He doesn't try anymore. My pants cuff snags a low branch and before I can reach down to unhook it, Clint's hand is there and now he's holding on to my ankle, kind of guiding me down safe.

"Hold out your hand," he says. "And close your eyes."

He sets something light and slick in the middle of my palm. It's warm from being in his pocket.

"Okay, open."

It's beautiful. Deep goldy yellow, clear, shaped and sized like a dinosaur's tear. Shiny and warm yellow with two tiny bubbles at one end, so I laugh because it makes me think of pee in the cup for Dr. Smythe.

"Do you know what it is?" he asks.

"Glass?"

"Amber. Look at the inside."

I hold it up to the sun and it shines its circle of light onto my wrist, then my arm, then Clint's cheek as I turn it above us.

"Look closer," he says, pulling my hand down toward my face.

I do. And there within this thing is the most magnificent blue fly I've ever seen. The eyes are soft with black fur.

"Do you like it?" he asks.

"It's mine?"

He nods, then takes my hand and we walk to the forsythia. He pulls back the leggy whips of bush and I am to go in first. There in the gully made by Vivvy, then Floey, then me, Clint and I sit and we kiss.

Francie

He slips a hand inside my nightgown, moves up the side of my waist. Where I've begun to swell. I feel his big toe in the arch of my left foot, nuzzling there. He kisses my shoulder, my neck. He works his way to my cheek, my lips. I shut my eyes, though it is dark enough here.

"Stop," I say. My hand, too, it's pushing him back, his chest, the center of his heart. He leans back. I can see his eyes well enough to know what he would say if he were saying anything.

I pull him close. *I love you*, my head is saying.

Forehead to forehead. My hands holding his cheeks, the bristling of his beard. His hand is still, holding me through the rumpling of flannel low on my side.

Tate's fingers inch down my thigh. "Soft," he says, and I push him down and turn away.

19

Francie

I come home bearing proper groceries to an empty house today. Floey peers into the first bags I set down just inside the porch door. When I come back with more, the new dog has tipped over one of the sacks and is dragging the plastic-covered loop of kielbasa across the porch floor. I pry that from him and manage to get the rest of the groceries on into the kitchen now. Celery, milk, a loaf of bread, peanut butter, the kielbasa (the plastic punctured and gnawed but mostly intact), green peppers, onion, Kleenex, toilet paper, and Minute Maid freezer cans. Floey lies down out of the way. The new dog gets in my way back and forth between the counter and the fridge, ever hopeful.

Saved for last, there is one more thing. A little reward for keeping on track: a bag of Chips Ahoy, which I will parcel out in the most reasoned, most minimal amounts. But not yet.

I go upstairs. I fiddle with the girls' toothbrushes, shaking them off at the sink and placing them in their holder. Their Crest spit is revolting: a pair of frothy aqua slicks, one on each side of the bowl. I look away, crumple Vivvy's nighttime paper cup and drop it into the trash on my way out. I consider tidying up their room but can't face it so I turn, instead, to ours. I yank our sheets down onto the floor and kick them toward the laundry basket. There is a bill on my desk. I pull out the chair but continue standing to write the check. I take down an envelope and write *Martin Greer, DDS,* then cap the pen. I leave the checkbook register facedown, open, to remember to record the amount.

I need a larger project to turn off my head. I get the cleaning bucket and cloths and head back to the girls' bathroom to scrub off the toothpaste spit. I need gloves and go down to the kitchen for them.

A moment later, I have a cookie on the scale. Twenty-five grams is way too much. I snap it in half and place the slightly smaller piece back on the scale. Twelve grams of butter and sugar and flour. Too much. I snap it again, repeat and repeat. With an eighth of the cookie on the scale, a sixteenth. Into smaller and smaller crumbs, I break the cookie. It is still so very much.

I'll just have a lick of the crumb on my finger. It's crisp but instantly yields nearly to dough when my tongue wets it. I smash all that remains of this cookie and I lick my thumb and press it into the sharp grit of crumbs. Before I'm done, my thumb feels twice the size—swollen for how I have sucked and gnawed at it.

Only one. I walk away.

Vivvy

There is a dead bear in Dawn's basement.

The first time I ride home on Dawn's bus, as soon as we walk down her basement steps, she shows me the bear. "Touch it," she says, her hand petting its back.

It is real: big, brown, has its head on and all its feet with toes and sharp, curved claws. The head is flat across the top and wide, really wide. What I touch are the eyes, which are yellowed, cold, hard, and glossy.

"The teeth are sharp, see?" She puts her hand flat inside, palm down on that awful tongue that is raised up in an arch like a yawn: pink and stiff, with little white bumps along the edges for tasting once, I suppose.

"Feel them," she insists, grabbing for my hand, but I take it back from her.

"I'm not afraid," I tell her, but it is the tongue. I don't want to touch the tongue.

"Well," she says, "we could play Indians."

"Okay."

I don't know what to do with my arms. She is still petting the top of the bear's head like Enid falling asleep with Floey. But the bear is stuck in mid-yawn and I can feel that yawn stick in me, too—back there, way at the back, one of those yawns that never fully come out. I knit my fingers behind my back; I shrug.

Dawn picks up the front of the bear by its two forepaws and scoots underneath it. "Come on," she says. "It's our hide. To keep us warm. Let's say it's nighttime."

"We don't have a fire?" I say. I don't tell her I saw her undies when she bent over. Rainbow candy hearts on pink.

We lie here on our backs. Quiet. Under the bear, which is felt-backed and smells like the deep corners of closets. I turn my nose away, toward Dawn. She is watching me.

"Dawn?"

She takes my hand, holds it at our sides between us, holds it beneath our hide. I look up, into the felt. The bear's head is heavy on us. For all my twisting and turning, it slips more onto me, my nose squashing beneath it. "Dawn," I say.

"Vivvy."

"Okay," I say. We are Indians safe in our tepee, warm under our hide, feeling the weight of death and each other's hand. I am the girl and she is the boy.

"Did you hear that?" she whispers.

"What?"

"They're coming!" She throws off the bear and suddenly I feel cold, naked. "Now I'm the cowboy. Scream."

I hold still, look at her a second.

"Scream!"

I do.

She grabs my arms and pulls me up. "I'm throwing you over my horse now."

I go with her.

"You have to scream, Vivvy."

"Help," I say, but too quietly.

For probably only two minutes she trots circles through the basement, her arms looped through mine, holding me tightly to her back like a human backpack, as I trot backward, trying not to trip her. Finally she stops behind the wet bar.

"Here we are, Indian princess. Home sweet home."

Enid

After school today, Vivvy rides our regular bus and we walk home—not together but not apart either, sort of diagonally from each other. Clint wasn't on the bus but we don't talk about that or anything, until we cut through his yard.

Now Vivvy says, "Dawn asked me over to her house again."

"What do you want, a cookie?"

"*You* do," Vivvy says and tries to pinch my side but I wriggle through the porch door first and she must not care because she goes straight upstairs.

I make a snack, which we can do now. I make cheese and crackers, cut the Muenster myself and arrange enough crackers on my plate, and stand with it at the big counter.

Now Ma comes. I hold my plate like maybe I'll run downstairs to hide. But I don't, this time. I set back down the snack and give her a little smile.

She looks at me and my plate. "How was school, Enid?"

She reaches across the counter and snitches a Muenster on Ritz and pops the whole thing smack in her mouth. Ma crunches once and gulp-swallows.

I have three Muensters on Ritz left.

I make a stack of them and chomp through like Daddy eats a Big Mac.

"Did you need all that?" says Ma. Her eyes are on my plate, the sheen of buttery crackers there and now gone, the flecks of salt. "You'll choke, Enid," she says. Ma's head always cocks down at me, and now she stands shaking it some. "Baby, you're crying," she says, but only the way she'd speak of the dogs rolling on their backs with their feet up in the air. Like you say of something cute or ridiculous.

I spit it out. Back onto the plate. I don't pick it up again, that orange buttery mushball. I want it but I don't.

Sometimes I know I'm gross. I think about it. Think: Do I sit up straight enough in the cafeteria? Because if not, I know what that looks like. I'm not that girl, with my arms wrapped around my lunch tray. I'm not afraid you'll take my fries or the last pepperoni off my single slice. I wouldn't like it, but I'm not afraid like Vivvy thinks I am.

Tate

By mid-September, I've driven to Dawn's house to retrieve Vivvy at least a dozen times. The girls are inseparable and tonight they have a group date with some of their other little friends. Vivvy thinks we don't know, but there was a phone call at dinner a couple of nights ago. She tied herself up in the cord and leaned into the corner to go unheard. She giggled and said "Oh my god" over and over.

Enid stared. Francie and I bit our lips to keep from laughing.

When Vivvy came back to the table, she popped a small broccoli floret into her mouth and chewed.

"I know who that was," said Enid.

"Do not," said Vivvy.

"Hush, girls," I said.

Vivvy looked off toward the kitchen. And Francie studied Vivvy as our middle child made grand movements with fork and knife. And then we were all done looking and each of us made just the noise of cutting, forks and knives scraping, and went on eating. Our first sign from the outside world: we are getting on with life.

Francie

Vivvy holds up a blue swan shirt inside an off-white wrap sweater with the hood and the sash that all the girls had two years ago, when these were the must-have. It makes her look homeless but this was the style and she hasn't outgrown it yet.

"Do you think this goes, Mother?"

I start to speak but find myself just standing here looking at this tiny girl who positively vibrates with hope and expectation.

"It has to be right," she says. "I need everything just right."

I sit on Enid's bunk and call Vivvy to me. She sits down and our thighs touch. I see, for the first time in years, our legs are different sizes. Vivvy's remain as tiny as birds' ankles. Mine, now, they spread beneath me. I lift my heels to raise them up off the mattress. I stand.

"You are such a good girl, Vivvy. Such a lovely, lovely girl."

"Why are you crying?" She swats my chin off of her head and runs back to the bathroom, her hands slipping off her blue headband to reapply at the mirror. "Oh my god."

Vivvy

When Dawn and I meet up at McDonald's, she looks like a high schooler. She's wearing her blue-and-yellow paisley shirt, the collared one that buttons and hangs to her knees because it's supposed to be that long. She has electric blue leggings beneath and her navy, point-toed MIAs.

Her mom lets her out at the drive-thru/employees-only door and pulls back out of the lot. She was singing to something but definitely not on K92. She would have flipped the station if I were in the car, too, but Dawn says when they're alone, her mom makes her listen to the God stations. One time, her mom picked her up at school and I was going home with her that day, too. When I got in the car, Dawn said, "Thank god!" and we started crying we laughed so hard. Her mom gave us dirty looks and didn't say much all the way home after that.

Right now, Dawn stands at the first real door she comes to and cups her hands around the outer edges of her eyes to block out the sun and the reflection of all the parked cars and me—*hello, I'm right here on the far curb if you will just turn around.* It doesn't even make sense that she's looking inside; we never go in.

"Oh my god," I say.

She spins around. "Vivvy! Hide why don't you." She steps back off the sidewalk and looks for traffic both ways. She fake-jogs over. Her hair swings out in front of her face.

I goof around, swatting at her behind up inside all the extra room of her shirt. "Oh my god," I say. I have been waiting here twenty minutes.

She reaches her hand down into the front pocket of my corduroys. It kind of jostles me and I stumble against her. She laughs, looking down like this is a private joke only for her. Her hair covers her face now.

"What are you doing?" She swats away my hand before I know it's mine and that it is going to touch her, to move her hair out of the way. "Aha!" she says and holds out the money I had in my pocket.

I don't try to swipe it back.

Now we walk together to the Wendy's parking lot. Wendy's is better than McDonald's for a date because of the stained glass lamps and because they clear your trays and trash when you're done. It is a bit swanky. She's going with Andy, because she has been going with him since the first week of school. She swears they've never even kissed, at least not frenched.

We cross at the light, come around the corner, and there they are: Andy sitting on the curb, one foot trailing into the gutter, Travis standing up, balance-walking along the edge of sidewalk.

Dawn drops my hand. She runs over to Andy and I walk behind, watching how she stops short of him, seems to stand outside a box he is in. And I smile.

Enid

"Tell me," I beg.

"No, Enid. Give it a rest!" says Vivvy, rolling onto her elbows to read.

"Did you do it?"

"Enid! I am not having this conversation," she says. "You are so gross. You're so disgusting. You don't even know what that is. God, you're stupid." She laughs.

"Did you kiss?"

She ignores me, goes back to her book.

"Like with Clint?"

Nothing.

"Like me with Clint?"

She peers down over the rim of the bunk bed at me. Vivvy studies me. Makes my skin feel hot and the bridge of my nose burn. "Clint didn't kiss you. When did Clint kiss you?"

"I told you before! A lot and for a while now," I say.

"How long a while?"

"*A while*—I don't know."

"Well I don't believe you."

"I don't care," I say. I take a book from our little half shelf by the far window. Any book, doesn't matter. I lie on my mattress, propped up on my elbows, and I look at it, every page.

"Be careful, Enid," she says.

"Who cares."

"Be careful."

"Why?"

"Because I said so, stupid baby."

"Jealous."

"Couldn't care less," she says.

"Ha."

"*Ha!*" she mimics me back. Then her whole head comes swinging down over the side of the bunk, her hair hanging half behind her, half in front of her face. "Think about it," she says and throws her book at me.

"I'm not a baby."

Tomorrow I'll go to Clint's house.

20

Francie

Sometimes I remember it wrong.

"They don't grow out of it," said Dr. Gibson. "They eat until they explode."

I bought Master locks, like for gym lockers, hung them from loops of dog chain and synchronized the combinations. Tate asked for the slip of paper on which I'd written *12-27-3*—no significance at all, and that was the point, because Tate's nothing if not a worrier of all puzzles and mysteries, until he's got them figured out. So when he asked for the slip, I placed it in my mouth, wet it really well on my tongue, and swallowed.

Vivvy

I wait for Dawn after school, stand just shy of her bus's doors and wait. Then I see her with Andy, holding hands and stepping up onto his bus. I go walk behind the school. Nobody is there anymore. The buses are leaving. I hear the air rush out of their brakes. The field behind school is big without kids running around on it. I lean against the bricks in the cubby where I first did with Evan, then Marco, then Travis.

The back door swings open, but it's the janitor. He stands in the doorway tossing trash sacks in the air. They clang down into the dumpster and rattle the flip-top lid against its side. I like the sound, how big it is. How long it goes on rattling. I kick the dumpster, kick it again as hard as humanly possible.

Francie

That was last night. I cleared every shelf. Anything in a box. Any mix or sack. But the butter and flour and sugar, too. Cookies and bread, the girls' graham crackers and oatmeal packs. None of it stayed but the carrots, the milk, and orange juice.

Today, I rebought it all and more.

I stood in the checkout pretending there was a party and I was trash who won't cook: store-made cookies, a quarter sheet cake, Doritos to stain my fingers orange. Pop-Tarts and Pringles, banana wafers, and caramel squares.

The house was empty so this lot I ate standing at the counter, looking out the windows to make sure no one would see. All the wrappers and boxes I bagged, double-bagged, and hid beneath old magazines in the trash. I gloved one hand in one more bag, walked out to the back corner of the yard where the dogs like best to shit between the wall and black currant bushes—I told Sheldon they were poison so many years ago; I don't know why I did that—and placed their mess on top. Just so to be sure.

•

"Come to bed," Tate whispers tonight.

He has already walked the dogs so they stretch out long on the carpet.

"In a bit." I'm trying to read.

"Francie, come to bed."

Enid lies belly-flopped on her baby blanket. She pretends to sleep so maybe we will let her be, let her stay down here. She squints one eye open to see, then flips her head the other way. Vivvy is puzzling through a crossword at my feet.

Tate has folded up his last section of the paper. He's highlighted what he likes in one of his texts he keeps stacked around the side of the chair. He leans my way. Pushes his lips to my ear: "Darling," he coos, "come to bed."

"I'm busy here. Dammit, Tate!"

"Da-ddy," says Vivvy, though she keeps to her page and pencil.

He lays aside his book. "It's late is all," he says to the room.

•

I hid the doughnuts in the basement toy chest because the girls are too big for sock puppets and building blocks.

Pink box. Glaze flaking overtop, gooed to the box on their bottoms. One cinnamon cake, one cruller, sour cream sugared, custard squishing out of chocolate. It's not impossible to taste glaze on the finger. It's also not impossible to gain 18 pounds in one week. And it's certainly not impossible to prefer carrot cake under cream cheese to anything a man can say or do.

I've hidden a sack of pretzels here amid the toys, too. A bag of peanut M&M's.

I kneel here at the chest, both hands buried in them now, and feeling, feeling—I touch the candy first, each piece's round slickness.

Down the steps come Floey's toenails clicking at the slippery painted wood she hates and fears. If the reward is right, it seems, we can all fight demons. I wait stock-still for Tate on her heels, but the house is quiet so I go back to the blocks and collapse to the floor there, my spine no longer bones pressing hard against the toy chest. I let the dog lick my face.

Eventually there are my own slow feet moving through the house. The water in the bathroom. The bedsprings.

He pretends I wake him. "I love you," he says.

Tate

When I pick up my office extension, I hear only the *clack* and *click* of Francie's rings sliding across the handset. It's an old habit; I wait.

Beside me sits a tidy stack of graded essays on the feminization of platonic love, each in its slick, transparent report sleeve of red, blue, yellow, green, or clear. By the light of only this desk lamp, they glow like a roll of Life Savers set on end and peeled clean of the foil and wax paper.

"Are you there?" she says.

"I'm here," I say and take down the top paper. The cover is red. I peel it open and the title page clings to it. I fold it back and smooth in the crisp crease I made in them all this week upon first reading.

"Francie," I say. "I'm here. What is it?"

"We're not on the same schedule," says Francie.

"Okay, I can't do this right now. I have more papers to grade. I'll be home later."

"Don't you think I'd be her again if I could?"

"I have to go now."

"You never have to think about it at all, you just live."

"I think about it plenty."

"Not the same."

"No, I'm sure it's not," I say.

"I don't know where I begin."

"How about with choosing to spend time with your girls and me?"

She is quiet. Just breathing there into the mouthpiece holes.

Francie

No more tonight.

Tomorrow, nothing until dinner and just one or two bites then.

21

Vivvy

October begins strangely: "Eat something, please," says Mom to Enid.

There are cheddar biscuits, beans, and potatoes done in the roasting pan, golden around the edges and crisp; pork Parmesan, which she invented when it was just Mom and Dad together.

"Won't you eat a bite?" she asks Enid again, moving her fork around in the beans on Enid's plate and skewering a potato for her. "It all looks so delicious, doesn't it?"

I pinch Enid's fatty inch, look at her and jut my head out at her: *Eat*, I'm telling her. I pass her the butter, which is still a perfect stick. That never happens in this house.

"Not hungry," whispers Enid.

Mom begins snatching our silverware and dumping each of our plates into her salad bowl. Floey stands up and the other dog comes jangling from his bed in the corner because she is using a knife to scrape the plates clean. She knocks her chair back, storming away from the table.

"Why didn't you eat it?" I ask. "What do you care? You could have eaten it, Enid."

Dad doesn't hush me. Mom has the faucet on full blast and clangs the dishes around in the sink before shoving them into the dishwasher.

"You could have made her happy," I say. "You are such a cow. Can't you at least eat when it matters?"

"I hate you, Vivvy!"

He does not say, *Go after your sister. Talk to her. Be her friend. You're in this together. Love her, baby.* He just stares.

But I do follow her. Enid is in the corner of our bedroom, where she has had a tippy stack of books leaning since she got them for Christmas. She is sitting with her knees up inside her T-shirt. I open my desk drawer where I hid Mom's good scissors and I pick up the top book, which is photographs of Black Beauty. I slide the open scissors beneath the cover and stand there in front of Enid.

She does not try to stop me. Enid's face is like Sheldon's but rounder. Her hair is straight and she has a cowlick over her left eyebrow along with a tiny scratch where she said the forsythia bush snagged her. She is not crying now. Not yet. And maybe she won't.

"Go ahead," she says.

"Who cares," I say. I throw the book at her and the scissors fall out across her feet. "Cow."

Enid picks up the scissors and stands. The shirt is stretched and gapes out from her body. "You can do anything—*anything!*—so easy," she says. "Nothing ever stops you. You have it so, so easy!"

I pummel her back to the floor, pound her stomach and pull her hair. Then I have the scissors in my hand and Enid holds perfectly still.

Enid

"What happened to your ear?" Clint asks, pointing at the bloody split separating my ear from my face.

"Dog bite."

"Very funny," he says, laughing. "What do you want?"

I shake my head because I don't know.

"You can come in," he says and walks back upstairs.

Clint's ugly. We always said so, Vivvy and me. Ma thinks his curly hair's cute.

"Well are you coming?"

I go upstairs. Basey heel-nips me and I sort of trip on the last step. Put a hand out to catch myself, land it right on Clint's sneaker. My whole weight. Crouching there on all fours, I look up, ready for it.

"You like that new kid, Ismael?" That's all he says.

"I don't know," I say.

"What kind of name is that?"

"Yeah, what kind of name?"

Clint tosses me a Rubik's Cube. "I can't undo it," he says.

I screw around the sides, make it worse, lots worse; he did have one side completely yellow.

"Want to see something?"

He tugs me down beside him. Pulls at the waistband of his blue jeans. "See that?"

There's a pink line along his side, from belly to hip. I touch it. He lets go the elastic of his underpants and it snaps at my finger. "Nobody said you could touch it."

"Sorry."

"Just kidding," he says. "But now I get to touch something."

Really fast, he sticks his hand where Floey's nose tries to go and I clamp my knees together. I can't help it; I wasn't ready and it tickles. He pushes at me, digs his fist down in there.

It feels a little good once he stops twisting so hard.

Clint moves on top of me now. My back's against the hardwood floor, my head on the end of his bedspread that's too long. Out his window is a shagbark hickory I know because Daddy showed me it every day he'd walk us to the bus stop before we were too big for that.

"Get up," Clint says.

"Okay." I pull my jeans back up my left leg, lean back to my elbows and lift my bum to get them on and button the waist—I used to have to be flat, elsewise they wouldn't button.

"I said get up!"

I put my left foot in its Top-Sider.

"Go on!"

I run down the stairs and out and Basey chases me through the pines.

•

I go to find my bag of chips in the basement but Ma is there, a stack of catalogues on her lap and little mailing boxes at her feet. Labels from Spiegel and Talbots and Penney's.

"Try them on," I say. "We'll play fashion plates."

"Nothing worked, sugar. I'm regrouping." She studies the description for a dress with a collar and belt.

"I like this one, Ma." It's blue and pink flowers on a wrap skirt. She likes wrap skirts because she can cinch them tight—so, I don't know, maybe now she won't like it?

"Mm-hmm." She turns the page.

"We could get matching ones. What size am I?"

She tips her head to one shoulder, looks at me. I suck in my middle. "Maybe women's ten now? Oh honey, I don't like the look of that ear," she says, touching her own earlobe.

I try to cover it with my hand but my fingers tug it once more.

"Don't, Enid," she says. "Quit messing with it. Come here." She takes my hand away to investigate. "I'll put more ointment on there when we go up. But you can't touch it, Enid. Your ear will get infected and fall off. And no more climbing trees in hoop earrings. Jesus," she says. "Jesus."

"What size are you?" I ask, touching the pages on her lap. "Do we match?"

"I don't quite know anymore." She leans back against the cushion, which she doesn't like to do because of how it's stinky like boy socks and rain. "Every other week I'm something new." She shuts the catalogue.

I reopen it to the wrap skirt. "But you could do this one," I say. "Please and thank yous forever. We could match. Look, it comes in a ten."

She takes the booklet from me. "Big girls don't get new clothes."

I turn to Ma and look at her. Really look at her. *She* is round and soft at her edges now, she is big. I don't know how it happened but I remember Ma before and Ma now. Where was the in-between?

Tate

Vivvy lies on her bunk looking at a glossy magazine.

"Where is your mother?" I ask her.

The new dog lifts his head from Enid's bed, looks at me, then lies back down.

"Laundry."

"What is she doing down there?"

She shrugs, her lips turning up in a tiny sneer.

"What are you reading there?"

"Nothing!" She shuts the magazine on her forearm. "She's down in the basement with Enid, Dad."

I head downstairs, smile to see the warm light coming in through the front door transom. It shines in boxes on the Persian rug at the bottom of the stairs. Francie said we shouldn't keep it there because it would fade—it already is striped in bands of paler silk—but that's a natural aspect of aging, is it not?

Floey is curled in her bed in the far corner of the kitchen. She peeks her nose out of her tail to see which one I am. I step into the pantry, rummage in her box, toss her a Milk-Bone, and grab a pretzel for me. She sidles her head over to the treat on the cushion. She grabs it with her tongue and chews lazily, unimpressed with what I have to offer. I suck the gooey crumbs from my fingers, wipe them, swallow really well, run my lips over my front teeth to be sure there's no trace, and clear my throat.

"Francie?" I call out, going down the basement steps.

Francie

We lie in bed. Tate and I both on top of the covers. He pinches the open pages of a Faulkner novel he rereads from time to time, holding the book up above his chest in the little bit of space allowed by propping his elbows.

"I'm going to just *be* now," I announce. "I need to just *be*. I'm going to just be."

"I think that's a good idea," he says, keeping his eyes to the page he's on.

"I can just let my body sort itself out, what it needs and doesn't."

"Right," he says. "You'll be just fine."

He will not look at me but I feel his eyes all the same these days. When he squeezes around me in the bathroom. When habit makes him tally up my empty dinner plate. And now when lying next to me, there is no denying his despair and revulsion.

"No matter what?" I say on the very verge. I breathe deeply, keep it in, keep it together.

"No matter."

And now he does look at me. Tate's eyes are lovely-blue. Soft and rich. He kisses my hair, the side of my head—kisses for little girls.

"I don't feel well," I say.

"You're upset," he says. "Why don't you sleep? Mornings are easier."

"I'll eat but only healthy. I'll take Enid to Jazzercise at the Y."

"Don't get too ahead of yourself. Put it out of your mind. Let it be. Let yourself *be*, like you said." His right hand still holds the Faulkner poised to return to.

"You have it so easy," I say.

"Don't do this."

"You *do*. Look at you. All your life. And you married me. And I was gorgeous."

He shuts his eyes. The book hand rests on top of the sheets. I stare at him. I sigh.

He opens his book, but looks back at me. "Vivvy had one of your *Elle*s today."

"Maybe she'll share it with Enid."

"Do you even hear yourself?" he says. "Do you know who you were two fucking minutes ago?"

22

Tate

In late October, I bring home a fan for Francie's side of the bed with a pizza from Angelo's for lunch. Francie claps three times fast like a baby and has me set up the fan right out of the box this instant.

I am tangling with the pieces and wordless instructions when she slips out of our room. "Be right back," she calls.

I am on the floor, feeding the power cord through the neck of the fan. I snap the head onto the rod and tighten two safety rings on either side, meant to keep the head from loosening all the way and flying off to kill someone. And I screw on the last section of the pole, with the tripod on it.

Francie comes up the stairs now, slowly, breathy, precariously balancing two beers, hot pepper flakes, and paper napkins galore on the pizza box. "A picnic," she says.

Francie

I wake in the middle of the night to the smell of melted chocolate.

The house is quiet. I am walking downstairs. Just this once because once doesn't mean always. The kitchen is clean but the air is thick yellow with flour and butter and eggs.

23

Tate

I stop at Shell's door. The dogs don't. On they go, down to their living room posts, but I linger.

I knock softly, then look behind me. Vivvy's head spins away, back to her book. Enid is sitting up and smiles. I motion for her to go back to what she was doing. She only waves. So I press my palms together and pantomime a pillow beneath my cocked head. She shrugs at me and keeps on smiling.

I mean to knock again but give up midway so the sound is just my hand slipping down the door and holding the knob.

"What?" says Francie. Her voice is so strangely close.

"Were you right here?" I say.

"Where?"

"Here at the door."

"No. Why would I be at the door? That would be dumb. Rickrack's unspooled everywhere in here."

"What?"

"For edging the shirtsleeves. The pirate's shirtsleeves."

"The costumes."

"Enid's."

"Oh." I press my face into the doorframe. I whisper, "Come say good night."

"I'm in the middle, Tate. Why can no one understand how much I'm doing here?"

"I know you are," I say. "Can I . . ." I cannot say it. My hand falls to the doorknob and holds on.

"Can you what?"

"Walk the dogs with me." It's all I can say.

"No. God no," she says. "There's just two days till Halloween. I have to finish."

"There's rickrack spilled everywhere in there?"

"Pretty much," she says.

"It would take just a minute," I say. "A literal minute to kiss your girls. A *short* walk?"

"How will I ever finish?"

"Okay," I say.

I go downstairs.

•

It is late. The girls are dreaming. Floey sneaks in next to Enid. I lift the other dog up to Vivvy's bunk and he curls up at her side. I go to check on her. Slowly, I open the door until the hinges squeak. The hall light falls upon her, head to toe. Francie is in the boy's bed. Under the bedspread. Between the sheets. Her shoulders bare.

Her back to the door, she does not move: lift her head, twitch a foot, sigh, or even flinch. It is, maybe, the first time in months I have seen her body at ease. She's so tired and has finally given up.

I go down to the basement and touch the telephone dial without lifting the handset.

Enid

Floey scratches her neck again and again until I'm awake and hot and can't fall back asleep. I go downstairs. She comes, too. I look in the refrigerator; Floey pricks her ears and wags. We choose a wrapped-up cheese and we take turns biting it off the half-moon. I climb the shelf in the pantry where she keeps special baking supplies hidden, and I eat from the jars of chocolate chips (just two chips), coconut shreds (one shred), and brown sugar (a licked pinky tip's worth). I put a tiny pinch of raw oatmeal from the tub onto my tongue. I replace the lid over the chocolate and hold the jar up to the kitchen light, wondering if she'll know the level is lower now.

Floey's toenails click on the floor.

I tell her, "Chocolate's not good for dogs," and find something she can have, a Meaty Bone and two Bonz.

Tate

"I'm sewing everything by hand," says Francie. "That's why you don't hear the machine."

"Is that right?" I say. "That's impressive. So they'll be done after all. Hear that, girls?"

"Of course they'll be done. How could you think they wouldn't be?" She looks at me expectantly, then turns back to the piece of soft sandwich bread she is picking at on her plate.

"They'll be so pleased," I say. "Girls, aren't you listening?"

Enid paws through her lunch sack. Vivvy looks at her mother attentively but with no real interest.

"Girls," I say, "that'll be special. That will be really special. Ma is making you such a gift of these costumes. Something you can really look back on for years to come."

"And they'll be ready, right?" says Enid. "To wear to school? To wear on the bus tomorrow morning?"

"May I be excused?" says Vivvy, already lifting her cereal bowl and milk glass.

Francie looks at Vivvy waiting for release.

"And you're sure they'll be done?" Enid's eyes shine with the gloss of only nearly holding herself together.

I touch Francie's shoulder. "Hon," I say and nod toward Enid. Francie looks at Enid. "Hmm? Oh, yes. Of course they will."

She heads upstairs to sew. The girls come back down, backpacks on but unzipped. I set the washcloth on the counter and wipe up with the dish towel. I hand them their lunches, which is apparently the wrong thing to do. They steal sideways glances, swap the bags, and turn around one by one to drop them in each other's backpack, then zip each shut.

"Have a good day," I say, kissing each girl's forehead.

They stand in place. Enid's brow crinkles up. Vivvy hugs her arms around herself.

I wait, but no one says a thing. "Did I miss something?"

Enid shuts her eyes and puffs out her cheeks a little.

"Will we ever go to live with you?" asks Vivvy.

"No," I say. "No. That's not how families are. We are one, single family so we are together again—and forever—so you don't need to think about that at all anymore." I blot my forehead with the dish towel.

"Told you," says Vivvy smugly to her sister.

They leave for the bus stop. Vivvy holds out one pinky finger and Enid takes it.

24

Francie

It's two in the morning. Dark inside here, even darker outside. I go to the kitchen, turn on all the lights.

We have pita bread. I split one, slide it in to toast.

We have colby and Triscuits. Preheat. Foil a pan. Single layer. Give each cracker a square slice. Let corners overhang; some will melt crispy-chewy to peel from the foil. Bake.

We have peanut butter. Perfect: no bowl to clean or hide or admit. Just a spoon. Spoons are easy; spoons are nothing.

Nails click the linoleum: the new dog comes in, ears up, tail wagging.

"You're hungry? Here." I give a spoon of peanut butter but have to hold it until he finishes, which is long for being peanut butter but fast for being a dog. He bats his lashes, blinking shut with each lick of the spoon. I stroke his broad forehead. "Good dog," I tell him. "Good dog."

I rescoop the spoon into the jar. Try to show him to pull the blob off of the spoon with his lips. Lick it, then suck on it to get it clean. "Now you," I say. There are so many things to eat in this room and we've only just begun.

I look at him, say, "What kind of family doesn't name its dog?"
He wags and jangles his blank tag but runs off out of the
kitchen with the spoon.

I butter the pita.

I butter an English muffin.

I eat and eat and lick and chew.

Through the oven window, I watch cheese bubble over the
edges of the Triscuits.

There is a freezer pizza.

I restart the oven, find the instructions, and turn up the heat.

I step out onto the porch, get the box of Walkers shortbread
hidden in my bicycle basket. I go back in.

The butter is now deep in my stomach, churning, aching. I
mitigate and moderate. I eat cheesy Triscuit, shortbread, cheesy
Triscuit, shortbread, cheesy Triscuit, shortbread, cheesy Triscuit,
shortbread, cheesy Triscuit, shortbread until there are no more
shortbread fingers.

I appraise the packagings. All the world's empty cellophane,
cardboard, and foil across my counters—like the Sunoco's dumpster out on Prices Fork.

I didn't want any of this in me. And I don't want Tate's fucking
Crisp 'n Tasty pizza either. Where will I even tell him it's gone? I
count by 100s, 150s, 400s. I am an abacus of calorie calculations,
sliding beads along the wires. I carry the 7, the 17. The 77,000.

I fit the pot holder to my hand, take the sizzling pizza from
the oven.

Bare-fingered, I pinch the scalding cheese, suck it and the
sauce from my skin. I suck and suck until I realize I am gnawing
smooth the indentations of my own finger bone.

The floor comes alive overhead.

He begins to rouse, begins to move. The bedsprings creak beneath him, a man as large as Tate.

He's coming. Down the stairs. Now.

I snatch the pan, rush through the porch with it. Run barefooted through the screen door and out into the night. The screen taps in its frame—I can't think of everything at once!

And now I fling it.

Fling the freezer pizza stuck to its pan out into the dark.

I pass the carport trash can, and I can't stop myself.

Tate

My wife stands over the open garbage can. In smeared and sweaty nightshirt. She looks up, then grabs something and shoves it into her mouth. Her lips are wet, wet and smeared. Peanut butter and whatever else. She is gulping, smacking like an animal.

I can't take my eyes from her. All I can do is stand at the kitchen door's window on the sane side of the glass.

She looks up and sees me.

Francie

He is in the kitchen. The light through the porch door's nine windowpanes glances off the rim of this can, its contents entirely unlit. Yet the light moves, or something moves through it. Passing back and forth, the darkness moving through is him.

But now, now the light dims. He stands at the door watching.

I do not know what I taste. Little buttered potatoes. The dogs' stew cans. Sandwich crusts tinged with the blood of last night's pork chops. I do not stop. Each arm shovels as fast as I can swallow.

Faster, faster, until all my mouth knows is: smooth, slick, salty, crisp, putrid, wet.

The light goes out.

I replace the lid and go back inside, wipe each foot in the dog towel. I walk in through the darkened kitchen door. I wash my hands deep down in the sink, where Tate has stacked all my plates and bowls. I let the water run hot, hotter.

I heard a strange noise, I will tell him.

Or *I was cleaning out the fridge and pantry*, I can say. *I'm just not comfortable with all these foods you've brought in the house. Think of the girls for one second, would you?*

I couldn't sleep, I will say. *I went for a walk.*

The wrappers, the boxes are gone and the oven is off, cooling; its motor clicks and whirs.

I could say, *Help me.*

25

Vivvy

Halloween morning, I drop down onto Enid's bunk, my toes as close to her drooly face as I can aim them. Floey doesn't move but her eyes open and shine into the dark.

At the bathroom sink, I sip from a paper cup. I set it down on the counter and look at the toilet, gauging if I need to go.

My throat feels dry again and there is a tickle at the back.

Dawn has had cherry cough drops with her at school every day for the whole last week. I flick on the light and look at myself in the mirror. I cough and make myself cough again. I take down my toothbrush from the holder and stick it all the way to the back of my mouth, where the tickle is. I scrub hard at it, which makes me gag, so I scrub the insides of my cheeks and as far back as I can force it, which is pretty far, after a minute or so. I set my toothbrush down on the edge of the sink and look in the medicine cabinet and in the cupboard down below for cough drops but there aren't any. That is totally fine; Dawn and I love to share.

Francie

PRESCRIPTIVE: WHAT NEEDS RETRIEVING

pizza

pot holder

pan

Before true morning, I slip from the house. Tate snores on. The dogs stay with the girls.

Leaves *shush, shush, shush.* I touch the trunk of the girls' tree. Imagine their hair, their dangling ponies in the morning's chill air above me, their laughter young and dangly, too. Anymore, they stay inside or go in other people's houses. It's just as well.

Enid

"Don't ask her," says Vivvy, the suds of toothpaste pooling in her cheeks. "I'm warning you." She spits and looks at me in the bathroom mirror. "I mean it."

"But it's Halloween," I say.

She sticks out her tongue and tips her throat up to the light. "Does that look red to you?"

"You don't have to," I say, "but I'm *not* dressing until she gives me it. She promised."

"Oh please," says Vivvy. "You have to get dressed."

"Just wait."

"For what, Enid? Where do you think she is right now?"

I point toward Shelly's room, where the door is shut.

"You are so stupid!" Vivvy says to me. She snaps the elastic strap of my nightgown. "Look under the door. What do you think—that she's in there with her needles sewing you a stupid eye patch in the dark?"

I leave the yellow light of the bathroom and go to Shelly's door.

"Face facts," says Vivvy. She's followed me and gives a small push from behind but I can catch myself. "They weren't ready last night, they're not ready this morning, and they won't be ready tonight."

There is no strip of yellow beneath the door.

I wonder if dead is something or nothing, if he knows he is dead and if it hurts. I put my hand on the door. My hair moves along the surface of the wood. My breathing grows faster.

I suck in all of my breath in one large bubble and hold it inside my mouth, leaning into his door, the doorframe holding on to me.

"Space case!" Vivvy slams me hard against the door now, all points and hard angles jabbing me, and I do hit the door hard this time. "She's not in there, you know. Get over it. It's what grown-ups do. They lie."

I still don't breathe. The tingling comes to my lips first. My eyes are shut.

"Oh my god, retard," says Vivvy.

I open my eyes and Vivvy is in a dress I've never even seen before. "Are you going to Dawn's after school?"

"Of course I am," she says.

"But you'll be back for later, right?"

"I'm her best friend—what do you think?"

"You have to. We always go together. Please," I beg.

She rolls on her Kissing Slicks and smacks her lips together, twisting the lid back on. She is finished and goes downstairs. I pick up the hairbrush and yank it through my hair, which is going every whichaway. Ma likes a good, deep part so I run the comb under the faucet and use my fingertips to try to find where my hair can separate.

I unscrew the cap of her Kissing Slick. It's strawberry and smells just like the hard candies that come in little white tins from the Roanoke mall. I hold it to my nose and shut my eyes. It's like pie, like candy, like strawberry jam. Just barely, I stick out my tongue and touch it to the roller ball. It is greasy, gummy, and sweet all in one.

Tate

I set a hand to Shell's door. "Francie?" I say. "Are you in there?"

No answer. I head down to the kitchen.

"Where have you been?" says Vivvy without looking up. She is bent down in front of the toaster oven, her head propped up on the counter to watch her toast crisp.

The dogs are stretched out at the edge of the landing steps. Floey beats her tail against the linoleum. She gets herself up to a sit. The new dog's tail swishes the floor at me.

Across the kitchen, on the big peninsula counter, sits a stacked plate of no-bake peanut butter cookie balls. The sink overflows with every mixing bowl and spoon we had left after I cleaned up last night.

"What is all this?" I say, setting my satchel by the kitchen door.

Vivvy crosses her arms.

"Where is your ma?" I say.

"Not here," says Enid.

"Are you sick?" I ask her.

She shakes her head.

"Why aren't you dressed for school?"

She does not answer.

"I told her to," Vivvy says.

"Have you both eaten? Did she leave you breakfast or lunches?" I say. "Have you eaten, Enid?" I hold her forearm a moment.

Vivvy pulls at the hem of my nightshirt. "Is that what you're wearing to teach today?"

"Sorry, I slept past the alarm, I guess." I look at my watch. "You have twelve minutes. Vivvy, you're good with just that toast? Enid, what can you have?"

"Not hungry," mopes Enid.

"Go get dressed," I tell her. "Quickly."

She pouts but goes.

I tell Vivvy to throw in a slice of toast for her sister. I check the fridge, take out the milk, which feels light, and get down two glasses for them. "Who wants cereal?" I ask.

I grab the box but it's empty. I put it under my arm and get the kitchen trash sack, too, and take them to the outside can. I don't look in it, just drop these in and replace the lid.

And there she is.

Around the back of the porch, I see her from behind, standing against the screened wall.

"Francie," I call.

She is squeezed between the porch and the holly bushes there. I go to her but cannot reach her. Not without her also reaching out to me, which she does not do.

She stays behind the bushes, sidewinding along the back perimeter of the house. She is huffing and puffing, sweat dripping at her temples, brushed across her upper lip, the folds of her elbows, and sides of her neck where stray clumps of hair have stuck in fancy cursive *s*'s and *l*'s.

"What are you doing, exactly?"

"I thought I lost my—" She stops for a moment, then never continues.

"What did you lose?"

She isn't bent over searching the ground, just shuffling her tennis shoes side-together, side-together, how she must in the minimal space she has. "Nothing," she says.

"What do you mean?"

"It turns out I didn't lose it after all."

"But you're still looking?"

"No, I'm done," she says and begins to push her way out of the bushes in between two of the hollies.

"Careful," I say, offering her a hand so she does not lose her balance, "those hurt." The holly leaves snag her sweatpants and drag white lines across her arms.

I reach for a spot high on her arm, away from her hands— somewhere safe I might touch her and not recoil.

She looks up at me dumbly. "Everything hurts," she says and speeds off, back toward the porch door.

"Wait a minute," I say.

She turns around.

"I just—I want to say, we'll get through this. We can get through anything."

"Yes," she says, smiling quickly. "Of course we will." But now Francie is gone, back into the house.

"We already have," I say.

There are broken branches here where she stood and passed. Snapped but hanging in place. I step on them and pull to free them. I pick them up, still taking pains to avoid the thorns, and when I stand again, through the eating room window I see Francie holding both girls to her, her hands at Vivvy's back and Enid's hair.

I drop the branches, go back inside, but only the girls remain. "Did she go upstairs?" I ask.

Vivvy rolls her eyes. Enid's lower lip quivers.

"What happened?" I say. "Are you okay?"

"Ask Mom if you want to know so bad," says Vivvy. She drinks the last of her milk and sets the glass down by the toaster oven.

I take it to the sink but now I go back to Vivvy, pull her aside into the eating room. "What happened to your sister?"

"Really, Dad?" says Vivvy. "It's Halloween! And Mom said we'll both look so pretty no matter what we wear tonight."

Enid erupts in sobs. Vivvy sighs and runs upstairs.

"Well that's, that's very nice," I say. "What's wrong with that?" I look at the oven clock. "Only a few minutes before the bus stop," I call after Vivvy.

Enid stands sniffling in front of her dry toast. She has picked off the crust but not eaten. I hand her a wad of Kleenex and slip her an extra couple of dollars for a treat at lunch.

"I love you, bug. Want to take some of Ma's cookies for lunch?"

Enid shakes her head no. She snorts and wipes at her nose. The tears keep falling but she is quiet now.

"Not even one?" I say, holding a greasy little ball up to her.

"I will if you want me to." Her eyes grow trembly again.

"Oh honey, no, I don't want to force them on you." I stroke Enid's hair and hold her to my belly. "Your ma is trying her best," I tell her.

Enid tightens her arms around my stomach as far as they will reach.

"Maybe she will be done with the costume for tonight."

"She won't," says Enid.

"We can hope."

Enid folds the two dollar bills and presses them into her rubber coin pouch. "She promised."

"I know, love. She should not have done that."

"She's a liar."

I wipe the pads of my thumbs along the swollen undersides of her eyes. "But hey, look at your R2-D2 shirt; that's sort of like a costume, isn't it?"

She looks at the shirt she has chosen but cannot muster the hope that it might be costume enough, at least at school.

I go to the bottom of the staircase. "Vivvy, time to leave." I listen. "Francie?" I call.

"One . . . second. Okay, I'm coming." Vivvy is chipper now, coming down the steps with a quick rhythm and smile. In her hand, she has a note folded to one-eighth the size of the piece of paper it's written on. She has something larger, rounder in her other hand but holds it in such a way as to intend privacy. I don't ask. She has traded her usual ponytail for a headband.

"You look very pretty today, Vivvy."

"Oh my god, broken record," she says. She looks down at her green dress, then up at me. "Besides, in this thing? Couldn't you have bought the real alligator one, the Izod?"

I follow her back to the kitchen, where Enid is ready—backpack on, mysteriously filled lunch sack in hand, and red eyes mostly dry. She is chewing something and turns her back to Vivvy. I don't press it but notice the plate of cookies is missing a few.

"Have a great day," I tell them, doling out hugs. I watch them cut through the Thomsons' yard as far as I can still see.

Francie

When I hear his shower water run, I come from Sheldon's room. In my hands are filled picture frames I boxed up long ago. I stand each one in tidy rows across my dresser. The ones of my brother and my daddy and mother. Of Floey and the cat we had once. And of us, too, as we were before—these I arrange in the first two rows. Tucked in between the last is a little, chipped sand dollar I've had since then, too, when we were at the shore and I saw it and picked it up. Tate cleaned it in the surf. It was perfect then.

26

Enid

Most everybody wears a costume in Mrs. Moss's room today. Laurel White is all fancy-pants in her real ballerina leotard, tutu, and feather crown she wore in the recital last spring, so that doesn't even count as a costume. And Laurel Davies wears a blue bathrobe over regular pants and shirt. She is Yoda, with a rubbery mask. The eyeholes are set too low in it so she looks more like a zombie with weird green ears.

I put my face down into my backpack and set one cookie ball into my mouth. I lift my head out and hold up a sharp pencil. I smoosh the cookie and swallow it fast. Or I try. Most of it sticks to the roof of my mouth and once it's out of there, it globs in the back of my throat. *Please don't call on me!*

Vanessa looks at me. She whispers to Veronica.

I turn around. I give Veronica a look.

Vanessa makes a pig nose and shakes her curls at me.

"What is wrong with you?" says Veronica.

"What *isn't* wrong with her?" says Vanessa.

Francie

I drive the Datsun. Sun on my face. This is what I need: all day, all day, inch by inch in mud-packed earth. The grass.

Vivvy

Down the hall to assembly, I see Dawn's matching green dress up ahead. When I reach her I cover her eyes. "Guess who?"

She goes stiff. "That's pretty obvious," she says.

"Vivvy?" says Dawn's teacher, Miss Ramsey, giving me away. She holds a finger to her lips like a librarian. My teacher, Miss Nelson, and Dawn's teacher are best friends, too, so mostly they understand and let us sit together.

I take Dawn's hand to make sure we aren't separated. "You gave me your cold," I say and nudge my shoulder against hers. "Give me a Sucret."

"I don't have them," she says. "I'm fine now."

Justine comes up on Dawn's other side.

"Well, you put your germs in me."

"Oh my god," says Justine. She laughs and another girl, Danielle, comes up between her and Dawn. Justine whispers in Danielle's ear and they both laugh.

"Do you have to say it like that, Vivvy?" says Dawn.

I tell the other girls, "Do you mind? This is private."

"No it's not," says Dawn. She looks at Justine. "It's not," she insists.

Dawn's hand feels like a fish. A dead one or one that is almost dead.

"Why are you wearing that dress?" asks Danielle.

"Are you, like, twins?" Justine says. They laugh.

"No, no we're not," Dawn says.

"I looked for you this morning," I say. "I waited by our spot."

"My mom drove me. I was early."

"But you got my note and the thing, right?"

"What thing?" asks Justine.

"None of your business," I tell her, then say quietly just to Dawn, "Did you get it? Do you have it on?"

Dawn's hand tries to wriggle free. She pushes my arm away to get her hand free. She slides her tortoiseshell headband off the back of her head and combs it through her hair again. Once she has it in place, she pushes it forward to make the little loop of bangs out in front of the band. It looks just as perfect as it did before she dropped my hand.

"Why are you being like this, Dawn?"

"I'm not being like anything."

"Too loud, girls," says Miss Ramsey. "Vivian, go back to your class, please."

"But it wasn't me," I say.

It doesn't matter. Miss Ramsey points me to my class, standing in single file way behind Dawn's.

The girls whisper and giggle softly.

Tate

I have grading to finish. The last two midterms from feminist philosophy. I stand up to shut my door right as Sue Hammond, the new Aristotle specialist, leans in to say hello with a big wave. I wave back to her and sit right down again. If life were different, I would have liked to invite her to a dinner party at the house. I could see Francie liking her, even being friends, maybe. Years ago.

I slog through the second-to-last midterm, give it a generous C- / 70%. I uncover Holly's. Just like Enid with a roll she has buttered and set back on the plate for after she's eaten the lima beans or spinach or whatever else Francie used to serve, I always save Holly's work to grade last. I take hers off the stack and slip it to the bottom, the best for last and all that. Or sometimes I flip the pile and start from the back. And until the midterm, she had always been the slowest to finish, which made it easy.

I pick up her booklet and place it in front of me. I think of the door and decide to shut it. Lock it, even. I don't know why. I sit down and settle in.

Now I peel back the blank cover and what I see is an ivy wall of curlicues: scrollwork *s*'s like ironwork fence gates, like stylized half hearts. The next page, again, is absent of answers to the exam. More blue ballpoint doodling. I turn the next page and the next, reach the midway staples and fan through the pages until, on the very last page, she has written:

Dearest Dr. Sobel,

You know what I miss the most? Falling asleep with you in the middle of the day, all sticky and hot and gross. Then waking up just before suppertime, the sheets always felt so much cooler and we weren't sweaty anymore. Just smooth and soft and, well, together. That was my favorite. And you touching my hair. You should know that, I guess. In case your wife doesn't tell you or thank you, I think

It's been two months since we broke up and, to be honest,

232

*I knew we had no future but I wish missing you didn't hurt
so much.*

*Everyone around me right now is so scared of you and this
test, that I can fill this entire blue book with drawings and
no one will even notice. What's that like? To have an entire
(almost) roomful afraid of you?*

*And by the way, if you wish to challenge my mastery of
the material, please summon me to your office where I'll gladly
provide all the answers to you in oral form.*

Once,
Holly

Vivvy

After school today, I step up onto her bus and start down the
aisle. I smile to the driver. "Dawn Prescott is having me over today," I say. "We're trick-or-treating together." He always lets me
on because I ride home with Dawn like every day.

She looks up, Dawn does, from way in the back. All I can see
is her tortoise headband and that her eyes are smaller because she
likes whatever is being said near her.

I wave.

She stands up in the second-to-last seat on the right—back
where she always sits. She motions to me so I move quicker. "You
can't come today, Vivvy," she calls.

I stop where I am.

Danielle and Justine stand with her but so do two more girls
swarming from the seat across the aisle from her. Where have they all

come from? They look me up and down in their green satin headbands and double-layered, flipped-up-collar shirts and dresses, which all have alligators—not a single tiger, horse, or swan among them.

But Dawn is only goofing.

"Oh my god," say the girls, and "Make her stop," and "What's her problem?" They cluster tighter together, enclosing Dawn.

I squeeze the seat backs where I stand and move farther down the aisle.

"Please, Vivvy," says Dawn, looking right inside me.

I stop and where I stop there is a guy here I know from science, when the G&T kids leave their own classes and meet up for word problems in an empty kindergarten room, where the furniture is brightly colored but too little. That's what Dawn says, except she always adds, "But not for you, Vivvy. It would be perfect for you, if you were gifted and talented."

Around this bus, the other buses have started up their motors. Puffs of gray smoke roll onto the windshield of each bus behind another's tailpipe.

I sit down next to the guy—I think his name is Charles—and swing my legs into the aisle to show her it's okay, I'm still here, I'm not mad or anything.

Dawn does not look. She will not look.

The boy standing behind her in the back row starts flicking her hair. Dawn kneels backward on her seat now, trying to slap at the bus boy's hands. I watch her do it. The bus's motor rumbles through the floor, walls, and seats. Everything I feel, I know she feels it too, right this very second. She turns around, just looking over her shoulder like she knows I'm thinking of her. I sit up straighter and smile for her.

Dawn purses her lips; her eyes and eyebrows pinch together. I look straight ahead now. The buses begin to pull out and it is stupid, but I feel like I'm spinning in outer space. Totally bogus but my stomach flips every time I think her name.

Tate

Finally ready to hand back their midterms, I lurch and lumber into the fray, the narrowest aisles made narrower by student cargo: backpacks, purses, those enormous basket bags the women carry like they're Guatemalans toting baled sugarcane to market. I suck in my gut and breathe through my mouth but the humiliation can't really be minimized.

This is her class, feminist philosophy.

I try not to think of it this way, but no matter what, every class I have taught since Holly has been defined by either her presence on the roster or her absence from it.

She is wearing a long, full skirt today. I don't have to look at her to see that. She never leaves my periphery. Today it is blue in soft geometric smears over a creamy background. I know the skirt. There is a cord that ties at the waist. Tiny tassels at each of its ends.

I pass Holly's desk, see down in her straw bag an obscure, unmarked collection of French poems from my bookshelf. I'd forgotten she took it. A wave of heat blasts through me, accompanying the thought that perhaps she intends to return the book after class, today.

Nothing good can come of it.

I reach the front of the classroom, aware that I am midsentence but without any shred left of the train of thought. "And so . . ." I say, hoping time will jog my memory. I stand in place. I tug up my waistband in back, run two fingers just inside the cut of my belt to smooth the tucked portion of my shirttail.

Still nothing.

I shake my head and start anew.

Enid

On the bus, nearly everyone has store-boughts except me. And they look different than they did this morning: the folding lines have worked their way out of the stiff smocks that tie three times down everyone's backs. A couple of them are torn or crusty with sloppy joe sauce from lunch. Still, they are beautiful. The girls are Leia and Wonder Woman, with shiny plastic buns or the gold crowns and smooth black curls printed on the tops and sides of their masks. All of them make that special *rustle* sound coming down the aisle in the plastic capes and elastic-stringed masks their mothers bought them. The littlest kids who sit up front are Cabbage Patch dolls, Tweety Bird, and Raggedy Ann. One boy is C-3PO. Another wears E.T.

Foot-long Slim Jim at the checkout. Mr. Goodbar in snapped-off squares. Milk Duds smashed between my molars till they're stuck and I have to work to pry my jaw open. Hot Fries, Starburst squares and smoothing a stack of their waxy papers deep down in my pocket.

Tina sits with Rachel. Michelle sits with Caroline.

Corn Nuts. Pringles.

It's best when Vivvy rides home with Dawn. Without her here, I can be no one. Just slouch way down and drift away.

Star Crunch, Nutty Bars. Star Crunch, Nutty Bars.

Bubble Yum grape—two blocks at once.

Cheetos, Boston Baked Bean candies, cinnamon bears and chocolate-covered cinnamon bears, Bottle Caps, Laffy Taffy, Beer Nuts, Super Skrunch bars, Whatchamacallits, Hershey's Miniatures, Reese's PB Cups, Kit Kat, Twix, candy cigarettes, half-and-half powdered sugar and chocolate-covered little tiny doughnuts all lined up.

Mrs. Healey pulls the bus up to the stop and my belly flips over. I move down the aisle like flying. I picture myself invisible, which is picturing air with just a faint silvery outline. Corn Nuts, Corn Nuts, Corn Nuts. Red cherry licorice strings. Bugles and Whoppers and Big League Chew. I go down the last step and I'm free. I run my hand along the hedge I walk beside. The bus turns off.

"Hey, Jabba the Butt! Wait up."

It's Clint.

I keep walking.

"What's wrong?" He is beside me now. Dressed as an astronaut in an orange smock but no mask. "Don't you like your new name?"

I walk.

"Come on, it's just a joke," he says. His face is so close to mine I can smell his teeth.

I take a deep breath of air away from him and I hold it, start counting one, two, three, four, five, six, seven.

"Hey, want to come over?" he says. "I have a new magic trick to show you."

I keep my breath inside but my eyes kind of peek at him.

"See?" he says. "You know you love me."

"I do not!" My breath floods out and he laughs.

"Where's Vivvy today?" he says. He yanks me back by the loop of my backpack.

"Quit it," I say but he does it again. "Quit it!"

Once more I go stumbling back and this time I fall right on my behind. It hurts but I squeeze my eyes not to cry. We're nearly to his house so I cut through his neighbor's yard, instead of his, which also runs against the side end of our yard. Clint follows me. I start to run and he's running after me.

"I saw London, I saw France!" he calls out. "I poked Enid with no underpants!" He sings it loud, louder.

I'm in our yard but so is he.

"What's the matter, fat girl? Don't you like me anymore?"

Francie

I'm here with my boy. Daddy hollers from the upstairs window but does not come out. I hear him cough in the house. I don't want to leave this place to the girls or to Tate. This is a place of endings, of tree roots run too shallow and boxes of little boys.

I lie down above him, let my fingers fan through his grass. I shut my eyes, take the sand dollar from my pocket and hold it up to block the sun. But when I open my eyes, light shines through the notch Sheldon made, trying to eat something else I loved.

Enid

"Stop it!" I scream. I'm nearly home.

Basey lies panting near the forsythia. He licks at his front paws. He looks at me with horse eyes and growls. I scuff the dirt, kick pine needles at him. He growls again but it isn't him making the noise. It's in the bush, the forsythia. It's our dogs. The bush vibrates with their sound. I peel back the vines and scraggly whips to see all the way, and Basey's up now. Floey and the new dog are in the very middle, where everything happens. Floey's sitting. The little one makes a *grr* sound at me and licks Floey's coat. He stands next to her and his claws make a pinging sound on something metal in the dirt beneath them both.

I drop my backpack in the footsteps worn around the bush. I go in it. Basey follows me. Floey and the new dog bark. Basey snaps. He paws at the ground, scratching at what is there. It's one of Ma's big pans and his claws scrape it and catch on the edge. He gets this hump of fur on his shoulders and neck, like a buffalo or a warthog. So does the new dog, just exactly the same.

Everyone is teeth. Skin and lips scrunch up so high on their snouts, they look like ruffled petticoats if the teeth were ladies' legs.

They bark. Gnash jaws and teeth up in the air next to one another's faces. Something drips out of the new dog's butt. Basey sniffs at it. He goes nuts. He digs his front feet into the earth superfast. He jumps in the air, straight up from all four legs. The new dog hides behind Floey. She bares her teeth and points her snout up to the sky but right in Basey's face, so he does it back and now both of them are pushing their jaws and skulls hard against each other's.

I want to run inside but it's my Floey and I can't let Basey pick on her!

I reach in for her collar, feel my fingers grasping at it in the kinked white fur around her neck. Basey flops over. He jumps back up and growls again. I don't have a grip.

"Don't do that," I yell at him.

Basey moves closer, head low, growling.

I go at him, I stomp my sandal. A shovelful of dirt and dust slides in under my toes so I take off my shoe and shake it. "Rawr!" I scream. I shake my shoe in the air.

He's up when I move. His claws drag across my shin. Beneath my jeans, the skin stings.

I scream and try to kick him but miss. I reach for Floey again and grab hold of the bush to keep from falling. He gets behind me. Between me and Floey. They tussle in the branches and down into the dirt. Basey pushes Floey on her back and her eyes get big. The new dog stands behind Basey now.

"Do something," I tell the new dog but he just watches and whimpers from where he is.

Her back feet pedal and kick at Basey to get him off of her. Her tongue is long out the side of her mouth. Stiff like she's trying to reach something important but can't quite make it.

Basey tumbles back hard, yelping when he lands. Floey rolls over but stays down. She is panting now. I turn and see Basey jump at her. I scream and I don't even know what words I'm making. Her name and "no," and "stop!" She's just a mama-dog.

I slip my hand in between Floey's face and the others'.

There are necks in jaws. There is fire and blood in my hand. I have no idea who's done it but I am bit. I hold my breath until my cheeks buzz. I make myself look at my hand and there is so much blood.

"Crybaby, crybaby," Clint calls.

I back out of the bush the wrong way. The branches scrape but I don't feel them.

I hold my hand out to his face.

I hold it out to him, all the shine of blood and spit going crazy in between our eyes.

"Oh shit." He grabs Basey by the collar. "Let's go," he says.

I shake my hand, try to shake out the fire, and shriek out every bit of air I have. "Get away from me! Get away—I hate you!"

He yanks on Basey to drag him home but the stupid dog won't go. Clint slaps his hip but Basey splays his claws in the wispy grass. His toe knuckles dig in.

"He bit me!" I cry. "Ha-ha." I wipe my nose and up my arm is dirt, mud, and gooey red snot.

Clint keeps pulling at Basey's collar but the dog weasels and twists and they're only to the wood chips under our trees.

"He'll go to the pound!" I call. "They'll shoot him." I wipe at my tears and runny nose. "Forever!"

Clint's eyes look to mine for just a second. "Come on!" he yells. His voice goes high and small like his big sister Lisa's. He wraps his arms around Basey's ribs and keeps dragging, but the dog flops backwards so then he has him around the belly and the back legs are all that's keeping Clint's grip. He pulls him that way, though, backwards, into his yard, and keeps going. And now even Clint's crying, "Basey, come *on!*"

"And my ma's here. Her car's right there!" I call after him but he's gone now and there is just my voice and the wet licking of Floey and the new dog cleaning each other.

Ma knows. Ma saw everything.

I run to the porch. The Datsun isn't here, though, it's gone.

All the hurt is a volcano inside my hand. Throbbing like a car door slammed shut, burning like boiled water. Shredded skin like it will all fall off and all that's going to be left of my hand is bone so I'll have a skeleton hand.

I run through the house. I run.

"Ma!" I call out.

Tate

In the classroom's doorway stands the department secretary, Mrs. Leahy. She motions to me with a square of scratch paper she cuts down on the paper slicer from old memos and committee meeting minutes.

"Excuse me, please," I say to the room. I move briskly to her but when I'm nearly there, her expression changes: she smiles softly, nostrils flared, chin tucked slightly under, and lips pressing hard against each other.

This is how they all looked after Shell.

I take a step back.

"I'm so sorry to interrupt you, Dr. Sobel," says Mrs. Leahy. "Under normal circumstances, of course . . ."

I shake my head, meaning *it's okay*, meaning *get on with it*, and *please don't make this last any longer than it must*.

"Your little girl," she starts. "Enid—"

I start to walk. I pick up my satchel. It is heavy. I run toward my office, arrive covered in spittle and full-on lather of sweat. Winded, I fumble with the key in my office door.

I make it in but don't know how to order my tasks. Or what my tasks are. I pick up a scratch pad from the desk but am stumped as to what comes next.

I dump out my satchel over the desk chair, dump everything out to see what we're dealing with. There are books, folders, papers, a manila envelope gone soft around the form of chapter edits. Cough drops, sticks of gum. Thick yellow markers, red and black pens, they roll over the cracked edge of the chair cushion and are gone. Sweat in rivulets ferries down my neck, sticks me to my shirt collar. I wipe at it and lose track. Why have I dropped to my knees? Why am I staring at it all on the chair, trying to understand what any of it is, what it means. What I will say to them.

I look up and from nowhere, Holly is magically here.

Real or imagined, I don't care, I just want her to tell me what to do.

"Sorry," she says. "I don't mean to go back on what you said, but—are you okay?"

I shake my head. Lips tight together.

Her eyes grow round. She drops her bag, comes closer but not near enough to catch my thoughts. "Tate," she whispers. "You're . . ."

I shut my eyes.

"I need to go home," I say. "Enid is hurt . . ."

"Oh my god, yes." Holly lets go of her braid. "I'm sorry. Of course you need to go."

As we walk, I'm not thinking about Enid—I think about Shell and what happened directly after. I phoned the doctor. I held the girls beside me on the couch, waiting with him bundled up across my lap. I worried then that maybe they shouldn't see him like that. All these years later, maybe they should never have seen what Francie could do.

27

Enid

When the Plymouth turns up the driveway, Floey and the new
dog still haven't come out of the bush. I bust out crying again
and run barefooted out onto the rocks. Sunlight hits the windshield and bounces straight at me. The rocks carve their shapes
into my feet.

"Daddy!" I call.

The car's side door swings open and he gets out. He runs to
me and scoops me up into the sky. "You!" he says.

The bite pounds harder in the towel. Sharp and hotter. This is
how blood feels dropping out the holes in my skin.

"My girl."

"Daddy." I hold tight around his neck, squeezing the towel
behind his back, making it hurt much worse. I shut my eyes so
tight maybe I can forget how it burns.

"Vivvy, she's—"

"At Dawn's," I say.

He squeezes me to him. All I see is the heat of his skin and the wet curls dark on his neck. He smells like Floey wet from rain.

Now we're both crying and our faces are nasty with goop from our noses and sticky-cheek and sticky-beard tears.

"I don't even want to be a pirate anymore," I say.

He bristles his beard against me. Goose bumps prickle my shoulder and chin.

Now Daddy lets go and I'm sideways in the gravel. On my knees and one elbow, one foot over Daddy's shoulder, and he's down on all fours. The sounds we make are no sounds, like only emptiness where we used to hold air.

There is someone else. A driver, someone gets out of the Plymouth fast.

"Tate!" she yells, running to us.

She kneels down and she seems like she doesn't know which one of us to talk to first. She reaches for Daddy's back. She bends down and a long orange braid slips past her shoulder to hang between us. "Are you okay?" she says and tries to make a smile. She looks back at Daddy. "Are *you*?"

I know who she is.

I look at her cheeks, all those freckles like she needs to wash up. There is ribbon strung through her blouse at the neckline: baby-blue satin. Its ends hang down her front where the shirt could tie to close itself up. There's a snag on one of the ends so a blue string of it hangs down.

"Baby girl," he says to me, standing up, brushing off his palms. "And Vivvy's all right? What happened, then?"

Behind my back, I peel down the sleeve of my sweatshirt, fit it gently over the towel.

"Tate," says the girl, "she's bleeding."

"Am not," I say, keeping my right arm behind my back. I tug my sleeve over the cloth and over my entire hand and repinch the cuff and hold it between two of the stiff, curled fingers inside. I squeeze my right hand, squeeze the towel and feel a slow, cold trickling down through my knuckles.

"Right there," she says to him.

"I'm sorry, Daddy."

"Oh honey," says Daddy but he is looking at my leg and so is she. He kneels down. He works one of his giant fingers in through a new rip in the knee of my jeans. Seeing the fresh color coming up there makes it sting, though he is careful. "Are you sure you're okay?"

I nod.

"How did you do that? Did you fall from the tree?" He stands up now. He looks at our tree and out into the yard, where the forsythia is all snap-branched and mangled on one side and in the middle. "What's that?" he says. The dogs don't move.

I shrug my shoulders.

"So when are you going to show me what's behind your back?"

My eyes go wet. All at once there is new lightning in my hand. Feels like it cuts itself open all over again. I squeeze the blue towel hard, harder into the torn V between my thumb and hand.

"You need to let me see," he says.

He pushes up my sleeve and he is gentle but when he sees the stained towel, his hands go more slowly.

"I'm sorry, Daddy."

"What on earth for?" He is unwinding the layers of towel until finally he sees it. A half-inch-long slit runs along the side of my hand. It is sticky with dried and drying blood and now, without the towel to soak it up, new blood dribbles from the cut. There are no tooth marks, no fur or dog slobber.

"Looks like that hurts," he says.

I nod.

He holds my wrist in place, watching my hand bleed. "It's not too bad. We just need to clean it up properly. Where's your ma? Did she wash it? Did she give you this towel?"

"No and she'll be so mad at me," I say. "It's ruined."

He looks to the driveway where only the Plymouth sits. "She isn't here?"

"I think so?"

He holds my chin, tips my face up into the bright sun. "Please don't worry," he says and rewinds the towel loosely. "Can you do something? I know I have no right to ask."

He isn't talking to me, he's talking to her.

"Right," she says. "It's okay."

"It's not," he says.

"I know, yet here I am."

He blows his bangs up out of his eyes.

•

We hear knocking upstairs. He's looking for Ma. She's not here, but what if she does answer? What if she tells him I cried for her at first but then I stopped? What if she tells him I didn't go to her at all or that I screamed "I hate you" or any other thing she could say? He knows her car is not in the driveway, but he keeps knocking.

Holly is looking around and we haven't turned on the light in the eating room but the kitchen's is on so she is looking at the sink and after I called Daddy's office, I didn't want to but I kept thinking about that butter hiding behind the cabbage and Ma used to make me fold-over bread-and-butters when I was little, I think, so I made three—one right after the next even though I knew it was wrong.

After that I wiped Shelly's door and covered where I dripped in the rug so no one will see until the washcloths have soaked it all up. I sat at the top of the stairs in case Ma came out of Shelly's room or any other hidey-hole, and I picked at the dried blood on the top of my arm.

And now Holly is here, looking over the crumbly countertop and the butter knife holding over the edge of the sink.

"Those aren't mine," I say. "They're my ma's."

She kind of shrugs her head to the side and says, "Fine with me either way."

"Well, you can't go in there," I call. "Ma wouldn't like it."

"Oh?" she says. "Okay."

Daddy pounds and the whole house rattles, even my hand and it burns when it does. He's talking so loud now at Ma that I start to go to the front of the house, to the stairs.

"Hey now," says Holly. "Hey, Enid. Come on back in here with me, please." She follows me, so when I get to the dining room, I turn back.

In the eating room's bathroom, she flicks on the fan.

"We don't need that," I say, flicking the switch off, "because I'm not pooping with you in here and if you start to poop, I'll leave."

Her eyes go big but she kind of half giggles, then gets all serious again, then half giggles. "Thanks for the warning," she says. "I'll be sure to warn you before I suddenly poop in front of you."

I mash my lips together hard to keep from smiling. She sees.

"No matter who's pooping or not. I do have to warn you, though," she says and leans in almost close enough to kiss me. She whispers, "Sometimes I don't know when it's going to happen."

"Sick!"

"Gotcha," she says.

I roll my eyes like Vivvy would. She smirks.

And so I decide to ask her: "You're a grown-up, aren't you?"

"Yes," she says. "In most ways."

"Do you have to do everything my dad says?"

"Definitely not. Well, that all depends, I guess," she says. She reaches underhand behind her back with both arms now. When she moves just a tiny bit to the side, I can see why. She's holding the end of her braid, using the first and second fingers of both hands, straight like the scissors in Rock, Paper, Scissors, only she clamps the hair between her fingers and slides them down to the end of the braid. Over and over again, left hand, right hand, left hand, right.

"That's kind of weird. When you do that, it's kind of like you're petting yourself."

"Oh," she says and stops.

"Sorry," I say.

"That's okay. Sorry I was being weird."

"It's not a bad weird. You can still do it," I say. "It's fine."

"Okay, maybe another time."

She turns on the faucet and takes the little fringed towel off its ring. "Do you think your mother will mind?"

"I wouldn't if I were you."

"Hmm," she says. She goes out to look at the kitchen again. There are cleaning cloths in here under the sink and I don't tell her.

When she comes back, she has paper towels. The water is steamy on the bottom of the mirror. She turns both knobs and tests the temperature with her fingers. Now she tears off paper towels and crumples each one into a wad under the faucet, letting them get really soppy-wet, then wringing them out. She wets each one until she has a pile of wet, wadded towels on the counter.

"Hop up," she says. She pats the other side of the counter. Ma calls it *the vanity* because those are the kinds of words she's good at.

I scoot my butt up to the sink but with only one hand, all I can do is try to lean myself up onto it.

"Hold on," she says.

Her arms go around my middle and now I'm in the air and plopped right onto the counter. She doesn't say, *Oh my god, you weigh a ton! Oh my god, what have you been eating?*

I move my legs out of the way and tell her the stuff's down below me. She opens the cupboard and brings up Ma's box of first aid supplies. It's not an official box like the ones teachers have on the walls over their sinks at the back of the classrooms. It is an old shoe box with Ma's neat, black writing on one short edge of the lid: *Tan Peep-Toe*.

She opens it, looks over the tidy rows of bandage boxes arranged by size and shape, the cotton balls, Q-tips, gauze pads, and white tapes.

There are little bottles that sting so I say, "Ma never uses those."

She pushes at one side of a bottle and it spins to show the back label. "You have an awful lot, don't you?"

"Ma likes to be prepared."

"I guess so."

She pushes that bottle's side, slowly, purposefully spinning it back to face right side up again. Now she pushes the side of the next bottle and, when it first begins to spin, the bottles *clink* against each other. That's a Ma-sound; I've only ever heard it when Ma spins on the bottles to spin them—her baking extracts, too.

"We'll start small, shall we? The easy ones first." She rolls up the leg of my jeans just a bit. "You got really scraped up down here, didn't you?" She squeezes a little water out on my shin. One line is deeper, darker. She presses the towel to it and the blood turns the water pink. She wipes at it, soaks a cotton ball in one of the bottles, and daubs that on. "Sorry," she says. "Does it hurt?"

I shake my head but hold my breath through the burning. At least it makes me feel my hand less.

She cuts lengths of tape and makes a rectangle of gauze to cover the scratches. She tapes it down on all the edges and makes an X across the rectangle, too.

"Okay," she says. "Let's look at that knee." She rolls my jeans up over my knee, being careful not to touch the skinned and clawed part where four straight lines are scratched into me. She washes it and cleans it just the same but uses the biggest Band-Aid we have because it's special for knees. She checks my other leg but it's not bloody, just has a few white scuff marks on the knee. She blots at them with a clean, wet paper towel. The towels aren't warm anymore but I don't tell her.

"Look up," she says and daubs at something under my chin.

"Is it bleeding?" I say.

"No," she says, smearing it between two sides of the paper towel when she's done. "I think it's . . . spaghetti sauce?"

"Oh," I say, rubbing the spot away on the topside of my left hand. "Pizza."

"It's okay. Look." She lifts part of her skirt and hunts amid the blue-and-white paisleys and flowers of the fabric. "See?" She holds it out to me and there's a faint orange stain. "Everyone makes a mess every once in a while. Your dad on the other hand, well . . ." she says but that's all.

She takes my good hand, gently pushes up the sleeve. She turns it and lifts it up to inspect my whole arm. Now she holds it twisted so she can work on the elbow. When that's clean and bandaged, she says, "Last but definitely not least," and touches the cuff of the sweatshirt.

I nod.

She squats down, trying to replace some of the bandage boxes in the right spots of the jigsaw puzzle as Ma can always do super-speedily. There is a loud noise upstairs, like dropping Ma's double-volume dictionary flat to the linoleum. Maybe louder.

Holly's head spins from the box to look right at me. "It's okay. It will be okay."

"Now to your hand," she says. She gets her face down close to my hand and begins touching the end of the sleeve.

I take a deep breath and look away.

"I'm sorry," she says, "am I hurting you?"

I pinch my lips between my front teeth. I watch the loose blue thread snagged from her ribbon bend one way, then fold back at the kink in its middle and stand straight up. She moves out of focus and back in focus, bends over my hand again, and I notice she has the very end of her braid in her mouth.

Her hands stop moving. So I look down. My hand is still here and deep inside the towel, still looks like a hand. On the tops of my knuckles are circles of dried blood. My fingers stick together. I try to loosen them.

"Um, don't go anywhere, okay? Just sit tight. And don't pull anything apart just yet. Just give it a minute."

When she comes back, she brings trays of ice—all of them—and twists the cubes right into the sink. Now she runs cold water on the ice and stoppers the sink. The cubes crack, some breaking themselves apart.

"We're going to put that hand in here, soak it a bit, then unwrap it and soak it some more. Sound like a plan?"

I shrug. It's a plan but I don't know if it's a good one.

"You ready?" she says.

I nod.

Together, we lower my hand down in. The ice and water take on a faint pink cloud I know used to be in me. It's all so cold that, for a second, I can't even feel it. Until I do and now there is a new kind of pain I can't do anything about. She holds my arm just below the elbow and lifts it up from the water. The towel drips a steady stream of water. She undoes the towel from around my hand and it's okay. It comes off and I'm okay.

"It was the dogs," I say.

"Your dogs? Dogs you know?"

I nod.

"Ouch," says Holly. She moves my hand closer to inspect the cut. "It's not so bad, though you might get a little scar but that's okay, I've got a few of my own." She points to a white line across her elbow. "Glass window," she says.

Now she holds my hand again and together we move it back and forth in the water. There is a flap of skin where fresh blood swims from it like a fancy fish's tail. It isn't long or wide.

She is quiet.

We keep stirring. Side to side, front to back, in circles, then bobbing up and down.

"It's kind of like stirring a witch's cauldron, isn't it?" she says.

"It's Halloween," I say.

"I know. I guess I'd forgotten but yes, it sure is."

We stir. I look down at the water but also, I can see out the corners of her eyes she is looking at me. My cheeks feel hot and I look back at the water only.

"What are you going as tonight?"

I shrug.

"Haven't decided?" she asks.

"Don't know."

She lifts my hand out of the water and I try not to but I cry.

"I'm sorry," she says. "It will probably hurt awhile longer and maybe even worse for a little bit while you thaw out." She presses a wad of gauze to the V between my thumb and hand. "I'm really, really, really sorry," she says. She positions my hand in the air and has me hold it there. She pours the bubbling liquid over and tells me to scream "Yayayayayaya!" while it burns and she shouts it with me, shaking her head back and forth. Now she blots my arm dry and starts winding the spool of gauze around my hand, around my wrist, around and around, then tapes down where it could get loose.

"Now we have to keep it upright," she says. "What's your favorite place in your house?"

"Basement?" I say. My voice squeaks in the back of my throat.

"Lead the way."

Downstairs she has me lie on the sofa with my arm up in the air. She sits down next to my head and I can't get comfy without a pillow so I put my head on her lap and look at her to make sure it's okay.

"Do you like anyone special at school?" she asks, looking down at me.

I shake my head, ask, "Do you have a boyfriend?"

"No," she says. "Not anymore."

"Oh," I say. "Me neither."

She smiles down at me, says, "It's okay if you want to shut your eyes."

She begins to hum. I don't know if she knows it's out loud or not. Her right hand touches my hair and strokes my forehead. I stretch my pinky finger and tuck it into Holly's silky braid.

Vivvy

It is a free country. Dawn can't make me go home. She can say whatever she wants but the parking lot of Pizza Inn is public property, so there is nothing either one of them can do to make me leave. She and Andy aren't even eating and it's 4:10—*big date, heavy, heavy!* So what is the big deal?

His bike rests against a lamppost by the curb, not chained or anything. I straddle mine, which is really Dawn's, even though I have on a dress. Our dress, which we planned on the phone last night. Mine is just like Dawn's: a green alligator shirtdress with the drop waist so gathers of the skirt-part begin at our hips. Hers is Izod. Mine is not because Dad doesn't know anything. But also we both have on our penny loafers—mine are black, which Dawn says is so much cooler than her regular ones. We keep dimes in the penny slots and that is how one can see just how in the know a person really is.

Last night Dawn said she wasn't going to wear her sweater so I don't have mine, but she *is* wearing it. She sneaks about everything now. Pizza Inn is stupid. And she never, *never* said she was doing another date. I sat in the grass and weeds opposite her house today. I shut my eyes and pictured her fingers running through the scales I could hear. She did the same two over and over so much it was almost like its own song. Then Andy came riding down her street. He waved at me, then huffed up her driveway. He wasn't in our plan. Dressing in pajamas and trick-or-treating together, that was our plan. Riding off to Pizza Inn on his handlebars wasn't our plan.

They are so boring inside that I have to watch the traffic lights change in the metal fenders of Andy's wheels. Then that's so boring, I look back through the tinted window. They bought drinks at the counter and have been playing tabletop Centipede by the WAIT TO BE SEATED sign ever since. Andy's right hand jerks like a lunatic's over the rolling ball; his left moves so fast over the button it seems not to move at all. Dawn stands behind him, sipping her Pepsi through a straw, and sometimes she leans over the game to see it better. She bounces up and down because he must be good, then goes quiet and touches his shoulder.

It's her turn. Finally. I tiptoe the bike a few inches closer because the sun has moved since the last time she got to play. She sits down and her hand floats over the ball, delicate like a bee that can't decide what flower it wants to land on. Her button hand is fast. Andy gulps his drink and sets it down on the glass top. He leans over Dawn to watch the snaking centipede come at her, bracing himself with one arm, his big stupid hand all spread out on the edges of the screen. But now he jumps around like he's *Andy to the rescue*, and slips his hand overtop her button hand to shoot even faster. The colors are in their faces: yellow, blue, and green. He shifts side to side depending on whether she is doing well or not. The whole time, Dawn's mouth makes the letter *O*, her lips full and open like she is waiting for something.

28

Tate

"Are you okay, baby?" I call out before I can even see Enid from the basement steps.

"Shh," says Holly. She shuts her eyes and nods toward Enid.

I pass through the waiting piles of laundry, pretending they do not exist. I get to the hide-a-bed. "You are too good," I tell her quietly. "A saint."

Holly smiles but lets it go fast. "Are you okay?" she says.

I wave her off. "I know this has been awful. How can I make it up to you?"

"It's fine. She's lovely."

"Truly," I say. "Babysitting, nursing? How much do I owe for your services?"

She lowers her jaw. "That isn't funny, Tate."

"I'm sorry," I say. "I don't mean anything."

"Is she here?" Holly whispers.

"No," I say.

I kneel down where I can look at my girl, at Enid. I touch her hand and sit back on my feet. "I'm so sorry, Holly. Today has been . . . There are no words for today."

I shake my head and look at beautiful Enid's big, rose-flushed cheeks. Her blue jeans, always so long her toes just barely peek out, and the nails smudged and smeared in pink polish.

"Watch out your skirt doesn't get any of that on it." I nod to a bit of blood dried between Enid's toes.

Holly shrugs and smiles.

And all around Enid's face—at her hairline, her temples, and high on her cheeks—wet clumps, just a few hairs in each, have stuck in the sheen that covers her entire body. I touch one of the snaking loops, slip a finger beneath where the wisps sprout from her head, and slide beneath it, lifting as I go. Two or three or four more strands remain. I rub a circle into them and when I see my finger moving this way, I remember Francie holding Shell in the night.

"She looks like sunken wreckage on the ocean floor," I say. "Greek statue or something. Both of you, together."

Holly looks at me and at Enid. "Hmm?"

"The way she's sprawled. With her hand up." I nod at the wrapped hand. "And you just so . . ."

Holly smirks.

"Her hand," I say, "it's bad?"

"It's not so bad, not so good," Holly says. "She could need stitches. Has she had a tetanus shot?"

"I'm sure she has. Is that one kids always get? She's had all of those, I'm sure."

"Rabies?"

"What?"

"She said it was the dogs."

"*Our* dogs?"

"Well," says Holly, "the big white dog I've seen in your office picture, that's Floey, right? She was saving Floey."

"Floey wouldn't bite my daughter."

"The neighbor dog was there. The dogs had something, a pan or something, she said, and they didn't want him to have it? I don't know; that's what I got out of her."

"Basey," I say.

"Hmm?"

"The neighbor dog. So it's not enough that he impregnates our dog, but now he's viciously attacked Enid?"

"It's not vicious. It's just a little flap of skin here." She points to the side of her own hand near the thumb.

"At least his shots are up-to-date."

"How do you know?"

"I went over there once she gave birth. Pretty obvious signs of a beagle."

"Well, that's good."

I set a hand on Enid's cheek. Beneath her eyelids flicker dreams. "Should we wake her?"

"At some point, probably." Holly looks at Enid's face. "I kind of think she needs the rest more right now. I bet she'll tell you what she needs."

"What, like stitches?"

"No . . . no. I mean she'll either be in so much pain she's screaming and you'll know to get her to a doctor, or she'll just kind of say it hurts and you'll give her baby Bayer."

I nod.

"You look like you've shaved three years off your life today."

"That good, huh?"

She blushes and looks down at Enid's face. "I think I was asleep until I heard footsteps," she says. "I'm glad they were yours."

I want to ask her, *will you stay just like this?* But Francie must come home soon.

29

Enid

I wake to the smell of the porch when it rains. I'm still on the basement hide-a-bed but Holly is gone and Vivvy is home. She is poking me, shaking me, feels like she's wrapping me up in something, who knows what else she's done?

"What?" I say, wiping spit off the side of my mouth, back and forth on the cushion.

"Sick," she says.

"When did you get here?" I say.

"I've been here. You were out cold."

I try to sit up but Vivvy pushes me back down.

I roll back down, stop myself from falling, and sit upright. "I don't feel so good," I say.

"I know just the thing." When she returns, she has the Kahlúa.

"Oh no," I say.

"Just a wee little bitty." Vivvy holds her fingers up in a microscopic measurement. She unscrews the cap and hands the bottle to me.

I take it but can't hold it double-handed so I slosh a bit. Just one sip. When I look down I'm stuffed like lumpy sausage into Ma's royal-blue tennis dress. "Oh my god, Vivvy!"

And so is she, except hers hangs off with inches to spare and it's yellow. The shoulders are so wide, they flop and one side hangs way over down onto Vivvy's elbow. Every few seconds she pulls it back up. Now she's bent over one of Ma's special boxes we are never to touch. It's pulled out from under the TV counter and the flaps are wide open.

"Oh my god, there's *everything* in here!" she says.

"What are you doing?"

"What does it look like I'm doing, dummy?" She pulls out a pretty scarf that's dark blue with little red flowers all over it. Vivvy holds it end to end and folds a triangle. She bends over again—so does her dress, and no, she is not wearing a bra—with all her hair fluffed and hanging down, then sweeps it up in a bouffy bun she wraps the scarf around to hold in place. I go to the box to look for something that will work for me.

Vivvy goes into the laundry room and when she comes back she holds up two clothespins. "Hold still," she tells me.

"No, please, Vivvy." I cross my arms but can feel a pinch of my fatty skin on both sides of my chest as if she's already fastened the clips to me.

She pushes down on my shoulder until I'm kneeling and my knees feel like big yellow bruises. "Sit down," she says.

I jiggle my right hand to shake the throb right out of it. I could run upstairs. I could find Daddy or Floey.

"Just hold still." Vivvy places one pin between her lips just like Ma always does with a comb or ponytail holder when she fixes our hair.

I hold still.

Vivvy rakes her fingers through my hair, starting in my bangs and pulling all the way back. When she hits a tangle, she yanks right through it. She sections off a handful and snaps the pin's clamp right around the hair. She reopens the clothespin and clips it into place along the side of my head. I can't see it but it feels smooth.

"Is it good, Vivvy?" I say. "Is it pretty and smooth?" I put my good hand on it and try to touch every part of it without messing it up. "Should we be doing this?" I whisper.

Vivvy looks at me and laughs. Then she leans into my ear and yells, "Of course not!"

I jump back, rub at my ear. In the white wrapping over my hand, a faint pinkness has begun to show through.

"Oopsy," she says. "Should have had these in." She hands me cotton balls from the box. We stuff them in our ears like we've seen Ma do when she gets one of her headaches and everything we do is forty times too loud.

Vivvy picks up the Kahlúa and sips from it. She puts one hand on her hip and makes the other one flop around in the air while she yells, "Girls, girls! Could you please just hold still and please, oh please, not say another word, please!"

"Eh?" I say, cupping my ear. "I can't hear you. I've got the cotton in my head. Did you say something?"

Vivvy repeats Ma's line and we die laughing.

Now I try. Hand on waist, gauze hand swinging around at Vivvy, I say, "And do you think it possible, at all, for you two to make no sound at all?"

"And maybe, too," says Vivvy, "you could be a couple of dears and stop breathing? Do you think? Hmm? Hmm? A couple of dears?"

"Might you be a pair of pumpkins," I say, and Vivvy falls sideways on the sofa, banging her head on the far, chewed-up armrest, "and live down the street where I can't hear you?"

"Or smell you."

"Stop it," I say, "I'll pee."

"Wouldn't be the first time."

I can't help laughing so she keeps going: "Be a couple of platypuses—"

"Be a pair of orangutans," I say.

"Be two dolphins."

"Be seventy-two field mouses."

"Field *mice*," says Vivvy.

"Field mic*es*."

"Be a penguin. Be one tiny hummingbird."

"Be half a person," I say.

"Quarter person."

"A third—"

"One-nineteenth of a person," she says.

"Be someone else," I say.

"Yeah, someone else."

We collapse, panting and staring, at either end of the hide-a-bed. We look at the box and the dresses, frilly tennis underpants and padded sun visors strewn about the room, in colors like ice cream scoops and other families' cereal.

"What is that?" she says, pointing to my right hand.

"Nothing," I say.

Vivvy takes the cotton out of her ears. She tosses it on the floor. "*I* know!" she says, like she's had the best idea ever. Now she's up and fiddling with the TV. She yanks on the knob, turning on the set. It makes the *zap* noise that shocks her full of electricity. She likes that.

"That's it, that's it!" I say. "Oh, but it's not Sunday. *Alice* isn't on."

She's done and backs away just a little—way too little as far as Ma would say but what do I care about that? I mouth the station number, *seven, seven, seven,* and the first image we see is big-headed Ernest and one of his pickup trucks. He does his thing with the teeth and says what he says: "It's the epi-tome of excellence. Knowhutimean?" He's funny but Vivvy thinks he's stupid.

She turns around to look at me to be sure I'm not laughing.

"What?" I say it right to her.

"Nothing." She turns her head back to the TV.

I pinch the cotton out of my ears, too, now. I stand up to get hers and throw them in the laundry trash because Ma, but I think of touching them and it's disgusting, like licking a used Q-tip almost. I don't have to do it—I don't have to do anything, so I plop back onto the sofa.

"But turn it down," I whisper.

She drops to the floor, as close to the TV shelf as she can get, and leans back on her palms because that's how you have to do it if you want to see the set from there.

She looks over her shoulder at me. "Well come here," she says. I do.

She rubs her hands together, saying, "Now let's watch TV!" like it's the greatest secret plot ever.

Francie

Darkness falls through the trees and out across the length of me. I won't go into the house tonight but sleep here with him.

Vivvy

It's six o'clock. We can go out soon. Probably after two more episodes. We dig through more boxes and hit gold: all the fancy shoes Mom used to wear. I peel off my socks and throw them at Enid. She ducks the first but the second ricochets off her head.

She puts her left hand where it hit and feels around all over her clothespin hairdo. "Did you mess it up?"

"No."

"Everything's still smooth?"

"Here," I tell her, handing over a pair of silver high-heeled sandals.

Enid unfastens the buckles to widen them. Her fat foot jams into the front band of the shoe but her heel doesn't come close to being far enough back for the ankle strap. She looks at me now. "What will you wear?" Enid keeps rummaging in Mom's junk. "Oh, look!" she says, pulling out a shoe box marked *Yellow Patent.* "They go with your dress."

I open the box and the shoes are awesome and there is no way they are Mom's. They are yellow patent leather with tall skinny heels. I stand them on the carpet and get myself up, tugging up the top of my dress as I do. I step into one shoe and I'm no longer a midget. I step into the other shoe. I have to hold my arms out like a tightrope walker but I manage to stay up.

"Oh my god," says Enid. "You're almost as tall as you should be now!" She stands up, too, but her shoes have lower heels and she is wearing them like slippers, the backs of her feet squashing the ankle straps beneath them. She takes a step and another. We both do but Enid's have thick and low heels so I wind up grabbing for her just before falling. I take us both down into a pile of dirty clothes.

"Grody," I say.

Enid copies me now, saying, "Grody," too.

"Grody to the max."

Enid's feet are nearly up my nose and in between her toes are dried-on drizzles of blood. She swings her legs around the other way and we get ourselves back up and take a few more steps before toppling over again and again. Eventually, though, we can't get ourselves back up. We collapse in front of the TV, our legs stretched and splayed out in front of us.

"It's a marathon."

"How many?" she says.

"I guess until the Charlie Brown." I start up with our invisible microphone now, singing the theme song, "Early to rise . . ." now hold it in front of Enid.

She sings into it, too: "Early to bed." She leans back over to me and we do that, we swerve over onto whoever is singing. Back and forth we go. First me then Enid, me then her, until the chorus when we smash our sides together, our faces, too, and belt it out.

Now there is just my voice holding the last note. Enid is sobbing uncontrollably—like if a person can die from crying, bang: she's dead.

I stare at her, like *come on, lady; get it together.*

I pat her shoulder twice and say, "It's okay."

I crawl over to the bottle of Kahlúa, bring it back, and give Enid first offer. She shakes her head, wiping down her face one-handed, dragging more of the long pieces of her hair into the gooey mess of her cheeks and chin. I take a sip but keep the rim suctioned to my mouth, keep the liquid's burn against my lips until the suction breaks and a gulp's worth pours down the front of Mom's dress, dark and sticky.

I set down the bottle. "Oopsy," I say, holding the fabric out to show Enid.

She squints through gluey, gloppy eyelashes. "You're gonna get it," she says. Her cheeks fatten bigger with a smile, but on them old snot and tears that must have dried there who knows how many hours and layers ago have left these shiny slug trails running up and down and cracking open beneath the wet the more she smiles.

She holds on to her knees now and presses her face in deep.

I slip an arm around Enid and lean my head against hers. "You're okay," I whisper. "It will be all right."

Tate

I drop Holly at work for a late second shift, drive out to Peoples Drug and slip inside a minute or two before the manager spins the lock.

I nod to let him know I understand the protocol. "Apologies," I say. "I'll be quick."

"The pharmacy is shut," he says.

"That's not what I'm after. Where is your Halloween merchandise?"

He steps aside. Everything left is heaped on a table near the checkout. Black-and-orange half-price signs adorn the edges of the tabletop.

"The discount is for tomorrow," he says, "not tonight."

"Understood."

There isn't much here. Bags of candy corn, themed art packets of orange and black pipe cleaners and construction paper, candy bucket jack-o'-lanterns that, upon closer inspection, must be seconds; their printed faces don't match their embossed faces but are a few inches left or right of center.

I dig through the crap I cannot imagine anyone will ever buy to find what I want and pay for it.

"Thank you," I tell the manager when he spins the lock for me to get out.

Vivvy

There is a knock at the door. We scrabble upstairs and through the kitchen, gripping and propelling off countertops and dining room chairs, the dogs excited and following us, until we open the front door and stand there falling onto each other and tipping out of our high heels.

"Trick or treat!" It is a Smurf and a littler He-Man.

I can see their grown-up standing in the darkness under the trees at the bottom of our driveway. I turn on the porch light but it only helps me see right here on the steps.

The kids' eyes grow wide looking at us. Still they hold out their candy buckets.

"I like your costume," says Enid to the Smurf, who maybe smiles or maybe doesn't; I can't see anything through the fake mouth hole.

"Just a minute," I tell the kids and shut the door.

"What are you doing?" Enid asks.

I *clip-clop* to the kitchen and she follows. So do the dogs. I go to the pantry and Enid to the refrigerator. We stumble back to the door, me hoisting up the neck of my dress so it isn't down to my elbow or off both shoulders at once. Now I drop a sleeve of saltines into each bucket and Enid gives each kid a wilted carrot. We watch them run back down our driveway, the slimy green tops dangling over the edges of their candy buckets.

I shut the door and we laugh so hard Enid gets that look. If I push it, like I usually do, she will become an actively erupting pee volcano.

There is another knock at the door.

"Trick or treat!" call a Strawberry Shortcake, E.T., Chewbacca, ghost in a sheet with tiny flowers on it, and Snoopy.

"One minute, please," says Enid. She shuts the door and we run hobbling to the kitchen. This time we shake seven raisins and a leaf of lettuce into their buckets and bags.

"Are those clothespins?" one of them says but we can't tell whose mouth moved behind their masks and we ignore the question.

When we shut the door, though, Enid looks at herself in the dining room wall mirrors. "Is it still smooth?" she asks me and I tell her yes.

Next is Porky Pig and Daffy Duck with another E.T., Spider-Man, and G.I. Joe. Enid and I bring armfuls of food to the front door. We pass out a knife's scrape of peanut butter, a slice of bread, a handful of white sugar, and when those are gone, we get even more desperate with cans of chicken broth and kidney beans, whole boxes of noodles and mashed potato flakes. And when the shelves are bare, we open the freezer and carry Styrofoam trays of ground beef, flank steak, and chicken parts and drop those into their pillowcases and buckets.

Now there is nothing left. Enid and I sit on the bottom steps of the upstairs staircase, waiting for the next trick-or-treaters to knock so we can tell them they are too late.

"I know what!" says Enid. She *clacks* back into the kitchen. I hear her drag the pantry stool across the linoleum. She is in the cupboards, sliding plate stacks and wineglasses aside.

The dogs know the next trick-or-treaters are coming before I do. Floey lies upright, her tail sweeping the floor. She woofs once. The new dog stands at the door, wagging. I pull him back to the stairs to keep from tripping on him.

The trick-or-treaters knock. I open the door and the kids call out "Trick or treat!" like all the others but these two are different in every way. A little witch and something with green face paint, they aren't in store-bought costumes or masks, but in real clothes and makeup.

"What are you?" I ask the green one.

"A goblin."

"You're the Hulk," says the witch.

The noise of Enid's shoes startles them when they see it's only a girl. I pull up the sleeve of my dress.

"What are *you*?" says the witch.

I look at Enid, stuffed into Mom's tennis dress, the silver shoes, and blood soaking through her gauze bandage.

"A Francie," I say. "We both are."

At that, I see what Enid has in her arms and I smile so big.

273

"Hold out your bags," I tell them.

Enid's arms are too full so I pluck each treat from them and drop it into the witch's and Hulk's bags. First go in Mom's daily notecards of calories counted, recounted, and uncounted. I rain them down into the bags, half to the witch and half to the Hulk. Next her special thin marker for writing up all her lists and counts. I drop this in the bag of the witch. The Hulk gets her encyclopedia of calories and nutrition. And now, Enid hands me the last of it.

"Are you sure?" I ask.

"Positive," she says.

Who should get this one I don't know so I start in with, "Eeny, meeny, miny, mo—"

Enid grabs the food scale from me and drops it, clattering, into the witch's bag.

"We don't want all this junk," says the witch.

"Where's your candy?" says the Hulk.

"We don't have a mother," says Enid.

"She died," I say.

The green face crumples up. The witch sticks out her tongue at us and now they both go running down the porch steps and across our yard but there's no grown-up waiting there for them.

Enid slams the front door shut with the wrong hand. "Ow oh-oh-oh-oh-oh!" she squeals and looks at the blood making the bandage wetter and redder. "Stupid dog," she says.

She *click-clacks* to the kitchen. I collapse on the stairs laughing so hard I lean all the way back and shut my eyes. I hear Enid folding up the stool and slipping it against the broom and mop inside the pantry. She shuts all the cupboard doors and tidies up everything else we touched, I guess. She is good at that, at following rules or at least making it look like she has.

I grab hold of the railing and get my yellow shoes pointed forward and upright on the floor. Before hoisting myself up, though, I check the top of my dress, which is now all the way down to my elbow again on one side so I must have looked like the one-naked-booby lady on the Virginia flag to all the little kids coming by. That makes me laugh hard.

When I get to the kitchen, Enid isn't there. I go to the porch and see her just outside.

"What are you doing?" I say, pushing through the screen door.

She's weird. She doesn't turn around. I wobble through the gravel to her and put a hand on her back. In the darkness, I creep it around her side to find the fatty pinch but she already has it hard between her fingertips.

The new dog is out but stays farther up our street. We see him sniffing cars and mailboxes every few minutes, lifting his leg to pee on them just like Basey, and then off he goes into the night.

I link our arms but Enid stumbles so we both fall flat and just sit here at the end of the driveway. The rocks poke our butts. When trick-or-treaters get close, we cover our mouths and make ghost sounds they think are coming out of the trees.

"Come on, let's go get candy," I say. "Let's stay out forever!"

We crawl to our feet and me and Enid, arm in arm, walk around in the night as Francies.

30

Tate

When I pull up at home, the porch light is off. The driveway
floodlight has lost its tension and points straight down. But inside, it looks like a party is under way with nearly every downstairs light on. Upstairs, too, there is a light on in the back of the
house, in our bedroom—too bright because when it blew last
night I didn't first look at the wattage before I changed the bulb.
What any of it means, I cannot say.

"Hello?" I call.

Floey greets me at the kitchen door, whining to go out. I
set down the bags and look her over, touching the lines of her
slack belly and backbone, her ears, and underneath her collar.
She seems unscathed from whatever happened with the neighbor
dog so I let her out.

I unpack the bags on the counter. This morning's breakfast
dishes were minimal because the food was minimal but they and
their crumbs have not moved from the far counter and the baking
bonanza is still wedged into the sink. I clear the breakfast plates
and the oily plate the peanut butter balls were on, and I scrape

off the crumbs. No other plates are here. I check the fridge to see what they might have picked at for supper and it's empty. Not even pickles and condiments left. Francie strikes again.

Floey's wings are out on the counter for tonight. I push them and their debris out of the way. I set out the two least screwy jack-o'-lantern candy buckets the store had and inside each put one of the full-size peanut M&M's and Baby Ruth candy bars. Best of all, I lay out the two costumes. They are only first-movie stormtrooper costumes but they're still something.

•

In the laundry room, I scan the bulb boxes on the shelves over the washer and dryer. They are no longer neatly arranged and labeled—*V&E's Room, Hllwy, Upstairs, Kitchen Sink*—as they always have been. I guess on a seventy-five watt for the bedroom and grab that. I go stand among the laundry piles and picture Holly here with Enid on the couch.

I flip off all the lights and sit beneath the basement steps. I dial the shop. Diane, the manager, will be long gone by now. I count out our seven rings just as Holly is doing on the other end.

"Hello?"

"It's me," I say quietly.

"Is she okay?" We both whisper now.

"She's doing great," I say.

"I've been worried," she says. The sound of Holly whisking stops. "We are friends, after all. Aren't we?"

"Of course."

"Did it start bleeding again?"

"No," I say. "She and Vivvy are trick-or-treating right now."

"What did she go as?"

"What are you making right now?"

"Chocolate-peanut. Hey," she says, "what did she go as?"

"I don't know. I just missed them heading out."

"Shit. I'm sorry," says Holly. "I told you you needed to get home."

"I stopped back at campus for my things, then went to Peoples Drug for costumes. I just missed them."

"But you saw her hand," says Holly. "You checked how it's doing, right?"

"I—no."

"Oh my god. Dr. Sobel, why did you even call here?"

"I wasn't in time to see her, but I will. And it's good, right? That she felt good enough to go out with Vivvy for candy."

"Yes, but you need to look at it. That doesn't mean anything."

"I will. She'll be home any minute," I say, wishing I'd waited to call. "I'll check her hand first thing the minute she gets home. And if it is bad, if there's anything that seems slightly worrisome, I will take her to the hospital in Christiansburg."

I am quiet now and hear the slight tapping Holly gives the raised doughnuts. I've watched her enough to know she is flipping them over in the oil. Soon after, she'll run the dowel through all of their holes to remove them before they get too dark. In what seems a single motion, she will let each doughnut slide from the dowel onto its spot on the drying rack, where they drain.

"'Dr. Sobel,' huh?"

"We have to start proper salutations sometime."

"Right," I say. My eyes are still shut. What I see is Holly kneading, frying, glazing.

•

I take the bulb up with me and double-check that the kitchen door onto the porch is unlocked so the girls can get in. For a bit, I sit in the darkness of the screened porch with a beer and the leashes and flashlight.

I look into the night of the backyard, look into the dull gleam of slugs' trails through the gravel and across the pathway stones. I shine the light into the length of the backyard, at least as far as it will travel—maybe halfway. I scan the sides, the center, beneath the trees, and within all the shrubs. In the girls' tree, I come to two red dots like a digital clock. They move, slightly, slowly, sleepily. As soon as what it is registers, I move the light off the possum. I see nothing else alive, though surely there are plenty of squirrels and nesting birds in our yard.

I take the seventy-five watt bulb and beer upstairs to the bedroom but only set the bulb on Francie's desk. I flick on the desk lamp, though it isn't needed. She's not in the bedroom, of course. That is plain to see.

I move to the window, look at my car in the driveway. At the end of the hall, Shell's door hangs from its broken jamb.

She is truly gone.

Enid

"This way, this way," says Vivvy, pulling at me. She has her arm through mine, which mostly helps us both stay upright in the shoes. Plus I already have a bandage on one knee so just one gets skinned when we fall. Vivvy's knees are both dripping but she doesn't care.

"Let's go this way," she says. "I want to see what Jamie's wearing. And Cindy. I want to see what everyone is wearing. And that girl Monica."

"You just want everyone to see what *you're* wearing." I flick up the back of her skirt. "Or not wearing."

"Oh please," says Vivvy, rolling her eyes, but she hoists one of the sleeves back up onto her shoulder.

"I thought you were going with Dawn tonight."

"So?" says Vivvy. "Come on."

We try to run to catch up with a group of two sets of kids and one dad. The pink Care Bear and brown Care Bear, Raggedy Ann with yarn hair and a real dress, Kermit the Frog and Miss Piggy, and a Pac-Man. Without our high heels, we'd be shorter than the Pac-Man and Kermit, but we walk up to the next house's front door like we know them.

The bears get to the door first and just stand there. Raggedy Ann rings the doorbell and when the lady opens the door, everyone says, "Trick or treat." They hold out their candy buckets and pillowcases and the lady drops two Tootsie Rolls in each one. The other kids get off her front steps and go back to the sidewalk. When it's just us left, the lady says, "Where is your candy?"

"We don't have any," says Vivvy.

She holds out the Tootsie Rolls. "Well, here you go," she says.

"Thank you," we say and hobble down her walkway. I'm pretty sure there's a big yellow blister on the top of each of my big toes. The faster we go, the less I think about it, though, so we catch back up to the Pac-Man group.

"Look, Enid." Vivvy's pointing across the street.

We cross over to join up with Boss Hogg, a scarecrow, Batman, and a vampire. Even though we're tipping over next to them, we can tell how much bigger they are than us. At the first house, the lady doesn't even see us standing behind them all and she shuts the door without giving us any candy.

"What did you get?" asks Vivvy.

The vampire looks in his bag. "Two Reese's cups."

"Damn," says Vivvy.

I look at her face, which is the face she has at school.

"Here." Batman hands her one of his and hands me the other.

"Really?" I say.

"I can't eat them."

"Oh," I say. "Thank you."

We give him our Tootsie Rolls and tear into our peanut butter cups.

"Trick or treat!" we all say. This time Vivvy and I stand in the front.

"Well let me get a good look at you all," says the old man. "I know who you are, Batman." He drops a lollipop into every bag or bucket once he figures out their costumes. "And you make a fine scarecrow. Don't suck my blood, Dracula! This one and you two, I'm going to need some help on."

"I'm Boss Hogg," says the boy. "*Dukes of Hazzard*?"

"Heard of it, I've heard of it." He drops in the lollipop.

Now he sets down the bag of them. From his shirt pocket he takes a pair of glasses and slides them up his nose. The lenses are yellowed, the nose pads green with old, dead skin he's sloughed off. His eyeballs grow behind the glass. He leans down to us, his face closer than our own to each other. First he examines Vivvy.

She crosses her arms and holds both of her sleeves up onto her shoulders.

"Now how am I supposed to figure you out if I can't see you in your entirety?" he says.

Vivvy doesn't say anything. She drops one arm. The sleeve stays up. Her ankle flexes sideways in her shoe. I hold her free hand.

"I guess you have me stumped," he says. "What are you?"

I don't say Francies and neither does Vivvy.

Tate

I stand in the backyard, calling, "Enid, Vivvy, Floey!" as if they are three sisters, and I whistle again for the new dog. I'd call him, but how? I call out "Floey" once more but hear no snapping of branches or running of claws down asphalt. The girls probably lassoed the new dog and took him begging and now Floey's joined up with them.

I get in the car.

I know my way to Raymond's place well enough. I can bring Francie back. At least the girls will come home and see the costumes and candy.

I cross Preston and go slowly. So many kids are out still. I turn on a cross street, go down Draper then back up Main, driving in squares like this, up and down the neighborhood, street after street, block after block. Enid and Vivvy have been gone for hours, milking Halloween and its candy carte blanche. But the kids out now are all the middle schoolers, high schoolers, and college kids pranking. The sidewalks crawl with fortune-tellers, monsters, little girls dressed up like their mothers, and spies. No more fluffy bunny suits or Big Birds; these kids draw blood. I round and reround the blocks.

31

Enid

When Vivvy tries to veer me her way, I pull her back just as hard to mine.

"I want to go home," she says. "I can't even walk anymore."

And it's true. She has fallen three times just on this block. But I don't want to go back. I feel like I never want to go back.

"Fine," I say, "you can go if you want." She won't. I know she won't.

Vivvy lets go of my arm and teeters in her yellow shoes but then she gets going, sort of shuffling her steps along, her arms out at her sides. She'll come back, though. She's just teasing.

I watch her.

She gets all the way to the corner and stands underneath the stop sign. She grabs hold of its pole, turns around to see me, and motions for me to come with her.

I shake my head.

Vivvy crosses the street. It takes her about five times longer than a normal person and about three times longer than when we hold on to each other. Once she gets to the other side, though, she doesn't look back. She keeps on going.

"Wait!" I call after her and we head home.

Now we're trying to figure out how to walk up the gravel of our driveway. Crab walk sideways on all fours—or all threes for me—and I figure it out. Going backwards works best, so Vivvy copies me and we get to the screened porch.

"Hey," she says. She reaches out to me for balance but is close enough she pinches my twist of skin. She's looking back at the driveway and now I see it, too. The driveway is still empty.

We go inside, *clomp* up into the kitchen from the porch.

"Dad?" says Vivvy but in her usual voice, not like she needs to find someone.

"No one is here," I say.

"Not even Floey."

I see the countertop first. "Look!" Two stormtrooper costumes in boxes, with plastic masks and smocks that tie up the back. They're wonderful, except that they should have hair because I've always said I want the kind of costume with molded hair that is smooth and perfectly beautiful. I tear the soft cardboard of my costume's box trying to get it open.

"So cool," says Vivvy. She's already slipping on her smock and tying the strings behind her neck and waist. "You should put that in a sock."

She means my hand. So I slide my smock up my arms and we grab our pumpkin candy buckets and *click-clack* and *rustle-rustle* upstairs. I go into Daddy's sock drawer and take one of his thickest ones. It's navy blue and itchy but I put that over the gauze.

"Tie my strings," I say.

She comes to where I am in their room and messes with them. She yanks on the smock.

"Don't wreck it," I say.

"They don't reach."

"Don't be mean, Vivvy."

"For real."

Vivvy opens Ma's desk drawer and staples the ties together at their very ends so the smock will close. I stand in front of Ma and Daddy's mirror. The picture of the stormtrooper kind of sucks in and out of my folds down my front just a little bit. I slip the mask on over my clothespins, get the elastic over my ears, and line up the eyeholes and mouth. It's perfect. I could be anyone now and no one would know.

I follow Vivvy to our room. She stops at Shelly's door hanging broken and open. "Whoa," is all she says and she keeps walking.

"Daddy did it."

I sit on my bed. Vivvy clambers up the ladder to hers.

I touch the candy in my jack-o'-lantern, the M&M's and Baby Ruth. "Are you going to eat yours now?" I say, rustling the wrappers with my hand.

"Mom's not here. You better eat them while you still can." Vivvy takes off Ma's scarf from over her bouffy hairdo. It looks as good as when she first made it.

"I don't want them," I say.

"Me neither," says Vivvy. "If Shell were still here, Mom would have banned Halloween by now."

"Hasn't she?" I say. I sit on my bed and turn to the wall, tuck my fingers up into the space between the wall and Vivvy's bunk. "Do you miss him?"

"I don't even remember him."

I lie down.

In a minute, Vivvy peeks over the edge of her bunk and she's upside down, her ponytail dangling like she's hanging from our tree. "You're keeping on your mask?" she asks.

I nod. "Dad would say the mouth hole's perfect for M&M's." I stick a finger through the hole and bite the tip.

She looks back a second later and she's in her mask. "Why do you think Ma got us all this stuff?" asks Vivvy.

"To make us like her?" I say. I lift my right arm up over my head and prop my sock hand on the pillow just in case.

"Maybe," says Vivvy. "Fat like her."

"She knew we were gonna dress up like her tonight."

"Nuh-unh! There's no way."

"That's why she hugged us and said we'd be pretty."

Vivvy is quiet.

We lie in the quiet of nighttime dark without dogs, without parents, and without a brother still.

•

I wake. It's still nighttime. I touch my face to see the mask hasn't come off.

"Vivvy," I call. "Look at my hand." The gauze bandage glows in the dark of our hallway. And when I turn it palm side up, there is no more blood. Like it's all soaked back into my hand while I slept. "Look," I say, holding it out to her.

"What?" she says. She lifts her head a second. *"Be healed, child!"* says Vivvy loud and silly like a TV preacher. *"A miracle of the blood!"*

"It's a miracle!" I say.

"It's a miracle. Woo woo woo woo!"

"Could have been Daddy, I guess."

"Or Mom."

"I don't think so." I try to picture Ma sneaking in to change my bandage. I can't see it—can't see her sitting next to me on my bunk, the warm steam of her breath falling around me, and her peeling up the tape of the old one and replacing one so clean and perfect. Her doing it so soft I don't even wake.

"I wore my shoes to bed, did you?" says Vivvy. She pulls one leg out from under the sheet. Dangling from her toes is one of Ma's yellow high heels. As dark as it is, though, I can see the difference in what they were when we found them and what they are now: black scuffs and peeled leather.

"When Ma sees those, you're dead," I say.

"I'll just tell her *you* wore them."

"That's not—"

"Joking! Just joking." She pulls her leg back under the covers, shoe and all.

I get up, all rustly in the plastic smock. I step into my silver heels and *clomp* back to bed. "It still could have been Daddy," I say.

"Could have been Mom." She laughs softly so I laugh softly.

"Could have been Ma," I repeat.

Vivvy giggles. "It's a miracle!" she whispers.

I touch the gauze. It's dry. It isn't just a fresh layer taped over the old one. "Could have been Holly," I whisper and feel myself drift.

32

Tate

The decision not to drive to Boone, not to follow Francie, is made before I even see the dogs. I don't know when or if I ever intended to follow her again, actually, but all the way down on Main Street, loping through yards and even our dentist's parking lot, are the dogs. I pull over, push my seat forward, and call to them: "Floey! The new dog!"

I get some hoots from kids in the back of a pickup truck passing by, but the dogs, the dogs are amazing, textbook even. Floey perks her ears. She turns her head and the new dog sees me clearly and they both, free of any oncoming cars, bolt to me. Right into the backseat they go. I keep on Main and head around back to knock at the kitchen door at Carol Lee. It's cool out but I roll all the windows halfway down for the dogs anyway.

Holly comes eventually, wiping her hands in her apron. She opens the door a few inches, just enough for her face, says, "I'm not letting you in unless you can tell me Enid's hand is not spurting blood and that you've verified this fact with your own eyes."

"Let me in!" I beg. "It isn't, I swear."

So she steps back and I come in. She locks the door behind us and I follow her skirt back to the work area.

"She and Vivvy are zonked," I say. "They must have walked the entire Blacksburg grid. Do you know they're in their bunks right now, wearing their costumes—masks and all."

"Sleeping in them? What did you get them?"

"Stormtroopers."

"Really?" She's not impressed.

"I know, but it was all that was left. Truly."

"Masks and all," says Holly.

"I took pictures. But without flash it probably won't show much."

"So," she says, "the hand?"

"I changed the dressing. It's healing already."

Holly resumes the many processes of her second shift. I bask in the warmth of the ovens, fryers, and rising drawers, the sweet moist smell of sugar melting, crystallizing, and remelting.

"Like I said, she was asleep but I needed to get in there and look at it." I wink at Holly. "She was actually wearing one of my socks over the hand and had it up over her head, propped in her pillow, just like you hung it for her in your braid." I look to that spot in her hair.

Holly smiles and shows off the braid by letting it swing around her shoulder to rest down her front.

"Go on," she says.

"So I took off the sock and cut off your wrap. The bite wasn't even bleeding anymore. I rewrapped it with care."

"You're certain."

"Positive."

"Yay," says Holly with her hands in two happy little riotous fists. We stand on either side of the long metal worktable.

She is flirting with me, throwing her twists higher. She flings a long piece of dough in the air and with a single flick of both wrists the dough comes down to the tray, halved and twisted. These will rise again then fry, be painted with cinnamon then go under the glaze drizzler. I can always tell Holly's handmades from Diane's or Sheila's, whose are always uniform. Holly's are artistic, interpretive.

She places the twist she's just shaped and waits a moment before lifting the next length of dough, holding her hands up in front of her like the surgeons of *M*A*S*H*. "Tate," she says, looking directly at me and not surrendering the gaze. "What are you doing here?"

"I never expected to need or want to tell you this. Jesus, Holly, I thought you would tire of the novelty of dating your professor much sooner than now."

"Tate, you broke up with me like twelve weeks ago. And right now feels like the second time you've broken up with me today. You can stop, please. I know you've made your choice. Please don't think you need to explain anything more to me. That just kind of makes it hurt more."

"You asked me what's wrong—with me, with her, Francie. The answer is the same. But I couldn't tell you. He wasn't your son, you aren't a mother."

"I'm a human being," she says, "but if you don't trust I'll feel the *right way* about it, the *right kind* of sadness, then by all means keep it to yourself."

My eyes tear up all at once, spill wet and warm on my cheeks and beard. I tell her everything.

"When a child dies, all the papers cover it. They call it a *story*. They don't say everything but the university runs pictures of Francie's car and the gravel. The *Roanoke Times* sends someone to the house. The sun is in the trees and I sit reliving the answers to the shit reporter's questions. Some other grown kid knocks at the door; there is a rental on our block, a slim white house used by three to four students any given term. It is devoid of plantings, all visible upkeep—not even a sidewalk or path to the front door exists through its brambly front yard. So I think maybe, maybe this is one of its tenants come to ask for sugar.

"He asks where I was in the house, what I heard or felt or knew. He says, 'Sheldon, what an unusual name these days; was it a family name?' No, no tale to tell. Maybe we just liked the name, or maybe Francie decided and that was that. They ask to meet the girls but I say they're napping. They are five and three—no, two and a half—after all. Our entire conversation occurs on the front steps of the house. He looks over at the driveway. We buried him two days ago. Francie took him to Boone."

Holly reaches for both of my hands. She turns their palms to the light above this table. She brushes her own, dusty and white, against them, replacing my flour with hers and her flour with mine. She lays her hands out flat upon mine and in the silken wells of flour and sugar grit, we curl our fingers around each other's thumbs and hold on to each other.

"In the first year, at every neighborhood block party, faculty reception, and parent-teacher night, conversation stopped dead when I walked in. If the girls were with me, Vivvy was admired,

Enid's lingering baby cheeks squeezed. Francie never left the house except to exercise-shop." I mimic her like an aerobicizing robot skimming the cereal aisle for puffed wheat.

Holly giggles but we both fall quiet. She stands up a bit so I do the same. She pats her hands against her apron, sending up clouds of flour.

"Holly," I say, touching her cheek, her chin. My hand leaves a fine dusting of flour over her freckles so I rub to uncover them again. "Holly. Francie is gone. She had to go. Instead of chasing me out this time, she chased herself away. It's what she's always wanted, anyway. What she has always needed, I guess, and she's given it to the girls now, finally."

Holly looks up. "She's gone?"

"She's gone home. To her home at her dad's and with Shell. I don't expect she can come back from that again—I guess she never really did."

"I don't know what to think," Holly says, shifting her weight. "Why now? It's been years."

"I don't want this life with her and I don't want my old life with her. All her rules and upsets. I want my girls and to be allowed to walk into my son's room if I want to and to be allowed to say his name. I want my family, my whole family. Come here," I say, turning Holly to face me again, embracing her fully. I take hold of her braid a few inches below her neck. I grip the sturdy girth of it firmly, channeling all of what I want from Holly into my fist. "Can I kiss you?" I say, breathy and as ridiculous as a teenager.

"Yes," she whispers followed by a quick "No." She looks down and shakes her head. "No." Still, she slides an arm up my chest, its hand in my hair, finger and thumb squeezing my earlobe, touching my neck. "Not tonight," she says.

And she's right. That tonight doesn't mean anything for Holly. And it certainly doesn't make us any more viable.

Yet we hold together that much longer.

"Wait here," she tells me and when she returns it is with one of the pink cake boxes Enid covets whenever we come in here. Holly lifts the lid so I peek in. She playfully brings it down quick on my nose and fingers.

"Oh, okay," she says, now grinning, "you may look."

Inside are about a dozen of the most pristine and fresh chocolate-peanut, glazed, cake, cinnamon-sugar cake, blueberry cake, custard-filled, and chocolate raised doughnuts.

"The case is going to be light tomorrow," I say. "What will Diane say in the morning?"

"I made extra. And I can make more."

She slides things around, slips two special doughnuts, in the shapes of an *E* and a *V*, into the box, and tapes it shut. "Breakfast tomorrow." She leads me to the door, unlocks it, and hands me the box. Now she kisses my cheek and pushes me out the door. "Tell Enid the chocolate-peanut is for her," she says and pulls the door shut behind me.

"She'll be over the moon," I say. "Lock up." I motion a key turning and she turns the lock.

So I get in my car, wake the dogs up, and we drive on home. A block or so away, a thought comes to me: What if Francie is there? What if everything I told Holly was wrong?

I cut the lights coming up the driveway, aware now of the possum hanging in plain sight all these evenings.

The driveway is all mine. I get out and flip the seat back and the new dog is first out. Floey hops down, too. We go into the porch and I unlock the kitchen door.

"Daddy!"

I open the door and there is a little stormtrooper in her mother's high heels.

"New dog! You found the new dog!" Enid runs to him in her plastic costume with its apparently stapled ties, and throws herself on him. He gets his nose up behind the mask and nudges it around to the other side of her head so he can lick her up the front of her face like a lollipop, from the base of her neck to the top of her hairline.

"You better watch out, Enid, or he'll find out how many licks to the center of your Tootsie Pop."

But she is crying now, sobbing into the new dog's fur.

"What is it, baby girl?"

She hugs him tightly around his neck. "The whole trouble is that you should have a name," she cries to him. She scoots herself around to the front of him and looks face to face, eye to eye. "Lowell. That's your new name."

"Hey, uh . . . should we maybe the three of us talk about that, Enid?" I say. But she stops crying, wipes her eyes, and replaces the mask, so who am I to care if we have a dog named Lowell?

"Lowell, come over here," she says, *clomp*ing toward the sink, and he follows her. Not so much for the name, which he's never heard before, but for love of her. "Come over here now, Lowell." She crosses back to me and the countertop.

She sees Floey's fairy wings and picks them up but there's something else beneath them. A new set of small yellow wings.

Enid squeals. She holds the dog in place while wrestling the wings to his back. He takes a couple of steps away from us, then sits. The wings pleat and fold together down his back. Francie has actually finished something and managed to articulate this pair such that now when he trots in a small circle, the yellow wings open and shut.

"He's like a huge bird from a zoo," says Enid.

The other stormtrooper appears in the kitchen now. Vivvy giggles, watching the dog. Holding on to the kitchen sink behind her, she teeters in four-inch, bright-yellow high heels I doubt Francie ever wore even once. Vivvy rubs her eyes without removing her mask.

"You like the costumes, I see. I'm glad. And the shoes," I say, "are an interesting accessory choice. I like it—it's *inspired*."

"Wait till you see what Vivvy's done to hers."

"Shut up, Enid."

"I'm just saying." Enid pulls her mask back around to the front. Her silver shoes slap the bottoms of her feet with each step.

"All right, girls. I think your mom can spare two pairs of shoes she hasn't worn in . . . let's just say—"

"Forever," says Vivvy, I think. Behind the masks, it's hard to be certain who says what, but it sounds like Vivvy.

"What about the pumpkin-head buckets? I know they're sort of wonky. I just got them as backups. But I'm sure you noticed the candy inside was full-size!"

"We saw," one of them says.

"You don't want it?" I say. "You must have gotten a lot trick-or-treating, huh?"

They look at each other, shrug, and look away.

"No, no, no, no! Enough of that and the *dry toast* business," I say. "*I* got you those and the costumes you are wearing right now because I love you and it was Halloween. Take off the masks, girls."

"Aww."

"We're sleeping in them."

"Take them off," I say. "Please. I need to see my girls."

They do. Enid holds her mask at her side and the new dog, Lowell, licks the inside like her breath is liverwurst. Vivvy pushes hers to the top of her head like a scary headband.

I clap once and rub my hands together. "Don't go anywhere," I say. "And shut your eyes."

I go out to the porch and return with the pink box. I slide the costumes' packaging out of the way and set the box down on the counter. "No peeking," I say. I think I hear the tiny wind of Enid sucking in her breath but her eyes are closed. I look to Vivvy, who fusses with something under the sleeve of her costume.

"Now," I say, "I have an important question for you both and, as your father, I require that you answer me honestly."

Enid is worried; Vivvy looks mad.

"Are you hungry?" I say. "Have you eaten anything?"

The fight in each girl is plain on her face: to find somewhere she can live in between feast and famine, mother and dad.

"Have you eaten *anything*? Are you hungry?" I say.

I take Vivvy's hand. I take Enid's hand. And I pull my girls, hold tightly on to them in the center of the room. I put them right in front of the pink box and they open their eyes, see it laid out before them. Tomorrow we'll eat vegetables, but tonight is Holly's gift and their own special *V* and *E*.

"We should eat," I say.
We should eat.

Acknowledgments

I am indebted to the support of many writers, editors, and literary arts organizations for their generous support of this novel: Jubal Tiner, editor of *Pisgah Review*; Andrew Gifford, director of the Santa Fe Writers Project; and Mary Elizabeth Parker, founder of the Dana Awards. And to my patient and beloved editor at Tin House Books, Masie Cochran.

I offer great thanks to my small cast of experts: Nancy Reid, Todd Schroer, Okla Elliott, Ken Gillam and Shannon Wooden, Garret Merriam, and Maurice Hamington. Thank you for helping to fill in the cracks of memory and invention. And much gratitude to my best readers along the way: Patricia Beltran del Rio, Melissa Cossey, and Andy Mullins.

Book Club Questions

1. With which character do you most identify? Why, and in which moments of the book?

2. How would you characterize Enid and Vivvy's relationship as sisters? How does each girl affect the other in good and bad ways?

3. What is each character's relationship to food? How do their attitudes toward food and their bodies change over the course of the book?

4. How do Francie's food and body image obsessions affect Enid, Vivvy, and even Sheldon?

5. Francie leaves home twice in the book. What is it she wants back in Boone, North Carolina and does she get it?

6. Sheldon's death devastates Francie, but she doesn't leave until seven years later. Why?

7. Why does Tate make the choice not to follow Francie on Halloween?

8. Is it significant that the novel ends on Halloween? Why do you think the girls dress up as Francie?

9. If you were to give each family member a piece of advice, what would it be?

10. If this novel were a film, who would direct it and who would play the leads?

Dear Reader,

Pretend We Are Lovely began as a narrow crack of light. I was living the last weeks of a two-year fascination with shrinking my weight as far down as it could possibly go. I had lost 181 pounds in that time and the constant worry, scratchpad of daily calorie counts next to the kitchen scale, and nervous jumping jacks before bed, weren't worth the long string of all the wrong men that thinness bought me.

I can see this now, of course, but at the time, there was little more than pitch-dark grief in my life. I began to write the Sobel family, and I gave each character pieces of my fears about food and fat so that, maybe, they could make sense of them or at least carry the burdens away from me. It was all I could see then and certainly there were no easy, or even good, answers.

But as the book unfolded—the lives of Francie and Tate, Enid and Vivvy, and even poor Sheldon—my darkness crumbled and that narrow crack of light spread wider for me, just as I hoped it would for them, and hope for all of my book's readers, most especially you. Each of us finding our way to comfort and love and pretending we are lovely until we get there.

All the very best,

Noley Reid

NOLEY REID lives in Newburgh, Indiana, with her two best boys.